Distortion

C.S. MCMILLIAN

This book is a work of fiction. Names, characters, businesses, organizations, places, events, and incidents either are the product of the author's imagination or are used fictitiously. Any resemblance to actual persons, living or dead, events, or locales is entirely coincidental.

ISBN-13: 978-0-9912989-5-2
ISBN-10: 0-9912989-5-0

First Edition

Cover art by Angela McMillian

Edited by Charles Gulotta

For Rylee

See you soon, kiddo

Chapter 1

As I sit here gazing through the grimy vehicle window, my captor a few feet away, I ponder whether this was all planned out from the beginning. I have always considered the possibility that I might be just a token on a board for the Gamemakers to manipulate. Perhaps free-will, my choice of who I would become, was an illusion. My beliefs have changed over the years, evolving and digressing, straying into more and more complex tangles of confusion. How could I now know for sure which of those beliefs is correct?

I'm riding along on a new journey, one that I fear will likely put a kink in my future endeavors. Even so, I am comforted by the one constant in my life: my battle with the Gamemakers is an undeniable certainty. What I exhumed in New Orleans tested me, nearly unwinding the fabric beneath my feet and dropping me into the abyss of insanity. But I have held strong, realizing that it had to be snipped off if I were to survive. Let's just say that Dr. Randal was not the only player in the psychological war game, and things are more intricately weaved than I could have ever imagined them to be.

In the distance to the west, a wall of pernicious clouds is threatening a storm. I smile while my captor frowns and releases a long heavy sigh. After a few miles, rain begins to fall, lightly tapping the window beside me. The pain in my head has lessened, but lately it never completely stops; only the intensity changes. I stare longingly at each drop as it slides chaotically down the pane, somehow avoiding the grime and finding the path of least resistance. I should take notes from my watery friends and follow their lead of ease, but it doesn't matter anymore. My time is limited in this place.

I glance down at my watch, the one Lesley gave me for my birthday — an exact copy of the dark tarnished metal timekeeper that my mom found for my dad in Rome on their honeymoon. My dad passed it down to me after I graduated high school, and then somehow I lost it in paramedic school. Lesley always finds a way to haul me out of a slump, even when the edges are slick and twenty feet tall. Though I've never liked admitting it to myself, she has been a part of me since the moment we first spoke to one another. She caused a ripple in my neatly tailored life that has continued to expand as we've spent more time together.

It's hard to imagine my life without Lesley. Man, have things changed, no matter how much I struggled or attempted to ignore them. Would I have spoken to her that first time, knowing how things would turn out? We are all curious beings, and can't help but question our path and the decisions that brought us to where we are. How much control do we really have?

The light tapping has turned into steady sheets of soft musical rain. I lean my head against the window, shut my eyes, and think of Lesley.

• • •

When Lesley woke, dawn was approaching. My eyes were heavy from staring at the road all night, my head pounded from the array of potential complications sprouting every few minutes. An old nemesis of mine was back and yanking on my collared neck at opportune moments, keeping me awake. I suppose it was fitting that insomnia had returned, given that my life was again in constant turmoil. I never truly knew which one of us was in the driver's seat on that trip to New Orleans. Whichever it was, he told Lesley everything. Well, almost everything.

"What time is it?" she asked, yawning and stretching her left arm toward me and running her fingers along my neck. She had been asleep for the last few hours while I listened to late-night radio jocks yammer aimlessly, and occasionally crack a poorly-contrived joke.

"Five thirty," I said. We had left Shreveport at around two o'clock after spending the evening at Horseshoe Casino Hotel, using darkness as cover. We were about an hour from New Orleans.

She twisted the top off her bottled soda, took a sip, and returned her reclined seat back upright.

"Do you want me to drive the last part?" she offered.

"I'm doing okay," I said. "Wide awake actually, just finished an energy drink." I pointed to the empty can in the cup holder.

She let out a tired smile. "If you say so."

The energy drink and insomnia weren't the only things keeping me awake. I was intermittently glancing at the side mirrors for my Uncle Frank's police issue vehicle, along with local law enforcement patrol cars. He likely thought I ran alone, seeing only me in the lab before I crushed the cameras and stopped the feed. But it was only a matter of time before he figured out Lesley was with me. Though she called her parents and told them she was safely back at college, Frank was thorough and would use his resources to confirm it. I figured we probably had a few days before he learned the truth and that we were traveling in Lesley's car. Once we arrived in New Orleans, I planned on ditching the vehicle somewhere discreet so we could travel on foot until we decided our next destination.

The car was awkwardly silent, the radio station now mostly static since we were out of range from the last city's towers. After pressing the seek button on the radio, I glanced toward Lesley and noticed she was staring at me, her eyes locked and anticipating her next words.

"What is it?" I asked.

"Do you remember saying that you wanted to explain things to me? From the beginning?"

"I did?"

"Yeah... really, you don't remember?"

"I do," I said with a smirk. I did remember, but was it wise to tell her everything: my mom's journals, the completely insane plot Dr. Randal had formulated for his patients? I could handle telling her about me, but my mom and dad? That seemed like an unnecessarily awkward conversation, speaking about people she will never be able to form her own opinion about. She had never met my dad before he died, and had known my mom only briefly after her mental decline had already begun.

After a few seconds, I could no longer resist the way her penetrating eyes focused on my right temple. I gave in. She knew about my sister's death, so I started there. It was where all of this began, and the origin of the curious and vengeful Tryke. The Gamemakers, and my personal battle with them, I kept to myself. Eventually she would learn the truth, but I would not be the one to tell her. She would have to come to that conclusion on her own.

I summarized my life story and continued to stare through the front windshield, lost in thoughts about my dead family. Although risky, I had quickly visited my family's graves before leaving town, leaving a fresh begonia by each of their tombstones. Who knew if or when I would ever return? I knew it was a silly tradition, placing my mom's favorite flower on the place where their empty suits rested, but it made me feel better to know there were still physical remnants of them somewhere I could visit.

Lesley's sniffling and nose blowing brought me out of my trance. I cast a furtive glance over at her and realized she was crying. Was it because she had finally come to her senses and wanted to take back her decision to come along with me? Actually, that was the reason I had suggested we stop in Shreveport and stay the night instead of going straight to New Orleans. I wanted her to realize her mistake and go back to school. Sure it would hurt, but she would be safe. I had never intended to have a companion when the time came to flee. Unfortunately for her, she had found me in my lab just as I had hung up the phone with my uncle, who had also tracked me down. He had somehow found the hidden room in my house where I had a video feed to my lab, along with other sensitive material.

I never expected her to catch me, but if she had, I couldn't have imagined the response I got from her. Though she didn't condone what I had been doing, she didn't run back down the dark stairwell, screaming in disgust at the two empty suits in my lab. She told me that she loved me and wanted to run away with me. What was I going to say after I had just told her for the first time that I loved her? I know — how romantic of me to declare my most tender feelings in a cold, dark dwelling surrounded by death.

"What is it?" I asked softly, and then kept quiet. I knew better than to imply that her tears were a sign she was questioning her earlier decision.

She wadded the tissue in her hand and said, "It's so sad. You and your family have been through so much. I'm so sorry, Tryke." She grabbed my hand, rubbing it gingerly. "We'll get through this. Together. Whatever you need." Her eyes were sincere and the flow of tears only reinforced her commitment.

I lightly squeezed her hand and said, "Thank you." And I *was* thankful. Her sentiment was genuine, but it wasn't going to protect her from the danger now chasing us. That was up to me, and it was not going to be an easy task.

Chapter 2

It was a week after arriving in New Orleans before we ventured to the famous coffee shop.

Cafe du Monde was as crowded as I assumed a world-renowned coffee spot would be. Even on a cold, rainy Thursday morning the line out the door snaked around the building and down the sidewalk. Hungry poncho-wielding onlookers stared at the tables, eagerly waiting for patrons to take their last bite of beignet and sign their check. The coffee was hot and brewed strong, and the beignets were addictively tasty, but neither warranted a wait in the harsh weather. We got there early, before the crowd hit, so I could choose our table. I made it abundantly clear to Lesley that if we were going to hit every tourist trap in the city, we had to take precautions.

We sat under the green awning at a corner table next to the building, behind a table of four fervent elderly tourists describing their previous night on Bourbon Street. I needed a clear view of the entire block, just in case we had to take off in a hurry — the inside was way too crowded and didn't offer an easy exit. The awning and outside heaters did a decent job of shielding us from the elements, although Lesley had been less than optimistic when the waitress assured us of that fact.

When we first arrived in New Orleans, I suggested we change our appearance, if only slightly, so when the pictures of us began to surface we would not draw instant attention. She seemed to like the idea and dyed her hair dirty blonde, at first, until I reminded her that Dr. Kimberly — the Elderly Slayer's daughter — had had the same color hair. After glaring at me for a few moments and warning me to never bring up the woman again, she ultimately decided on crimson, pulled back in a ponytail. Once again, I found out how completely oblivious and ignorant I really was to the female perspective. I chose a more inconspicuous cover: a hat, a cap really, one with the Saints' logo on it. We were clearly a couple of world travelers in town for the sight-seeing, melding nicely with the surrounding crowd of tourists.

Lesley smiled at me, powdered sugar on her upper lip from the bite of beignet she had just taken. I reached across the table and quickly wiped it with my napkin, and she instantly unwrapped another smile, this one much broader. I smiled back at her, not giving my gesture a second thought. Our relationship had reached a point I'd never considered possible. Me, Tryke Harper, cutely cleaning a smidgeon of sugar from my girlfriend's mouth. Yes, I was officially part of the annoying couple club that showed affection in public. When I realized what I had done, I quickly changed my thoughts to something more practical and useful before the nausea set in.

I had a plan in place before we arrived. A preliminary one anyhow. It involved my picking up a folding map of the city at a gas station and pinpointing local spots and potential hiding areas if our situation deteriorated. And I knew that it most certainly would if we stayed in one place for too long. Lesley had already asked me a few times about our next stop and our length of stay in New Orleans, but I did not mention anything about a plan. Basically, I told her that we needed to evaluate our situation with the authorities — nightly news, fugitives on the run posters, APB's — before we just ran aimlessly from town to town. But a strong, confident facade would hold her questions at bay only for so long.

Our first plan of action, after the map, was ditching the red flag waving over our heads: Lesley's vehicle. On the way into town, I noticed a graveyard of waterlogged vehicles under the interstate that were left over from Hurricane Katrina. After a long-winded argument from me, Lesley finally agreed to stash her car. After removing the license plate, we placed the car selectively among the others. I kept the keys and the license plate in my backpack, which also held some sensitive items from my lab, and then pinpointed the car's location on the map, just in case we again found ourselves needing to make a quick getaway.

Lesley pushed her empty plate to the side and slid her coffee cup and saucer in front of her. She ruffled her jacket and pulled it snugly around her waist, and leaned in close.

"You know, I never told you why I came with you. Why I didn't run screaming from you when you showed me what you had been doing."

What was this? A secret of her own? But, her tone didn't match a coming revelation.

"Wait," I said, "it wasn't my charm? Or my sexy overalls?" I took a last sip of coffee and placed the cup on the table.

"Of course it was," she said, smiling again. "But that was only part of it." She crossed her legs and leaned forward once more. Her smile faded as she continued to speak. "There's something you should know about me, about my past. I never told you because —"

"Wait a second," I whispered while leaning forward,

matching her position. "Do you have a secret lab?" I was distracting her, but why? Was I scared to learn more about the girl I love? Was I content with her accepting me for who I am? Would I show her the same respect that she'd shown for me?

"No, it's nothing like that." She averted her eyes, her expression turning solemn. "My family has a past, too."

She had my full attention.

"I'm listening."

After a brief pause — a moment I suspected she was using to build her courage and choose her words — she looked back my way and said, "My grandmother was murdered when I was five years old." She was struggling with her next words, constantly swiping her hair from her face and sliding it around her ear while her other hand drummed her nails under the table. She took a deep breath, and then finally let it all out.

"The image of my mother when she told me is still as vivid as it was that day. It's crazy, I still see her streaked mascara, her frightened eyes, and her trembling hands when she reached out to me on my bed. It was three years later before I learned what had happened. My grandfather let it slip out during an argument with my mother. Once it was out, he looked relieved that I knew. Of course my mother objected, but he insisted it would be good for me to learn the truth about the world. Anyway... she was killed on her way home from the store, walking her normal route. She was robbed and beaten, dying later that night from massive head trauma." Her lips began to tremble. "My innocent, soft-spoken grandmother, beaten to death."

I saw an anger building inside of her that I had never seen before. A furious aching, deep within and eager to be released. It was refreshing, and sort of a turn-on to see a passion similar to my own. Without thinking I reached out my hand and grabbed hold of hers underneath the table and squeezed her soft fingers. The grateful sentiment stained across her red-streaked eyes let me know I was handling the situation like a good boyfriend. It had always been hit-or-miss on my part, but I was obviously getting better.

She quickly regained her composure, shifting in her chair and peering around for onlookers, and then continued. "I was so mad at the time, unable to express my feelings, not knowing how. I was so vulnerable, Tryke, like I could crumble at any moment. A child breaking down from a broken heart, imagine that." She sighed and looked away, wiping a remaining tear from the corner of her eye. "The innocence of my childhood, the one where everything in the world is soft and fuzzy, was shattered. Nothing is supposed to harm you when you're a child. Your parents protect you from the cruel world. Only adults are supposed to mourn in anguish."

I sat quietly for a minute, allowing her to lament. "I'm sorry you had to learn about the world so young," I said.

"I've learned to adapt, but it wasn't always easy. I did what I thought was necessary to survive. I suppressed the memory, never talking about it after my grandfather told me that day. Until now. What else do you do when there are no answers?"

Build a lab, experiment, battle the evil. "Now we're even," I said.

"Not yet."

"What do you mean?"

She slid her chair next to mine and whispered. "I have a request, one more buried desire, and then we'll be even." In the short time we had been talking, her demeanor had changed from a sullen despair, to anger, to dark exhilaration.

"Okay…?" I said, unsure of the direction she was going. Her next words surprised me.

"I want to watch," she said without hesitation.

"Watch? What do you want to watch?" I knew the

answer, at least subconsciously.

"A release."

It took a minute for me to process her words. I sat there dumbfounded, unable to speak. Thankfully, she spoke first.

"I know it isn't convenient at the moment. I don't even know how it all works, and we're on the run… Just forget —"

"Okay," I said, regretting the word the second it left my mouth.

"Really?" She looked as shocked as I'd felt just a few seconds earlier.

I wanted her far away from me, in a safe warm place. Now I had pulled her in closer and committed her to more danger. It wasn't enough that she was with a fugitive, but now she was asking for more involvement. And if that wasn't stressful enough, how was I even going to pull off this feat I'd so hastily agreed to? This was an unfamiliar city, and I had no safe haven, no private lab, in which to perform a release. One thing I did have going for me was easy access to a suitable specimen. New Orleans was a breeding ground for dirty souls, especially with Mardi Gras around the corner.

As I sat there, contemplating the complications and avoiding Lesley's overzealous eyes, I couldn't help but wonder how much vengeance she carried in her heart to seek such a request. It was obviously more than curiosity about her boyfriend's extracurricular activities. This was a deep-seated rage that had been brewing for some time, waiting to be tapped and let loose. What was next, after she had seen a release? And would I allow it to go that far?

There were many variables to consider with this venture and it was more than risky, but I had to admit, there was a thrum of excitement sneaking around in the pit of my stomach at the unfolding possibilities.

Chapter 3

Lesley's request weighed heavily on my thoughts the rest of the morning. Why had I agreed to it so easily? In the beginning, one of my greatest fears was that she would discover the truth. Now I offer her to be part of it? Did my subconscious secretly want her involved? I wasn't convinced. Maybe I was just curious to see how far she would take it.

I had an idea, and that night before bed I pried a little deeper into what she knew about her grandmother's death. I needed more time to mull over the situation I had gotten myself into, and this was an easy way to distract her attention.

"Hey, you never finished telling me about your grandmother," I said.

"What do you mean? I told you how she was murdered."

"Didn't you ever ask who murdered her, and if they were ever caught?"

"I wasn't lying when I said I suppressed the memory."

"Don't you want to know? Now that the memory has

surfaced, I mean?"

"It crossed my mind, yes, but I wouldn't know where to start. I can't just call up my mother right now," she said, glancing around the area as if I had forgotten where we were.

"What about newspaper clippings?" I asked.

"Right," she said. I could tell I had sparked intrigue when her eyes remained focused on the blank wall in front of her. "I am curious, but we have enough going on at the moment. Besides, what good would it do?"

"I'm not saying we're going to hunt the person down. It's just a little research. You may get some closure in the end."

She thought about it briefly, then nodded and said, "All right. I suppose a little research won't hurt anything."

"There we go, see, get to solving that mystery. It will make you feel better, or at least keep your mind occupied while I do a little investigation of my own."

"You mean…?" she whispered as if we were surrounded by prying eyes.

"Yeah… that," I whispered back, laughing. "It's going to take some time, so please don't rush me."

"I won't," she said smiling, and then kissed me goodnight. Her excitement would soon be put to the test and I had a strong suspicion it would be matched with many more emotions. The reading light on her side of the bed stayed on longer than normal, and the reason was still plastered on her face when I turned off my own light for the long sleepless night ahead.

I was surprised to learn Lesley had never searched for information about her grandmother's case, considering how passionate she now seemed about the murder. The killer was likely in prison or dead. The odds of such a person living in New Orleans as a productive citizen were tenuous at best. Opening up old wounds was always a risky venture, with a potential to crumble the original memory into chaos, resulting in unintended consequences. But I wasn't one to stay hidden behind a door, too frightened to open it. We would take on whatever came our way, together.

• • •

Lesley and I sat in a small, semi-secluded Internet cafe. It was a local hangout on Magazine Street that a waitress told us about during lunch. Lesley was sitting across from me, intently studying archived newspaper clippings for her grandmother's killer, while I did online searches on my new prepaid phone for the number to Mercy General hospital. I realized I had not checked on my old partner and friend, Dave Higgins, since I left Dallas. I was the reason he was poisoned and now lay in a coma. My latest specimen — The Elderly Slayer — injured him to get to me. His daughter and accomplice, Dr. Kimberly, had also used him to get to me. She hadn't injured him physically, but the emotional impact of her actions had been detrimental to his feeble ego, especially as it related to women.

I slipped on my jacket and stepped outside the entrance door, dialing the hospital's number. It would have been easier to simply call the station and ask my fellow paramedics about Dave's condition, but that was definitely out of the question. I was sure that by now I was a known fugitive, and any contact with me would be seen as aiding and abetting. I could just imagine the chatter around the station as my picture popped up on the local news: "He was such a nice, quiet guy. They have the wrong person, I know they do." Or the other end of the spectrum. Dave's first ex-wife, Claire: "I knew it all along. I hope they catch that son of a bitch." But none of it mattered at that point, what people back home thought about me. I wouldn't be returning to my life as a paramedic for the city of Dallas.

Oddly enough, I thought, I had yet to see any pictures of Lesley or me on the news. But I knew it was only a matter of time, which is why I stayed vigilant, and borderline paranoid. I was constantly thinking about our next location, because once our pictures hit the national media my frame of mind would be in survival mode. I would need a plan to follow. The one I had recently formulated, which was still in the preliminary stages, was to make our way along the Gulf Coast, ultimately landing in Florida — and depending on the situation, maybe even one of the Caribbean islands. However, once the heat was off, I knew I would have to head back to Dallas to complete unfinished business with Dr. Randal.

"Can you connect me to the Intensive Care Unit?" I asked the operator.

"One second, please."

The phone went briefly silent and then began ringing. A female picked up on the second ring.

"ICU," she said with a mild twang in her voice.

"Yes, ma'am, I'm a paramedic from station fifteen. I was — we were just checking to see if it would be okay to bring our fellow paramedic, Mr. Higgins, a few items? Just in case he wakes up."

"Of course, you know you guys are always welcome up here. He could use some visitors."

"He hasn't had any lately? Sorry, I'm on the other shift and I haven't been able to make it up there yet. Pardon me for asking, but isn't his family staying with him?"

"Only the one time, very briefly. I feel so sorry for him."

I knew the answer before she said it, that he had been alone most of the time. Being partners on the rig for years, we learned a lot about one another, though I did manage to keep my activities outside of work a secret. At least until the most recent incident. I became proficient at simulating certain mannerisms to divert attention. Dave, on the other hand, was more overt about his life, offering bits and pieces at a time. He was passionate, to say the least, animated and loud and often relaying stories of greatness. But one thing he didn't speak of often was his parents and his relationship with them. When he did occasionally mention them, the words were never derogatory or angry, but were solemn and seemed to hold a wishful longing for his parents to change. They weren't at the hospital when he was first admitted, and likely never brought his daughter to see him. Of course, I didn't expect his two previous cheating wives to pay him a visit. Without Lesley or me there, he was stuck battling the mind's abyss by himself.

"Has he moved at all, shown any positive neurological signs lately?" I asked.

"Once in a while he'll move his right index finger. I try and talk to him every chance I get. I'm not bragging, but he seems to like my voice. That's when he moves his finger."

"Please keep it up, will you? And thank you for taking care of him... What's your name?"

"Elizabeth."

"Elizabeth, tell him his friends miss him, and that we'll be up there as soon as we can."

I pressed End on my phone. I was livid at the idea of his parents not visiting him. More than that, I was pissed off at myself all over again for allowing the events that had put him there in the first place. Whether it was part of the Gamemakers' scheme or the possibility that Dave was just an unfortunate fluke casualty, I was mixed up in the middle. I didn't know how I was going to make it right, but somehow, someday, I was going to.

Once I cooled off, I went back inside. Lesley was glued to my laptop screen, immersed in an article.

"You find anything yet?" I asked, plopping down next to her.

"I think so," she said, not removing her eyes from the screen.

"What do you mean, you think so?"

"I mean, I did, but nothing further than the description of the murder scene. By the way who'd you call?"

"The hospital, to find out about Dave's status."

She instantly removed her gaze from the computer to me, her eyes holding mournful anticipation.

"Not much change," I said. "The nurse said he moved his index finger. I guess that's progress, but certainly not enough. Oh, and he hasn't had any visits from his family. Shocker."

She shook her head and said, "So sad. Who are those people, not to go see their son in the hospital? Doesn't make any sense. I wish we could see him, let him know he's not forgotten. At the very least, he could feel the touch of someone who cares for him."

"Yeah, me too. But, at least there's a nurse with him who sounds like she has empathy in her voice. She actually seems to have taken a liking to him."

"That's good, she said and then nodded, disappointment and sympathy still slathered on her face.

Dave's situation with his parents made me think of my own parents and sister. I was lucky to have the family that I did. Sure, every family has issues, but at least mine cared enough to protect me until they were dead. Why one and not another? Why must one suffer and another empathize, while still another attempts to make sense of tragedy? All the while the apathetic and emotionless dark souls ravage the land unhindered, unbothered by the sickness smothering the world. Some don't even realize they are part of the plague, or don't want to admit their role in mankind's demise.

Our ability to recognize this injustice in the world is both a favor and a curse. Only the Gamemakers have the real answers. Meanwhile, until my time was over, I could at least play my part. I actually considered it an advantage, an attribute that would help build my mental army for the day-to-day struggle. I'd need endurance for when the final battle emerged.

Chapter 4

Lesley didn't have much luck with her search, continuing it
back at the hotel late into the night. I wondered how long
the pursuit would keep her busy, and how long until she
came to her senses and realized the depth of her request.
But something inside me felt she had considered the matter
thoroughly before she decided to ask for my help.
Eventually, I knew, I would have to fulfill her need. Which
made me realize that I had yet to figure out a plan. I
needed a day out on the streets to roam around and think
— a direct violation of my code for keeping us safe.

I was sitting on the balcony the next morning, my hat
tilted down, staring toward the array of umbrellas bouncing
along the street. Lesley slept soundly. At least one of us
would be well rested. Rain, the one thing that I could
always count on. Even when my arch nemesis is visiting,
wet weather can soothe my aggravated nerve endings
enough to ease his grip and allow brief naps. I was more
than grateful for the few that he'd allowed me the night
before.

I was on my third cup of coffee when Lesley slid the glass door open to the balcony and greeted me with a soft hug around the neck.

"How long have you been up?" she asked, concerned.

"Didn't really fall asleep," I said.

"I'm sorry." She sighed. "It doesn't surprise me that your insomnia has returned, with everything that's going on."

"Yeah… but at least it's raining."

She pulled her robe in close, crossing her arms, and sat in the chair next to mine. "Yeah, what's with all the rain? I thought hurricane season was over. I know you enjoy it, but it doesn't make for a pleasant day out."

I shrugged. "Maybe it's a cleansing before the Mardi Gras debauchery begins. Whatever the cause, I'm thankful. The rhythm is soothing."

"Okay, fine, the rain has its moments."

I glanced over and found myself leering at her. She was most beautiful when she first woke up. Unhindered, unfettered by the social norm. Her natural beauty always stuns me.

"What?" She covered her face and looked down. "Don't stare at me. I haven't put on my makeup yet."

I smiled and grabbed her bare right foot. "You don't need it." She lightly yanked her foot away, revealing her porcelain toned thighs. "Tryke!" She quickly covered up.

Smiling, she leaned up and glanced over the edge of the balcony for onlookers. "Lucky for them it's raining. I can't disgust anyone with my dry, pale legs. Anyway, what are we doing today?" She scooted her chair close to mine.

"They would be lucky for even a glimpse of such a perfectly sculpted piece of art," I said. She blushed, briefly turning a shade lighter than her dyed hair. "As for today, I haven't thought much past my coffee."

"Well, I slept way too long. I need to go take a quick shower."

"Lucky you."

"I'm sorry, maybe you can get a nap in this afternoon. The rain may continue throughout the day."

"Wishful thinking," I said. "I'm not that lucky."

"I beg to differ," she said, getting up from her chair and pushing it back under the table. "You got me, didn't you?" She kissed my disheveled hair in the back and re-opened the sliding door.

I smiled and took another sip of my coffee. "Good point."

"Think about it, will you please?"

"Huh?"

"Today. What we're doing."

"Yeah, sure. Okay."

She left the door cracked, and I could hear her humming. I glanced back and saw her moving around the room, gathering her clothes for the day and placing them neatly onto the bed. I was adamant about not fully unpacking in the room, just in case we had to flee in a hurry. She tried giving me grief about it at first, but I reiterated our situation and she gave in.

My thoughts were not currently on the day's activities, as Lesley would have liked them to be. I was more concerned with her demeanor, acting as if we were on vacation. As if we could leisurely stroll around town without a care in the world. The human brain has a bad habit of placing us in a state of denial when we are surrounded by endless chaos. It attempts to seek out normalcy whenever possible.

I finished my coffee, not giving a second thought to leisure activity for the day. For some reason, my brain would not even allow normalcy in the front foyer. Maybe it was the insomnia that prevented such an idea from developing, leaving me in a constant state of paranoia. It had been two weeks since my brief conversation on the phone with my Uncle Frank, and there was nothing on the news channels about us, and no pictures posted anywhere. I knew better than to think he had forgotten about me, or had decided to shrug me off as an annoyance. He was biding his time, lurking in the shadows, waiting for me to slip up, likely working behind the scenes with different police agencies. If there was one thing I knew about my uncle, it's that he was tenacious.

Lesley was sitting cross-legged on the bed in her robe, her wet hair pulled back, surrounded by a plethora of makeup. The television was set to The Weather Channel. On the nightstand beside her I noticed that the brochures of local hot spots had been shuffled around, a particular one beside her in the center of the bed.

"I had an idea," she said, massaging skin cream into her face.

"I'm listening."

"If the rain lets up, what would you think about taking a cemetery tour? And before you answer, I know we have to be careful. This is the last touristy thing for a while. I promise." She pouted her lips.

"Being a tourist and blending in is okay," I said. "I just don't want to stay in the spotlight for long. Anyway, the big Mardi Gras parades start next weekend, which will give us plenty of cover."

"So you're okay with going to the cemetery?" she asked.

I considered the risk. People had started to crowd the city the last few days, anticipating the big celebration. If the rain let up, the tour would probably be full.

"I suppose it will be all right. What time does it start?"

"Ten o'clock, and they have another at one o'clock. They don't offer night tours."

Not surprising with the amount of crime on the streets. Tourists being mugged on tours would be bad for business.

"One o'clock, I guess, since it's already nine and still raining."

I lay down on the bed and stretched my legs, letting out a much needed yawn. I slid my hands behind my head and shut my eyes, listening to the melodic rain and the sound of

Lesley shuffling around her gaggle of makeup paraphernalia.

I felt a sudden pressure all over the insides of my body. My vessels felt like they were going to implode at any moment. With my eyes still shut I felt paralyzed, the pressure ruling out any choice movements. I wanted to yell for help, but I couldn't find my voice. I wasn't even sure Lesley was still there beside me. The only sound I could detect was coming from inside me — a crumbling, stretching sound vibrating throughout. A second later, I was able to open my eyes, but a black darkness surrounded me. I couldn't make out any shapes. I could move my arms, but only up and down. I seemed to be enclosed in some type of container.

My heart pounded like a crazed drummer when I realized where I was — in a coffin. I began flailing my arms, rapping them on the inside of the box and shouting for help. In my mind, I knew it was impossible to yell through six feet of dirt, but panic outranked logic. I could feel my lungs screaming for relief as my breathing became more and more erratic.

When I finally forced opened my eyes, Lesley was standing over me with a damp towel in her hand, but I couldn't quite put the situation together. I was still attempting to claw my way out from the mind's sharp clutch.

"Tryke. Tryke…" Lesley said softly.

Panic filled me again as I struggled more and more to find my way back. I jerked up and stared at the wall ahead of me. Lesley was still there, but was keeping her distance. "I'm okay," I said, unconvincingly, as I began to comprehend my surroundings, piecing my existence slowly back together. She came around the bed and sat next to me, wiping the cool towel across my forehead. "How long was I out?"

"Just a few minutes," she said.

"Really, huh…" I said, relieved and taking a much needed breath of air. "That's disappointing."

"I thought you might be happier to be awake, considering the yelling and flailing you were doing. Do you want to talk about it?"

"I don't really remember much," I said, sliding my butt back in the bed and propping myself against the headboard. "Besides, there's enough to worry about without dwelling on my fictitious dreams." But I wasn't truly convinced that they *were* fictitious. A lingering fear had haunted me for many years that the dreams were a foreshadowing to my future. Since then, I have felt them inching closer, gnawing and clawing, whispering that they were growing near.

"What do think about skipping the cemetery tour and going to an urgent care to get you some sleeping pills?" Lesley asked. "And you can also tell them about the headaches."

"I'm fine, really. I doubt the doc at an urgent care would prescribe what I need. Besides, I have to stay vigilant. As for the headaches, they're just part of not sleeping."

She reluctantly agreed with me and lay down beside me on the bed. Maybe it was the recent bout with my recurring childhood nightmare. Maybe it was the adrenaline still pumping through my veins. Maybe it was the brief glimpse of her inner thighs as she snuggled up against me. Whatever it was, I was in a rare mood, especially since arriving in the city. I let my guard down long enough to actually enjoy myself. With the sound of a steady downpour and a softly ruffling sheer curtain, Lesley and I made love.

Chapter 5

The rain tapered off and then, to my dismay, stopped altogether, but a gathering of dark grey clouds still lingered low in the sky. That gave me hope that more downpours were in the near future. Though I had agreed to the tourist outing, I wasn't optimistic about finding Lesley's first specimen, much less a temporary lab on a cemetery tour. However, a graveyard was a perfect disposal area for dirty empty suits. If only it hadn't been so overused in the movies. Maybe it's had enough time to make a full turn, and was now back in style.

There were at least twenty of us waiting for the tour guide — a tall, lanky black man in his early fifties with a shiny, shaved head — to finish his spiel about the rules of the tour. These included warnings of the surrounding neighborhood. His rant ended up being less about our safety and more self-inflation, as he hinted of his vast knowledge of the city's crime, including his personal run-ins. All lightly mentioned while wearing a wily grin, so as not to incriminate himself. And his poorly contrived

Jamaican accent was annoying at best. This was going to be a long hour.

Lesley and I were standing in the rear of the group, next to an older couple dressed in typical tourist attire: camera, straw hat, boat shoes, and khaki shorts with black socks, despite the cold weather. They seemed determined to look like tourists, no matter the cost, as they shoved a middle finger into the face of the elderly stereotype of always being chilly.

"You know why I chose this particular graveyard, don't you?" Lesley asked. I was captivated by the brick walls surrounding the cemetery that appeared to have graves built into them.

"No," I said. "Why, are there multiple tours?"

"Of course there are." I didn't look over at her but I heard the fling of her hair. "Anyway, I chose it because of Marie Leveau."

"Who?" Fascinating, I thought, what a clever use of space.

"Only the voodoo queen herself. Really, you've never heard of her?"

"No. Oh wait… Yeah, maybe I have." I turned and looked at Lesley. "Is she buried here or something?"

"Yeah, cool huh? There are some really creepy stories about this graveyard, but I don't know how much I believe."

"Yeah…" I said turning my attention back toward the wall. "Have you seen the graves set into the surrounding wall? Why do you suppose they built them all the way up?"

"I saw them on the way in. They're neat, but…" Lesley was interrupted when a guy elbowed her right arm and nearly knocked over an elderly man standing beside us. I turned around just in time and caught the elderly man by the belt. He thanked me, shaking his head and staring at the rude young man, who did not apologize, but rather blamed his two friends for the intrusion. All three — two guys and a girl — looked no older than eighteen. I'd noticed them when we entered: loud drunken slurs and obnoxious shoving. Not out of the ordinary for New Orleans, I figured, but on a history tour that costs money? Maybe they slipped in without paying.

Lesley grabbed my arm and moved us farther back, not letting me engage the obnoxious teenagers. She was still in her vacation mood and was not going to allow a few drunks to ruin her tour.

"It kind of gives me an uneasy feeling," she said, as if the incident had never occurred. "You know, the ambience of the city and its creepy history."

"Along with the actual creeps around every corner," I said, glaring at the young group out of the corner of my eye.

As we made our way to the first gathering of tombs, my attention switched to the guide, who had begun to explain the different types of graves. I was so intrigued I even managed to ignore his exaggerated animation and poor accent. Who knew that such a variety of death boxes existed? The surrounding brick wall that I had been so fascinated by was filled with tombs called Oven Vaults, commonly called "ovens" by the locals, so named because of their arches. Fitting, I thought, considering the southern heat during the summer. The ovens' elevation was a necessary result of the water table. They were also economical; not everyone could afford large ornate tombs with crypts.

Other graves included parapet tombs, pitched, coping, pyramid, and my favorite — "boxed" — because it was made to fool grave robbers into thinking the body was inside the above-ground box when it was actually buried deep below. Cleverly simple.

As I peered around at the eclectic homes for the dead, I appreciated their morbid beauty: ornate craftsmanship, sun-bleached and ivy-covered surfaces, beautifully crafted words, and of course the aging and rust along the sporadic iron gates. Lesley's comment – that she felt as though she were walking beneath a graveyard, with the ability to see through dirt and smothered by decay and history — was a little less poetic than her norm. Maybe it was the dark gothic feel of the place, combined with the gloomy grey clouds, that interfered with her usual wit.

Our walking slowed as the guide perched himself on top of a crumbling wall of cement. "Everyone gather round, make room," he said. "You three. Yeah, you." He was referring to the three teenagers. They moved aside, holding back laughs and nudging one another in blame for being called out in the group. "Let the lovely couple around." He looked right at Lesley and me. I grabbed Lesley's hand and guided us as far away from the three as possible, stopping next to another older couple, who were beaming at us like proud grandparents. "We're about to enter a very haunted section of the graveyard," he said. "Though it be light outside, restless spirits don't care. They roam and torment whenever dey feel like it."

"Are they hot!?" the female from the threesome asked loudly, and then giggled like a schoolgirl.

The guide laughed and said, "Of course dey are. They be stuck in an oven." He winked and lowered his voice. "But we must show respect or all of us be doomed. The patience of deh dead shouldn't be tested."

"That means you, Tryke," Lesley whispered to me, heeding the guide's poor attempt at parlor tricks.

"Don't worry, I'll play along," I said.

We approached the gravesite of Marie Laveau. The guide began his spiel in a low whisper, tiptoeing around the grave to face the crowd, and careful not to disturb the plethora of gifts that littered the front: votive candles, flowers, Mardi Gras beads.

It was a pediment tomb, three stacked crypts with a receiving vault below. When enough time passed, these were designed so that the deceased body could be lowered further and another could be placed above it. I noticed many X's all over the tomb and broken pieces of cement scattered about. The guide explained that slivers from nearby tombs were broken off and used to make the "X" marks. For Laveau to grant them a wish they marked an "X", turned around three times, knocked on the tomb, and then yelled out their wish. If the wish were granted, they returned later, circled the "X," and left an offering.

"Though this grave be marked as Marie Leveau, a legend survives that speaks differently," the guide said, moving his eyes among the crowd. "Some say she never died." The crowd was silent and motionless. Even the three teenagers were hanging onto the guide's next words. The only sound came from the cool gusts of wind whipping through the maze of graves. "Dey say she changed herself into a huge black crow and still flies over the cemetery today." Half of the crowd looked around frantically. "Caw, Caw," he said, and then let out a boisterous laugh.

After the crowd settled back down, the guide continued. "It is true that many have seen a mysterious crow, and others claim to have seen Marie herself. Whatever be deh truth, there is no doubt dis place be haunted. Let's move on. There's much more to see."

As the crowd filed to the next area, Lesley pulled me to the side and waited until the final few passed. "What are we doing?" I asked. "Wait a second. You aren't doing what I think you're about to do. Are you?"

Ignoring my words, she knelt next to the tomb. She was contemplating the wishing ritual, staring up and waiting for me to say something.

"What? Really?" I said.

"It can't hurt. Maybe we should."

"You know what the guide said," I warned. It's vandalism. We can't afford to have any run-ins with the law."

"Real quick, no one will see. Besides, the guide was smiling when he said that, like it was no big deal."

I heaved a heavy sigh. "Fine, but don't yell out the wish. Loudly whisper it, please. And hurry. I'll keep watch."

She picked up a piece of broken stone from the ground nearby and started the ritual. I stepped a grave over and perched on a step so I could get a better view, just in case someone approached. The wind was beginning to pick up, brushing debris and leaves along the concrete, which made it hard for me to hear her. Though my attention was rightly set on potential intruders, I couldn't help but be curious about her wish. I leaned down below the grave in order to block the wind. To be honest, I don't know what I was expecting her to ask for, but I certainly wasn't anticipating the words that followed.

• • •

I couldn't hear everything she said, but I didn't need to. The one word that amplified like an announcement over a loud speaker in a library was definitely enough to cause my entire insides to rattle. It was the last word I thought she would utter. *Married.* Sure, I had thought about what it would be like to tie the knot, and if I ever were to take that leap, Lesley was the only woman I would even consider. But now? On the run, where everything is uncertain? And no future to plan, other than not being arrested? At the same time, there was a tiny twinge inside of me vibrating its way loose, urging me to entertain the thought. Nothing in this life is certain, and time doesn't stop for any of us. What if…

I lifted my head and turned back toward the tour group as I heard Lesley approach. I hurriedly removed any expression from my face, pretending I had been diligently keeping watch at my post.

"What did you wish for?" I asked, trying to sound prying.

She had a smirk on her face that said 'none of your

business,' although in a playful way. "Wouldn't you want to know? Remember the rules about wishes."

"Of course," I said. "How could I forget?"

She walked in front of me and I noticed a little more bounce in her step. She was leading me to the aisle, and I was letting her. I had been completely absorbed by our teetering situation, and she saw an opening, taking the upper hand in our relationship. I allowed myself to smile for a moment.

We settled into the back of the group for the rest of the tour. We were at the end, and the guide had just finished giving his last piece of advice about avoiding dark corners in the city. While Lesley was conversing with an older lady about Texas — she was from Denton and was apparently ecstatic over how small the world was — I was eavesdropping on the side conversation taking place between the guide and the three rude teens.

His accent miraculously disappeared as he whispered to them. "I own a voodoo shop not far from here where we can meet. I have plenty of gifts there to purchase, or you can bring your own." He was luring them there, but why? He wasn't going to give them an after-hours tour because he was a nice guy. Or sell them cheap gifts. "How is ten o'clock?"

They all nodded their heads in unison. The girl whispered excitedly to her two companions, "We'll be done just in time for the bar."

"The tour was sort of romantic, don't you think?" Lesley said, grabbing my hand and nudging her shoulder into mine.

"I suppose," I said.

"What is it? What has your attention over your own girlfriend?" She turned my chin toward her, and I looked at her vacantly.

"Them," I said, motioning my head toward the three teenagers.

"Again? What did they do now?

"Nothing," I said dismissively.

"Come on, don't let a few annoying teens spoil our time together."

"It's not them. It's the tour guide."

"What do you mean?" she asked.

"There's something not right about him."

"I admit he's a little odd, but no more so than most of the others around here."

Something clicked — I could almost hear the switch being flipped inside her head — and she leaned in and whispered loudly, "Wait a second. Are you working? You know... trying to find someone...?"

"Sort of... but I'm not convinced just yet. Don't get too excited."

"Really? What? Come on, tell me what you look for," she said vehemently, pulling me back a few steps away from the couple in front of us. "I want to know."

"Not sure yet," I said. "Relax. Just intuition at the moment. I'd have to do some research first."

She huffed, clearly disappointed by my vagueness. If I were to tell her about the Gamemakers, and what they had instilled in me, she wouldn't have understood. Or would she? I suddenly had a curious thought — one that had slipped my mind when she told me about her interest. Probably pushed to the side because of my attention to our relationship. What if Lesley were just like me? What if she were a fellow player on the battlefield, just waiting for an 'incident' to trigger her start? My own began with the death of my sister. Lesley's could well have begun back when her grandmother died, never developing because she suppressed it. What if?

Chapter 6

I left Lesley slumbering in the room. After dinner, we had a few drinks in our hotel room while playing cards and discussing a few plans about our shaky future. The port mixed with the excitement, and the combination got the better of her. She passed out a little after nine o'clock. I would be lying if I said it wasn't my idea to buy her favorite brand of port and discuss our future. I needed to be sure about this guy, and I had to do it alone. There were too many avenues to consider, and I had to determine if she were truly like me. It was much too early to mention the Gamemakers, but what harm could it cause to intervene in her development? On the other hand, if I were to teach her, I would be interrupting the process. I never had assistance or a guide to help me along, and look how I turned out. Okay, I thought, she may need my help after all.

The streets of New Orleans are never empty. Individuals, couples, and groups of every variety all united for one simple purpose: to get highly inebriated and celebrate the night. That was one of the reasons I chose this place. Anonymity would not be an issue. Wandering eyes would not scrutinize the lone man walking the streets at night. There were plenty of shady characters ahead of me on the scale of creepiness, figures who warranted a second glance as much as I did. However, I was careful to avoid Bourbon Street because of the drunken mass of potential complications.

I made my way down a side street toward the address of the guide's voodoo shop — which I'd memorized when he told the teens — admiring the charming soft glow of street lamps and aged faded brick road, all the while doing my best to ignore the mysterious lingering acrid smell. Though the appeal of the city was obscured, the potential could be felt beneath the soft mist hanging in the air. As I walked, I replaced the cars, backward baseball caps, and scarcely covered women with horse-drawn buggies, top hats, and elegantly-dressed ladies holding umbrellas and speaking with a delicate French accent. 'What's up, man?' was replaced by 'Good day, sir', and a nod of the head by a fellow traveler, followed by a twist of a gentleman's cane.

The thought quickly faded once I approached the dank desolate area where the voodoo shop was supposed to be. The place was not exactly where you would expect to find a profitable business. But if my suspicions were correct, this was not a tourist attraction representing the city of New Orleans. Once off the main road, I slowed my pace from that of a night roamer to a cautious wanderer. The alley was dark and narrow, with no windows along the damp rust-colored brick walls. Ahead, three quarters of the way down the alley, I saw a dim crimson light flickering under an aluminum shade that teetered from the occasional gust of cool wind. Other than one lone dumpster, there weren't many hiding places for lurking predators to surprise me, which was both good and bad. I wouldn't have many options if I were to come into direct contact with the tour guide.

There weren't any identifying marks on the grime-covered glass door, or anywhere else on the building, except for a worn wooden sign leaning against the wall with the words "Voodoo Shop" crudely sketched in white paint. The rest of the wording had either faded away or this was the extent of his marketing skills. The two address letters above the door were intact.

There was no mistaking. This was it.

I glanced down at my watch; it was fifteen minutes past ten. Promptness wasn't usually a teenager's first priority, but I wasn't taking any chances that they might arrive early and potentially recognize me from the tour. I did a quick sweep on the rest of the alley past the small shop, looking for a way out if things took another direction. There was a smaller alley to the left, but it was a dead-end that led into what appeared to be a deserted shop. I lightly shook the door knob. It was loose, but locked. It felt fragile enough that if I had to kick it in for a quick hiding spot, it wouldn't be a problem. I glanced above my head again along the brick wall, hoping that a variety of fire escape ladders had miraculously appeared, but no such luck.

I was out of my element, out of my city, leaving me with limited choices and means. But I had always been good at adapting, acclimating to strenuous situations, or at least it seemed that way. Of course there was always the other explanation, that the Gamemakers had manifested it all that way just to boost my confidence, and to move the game forward. Whatever the reason, that apparent resilience was pertinent to my survival.

Now that I had secured a less-than-optimum exit plan, it was time to enter the shop. Thanks to the poor cleaning habits of the guide — which I suspected were a combination of laziness and shadiness — I had a very minimum view of the entrance room through the glass door. I cautiously twisted the knob and to my surprise the door was unlocked. Was he careless, or foolishly trusting? I nudged it open a few inches, attempting to reduce the soft creaking, and then slid my hand around the inside to search for hanging bells or beads that most small shops dangled to alert the owner of incoming guests. Nothing there. I took a few steps in and quietly closed the door behind me. Immediately, an intense smell of incense hit my nose, along with another smell that was strangely familiar, though I couldn't quite place it at the moment.

I let my eyes slowly adjust to the darkness. The few box-shaped items I could make out in the shadows were scattered about in the entrance room. The place appeared mostly empty, which meant fewer places for shadowy figures to hide. I felt along the wall, following a right-handed pattern, until I reached a cracked door. Room to room I went, carefully using my phone as a light and briefly examining the contents as I passed them. I had found nothing of interest. There was minimal furniture and cluttered shelves of various items — none of which were packaged for retail distribution, giving legitimacy to my original qualms about this guy.

It was awkwardly silent, and empty, for a place that was supposedly a meeting spot to do business. My remaining prickle of optimism thought my original instincts might be wrong, and that the guide was simply using his parlor tricks and fake accent to entertain the teenagers. He could quite possibly be taking them for a night tour of the cemetery. Or maybe they had gone already, spooked by the creepiness the place exuded. I had an ominous vibe trekking along my own insides at the moment. Every sense I had was edging me toward a horrible outcome. Nothing good was emanating from these walls, but I wasn't leaving until I searched the entire place.

Ahead, another door was cracked open, giving off a faint flickering glow from the other side. Finally, I thought, we're getting somewhere. I pocketed my phone and hurriedly made my way to the door, just in case someone came barreling through, and knelt down against the wall. I listened at the door for a brief moment before taking a peek inside. Nothing. Just as I was about to edge the door open, I heard the sound of mumbling. I immediately retracted my hand and returned to my original position with my back snugly pressed against the wall. I attempted to discern the words being spoken, but I couldn't.

After a minute the mumbling had suddenly switched into a familiar man's voice. There was no doubt it was the tour guide, and he sounded like he was... chanting. I was still unable to make out the words, but I could easily picture him performing for his audience of three on the other side of the door. They probably purchased some fake objects that he explained were archaic and ritualistic — and that had a *Made in China* sticker on the back — and they were wielding them in hopeful anticipation as he flailed his arms and scooted around the room while spouting indiscernible nonsense. He probably even had a dead chicken and some fake blood in bowls. He was a common street performer and a crook, with no actual connection to voodoo.

I nearly laughed when I heard him say, "Let the offering be true, and my soul be cleansed." Was he passing around an offering plate? But then, out of nowhere, he started yelling. Not at someone, or in anger, but as a continued part of his fake ritual.

"Heal and rise! Take your rightful place at my side! Rise! Rise!"

Was he attempting to raise the chicken from the dead? And then it sounded as if he had begun to shake something. A rattle? And then some pounding on the floor. With his feet?

I couldn't wait any longer. I had to see this for myself.

• • •

I didn't need to open the door all the way to observe the spectacle taking place behind it. Through the cracked door, a huge mirror spanned the wall and reflected the dimly-lit room. The three teenagers were definitely there, but not at all how I pictured them, or how I'd expected this scenario to play out. This was worse, far worse. To put it simply, it was insane. All three, the girl in the center and the two boys on each side, were suspended from the ceiling by their feet. Their throats had been sliced open, and blood drained into three large wooden bowls beneath them. Scarlet spatters covered the far wall and the surrounding floor.

I found myself unable to look away, entranced by the crazy spectacle. I was disgusted, but intrigued, by this piece the Gamemakers had tossed onto the board. This was old school, ancient tradition, using ritual to murder the innocent. Was this a way to make me see the horror of what I do? Was the reflection on the wall a reflection of me and my own ritual? Yes, I use a room. I follow a procedure. But my specimens are far from innocent. They are not sacrifices. They are part of a never-ending evil, one I was sent here to remove.

Snapping back to the scene in front of me, I remembered the guide. I hadn't seen him yet, though I could still hear his soft chanting. He was at an angle the mirror wouldn't allow me to glimpse. I leaned forward and inched the door open. He was crouched down and facing the three dead kids, his face soaked in their blood. He was surrounded by a circle of flickering candles and other ritual paraphernalia I couldn't make out. On the wall behind him, there was a variety of symbols sketched in what I suspected were his past victims' blood.

From what little I knew about voodoo, it revolved around healing. The sacrifice was usually that of an animal, which was consumed in a feast to honor spirits. No, this was no voodoo ritual. Rather, this guy was hiding his true identity behind the *mask* of voodoo. The Gamemakers really outdid themselves on this one, I thought.

He suddenly jerked his head toward the mirror. His mouth was still moving, but no words were exiting. Only the whites of his eyes were visible, hiding the black pupils that I had seen earlier on the tour. It was like staring into an empty room lit by a soft black light.

Stuck in thought, it took me a second to realize that if I could see his face, he could see mine. I stumbled back a few feet into the shadow of the room I was in, all the while keeping an eye on the door. I wasn't sure if he had seen me, so I kept hidden in my position and listened. No sound of movement. It was time to go. I was observing and collecting data only, and I definitely had enough. Besides, even if I had wanted to release this guy, I didn't have my equipment with me.

I felt along the walls to the next room, trying to quickly make my way out without knocking anything over. Maybe he had been too absorbed in his ritual and hadn't noticed me. Or maybe I startled him, and there was a back door and he'd booked it out. All wishful thinking, and I wasn't taking any chances.

Once I made it through the dark labyrinth to the front door, I exited and quickly scanned the alley for any threats. It was empty and quiet. If indeed he had seen me, I wouldn't have time to run the full length of the alley to the street, so I slid around the corner to the small pathway I had mapped out earlier, the one with the deserted shop. I took a second to catch my breath, and then peered back around the corner, making sure I stayed within the shadows. Would he come bursting out of the door, wielding the same knife he had used to slit the throats of the three teenagers? Or would he cautiously lock the door and slip back into his makeshift ritual?

This guy's evil was tangible. I was pretty sure Lesley wouldn't object to what I now wanted to do. He was an obvious candidate to be her first specimen, although she would be only watching and not participating just yet. True, I had agreed to her request, but it was still up to me to make it happen. I had been postponing it for obvious reasons: we lacked a suitable specimen, as well as a private space in which to perform the procedure. But there had been something else — besides keeping her safe, a part of me wanted her to retain her innocence. Then again, that was not for me to decide. It was her choice, and she had already made the decision.

The door never opened.

Chapter 7

Lesley and I had lunch the next day at a cafe close to the hotel. Before I had a chance to tell her the exciting news about her first release, she took a long drink of her water — attempting to nurse a mild hangover from the previous night's bottle of port — and spoke first.

"I know you left last night after I fell asleep." She had been quiet all morning. I should have known it was more than the hangover.

"Don't you mean passed out?" I said with a wry grin.

Her lips didn't so much as twitch. She held her glare with crossed arms. "Stop diverting," she said. And then out of nowhere she let out a half smile, lightening her demeanor. "Tryke, I thought we were on the same page with all of this. Together, remember?"

"We are... I mean — "

"I know you went out searching for that tour guide. So why didn't you bring me?"

"I don't know. Old habits, I guess." She continued to stare at me. Thankfully the glare was gone, but so was the half-smile. She tilted her head slightly, as if pushing me to reveal more. Wrong answer. "Okay." I sighed heavily. "The truth... I worry about you. Look, I'm pretty good at taking care of myself, but I don't know how good I'll be at watching over you while I'm working. This is all new, having an observer. Especially one I care about. You could get hurt, or worse. You could get killed."

We all know how my last so-called companion turned out last year. I had been played for a fool, stalked, made to think I was the one leading. But this was different. This could work. This was love after all, right? Is there anything more powerful and loyal? Romantic love was still new to me, but if the rumors were true, it could go either way: really good, or horribly wrong. It was a risk no matter how I looked at it.

She sighed and brushed her dyed hair to the side. "You've done pretty good so far, watching over me."

"Lucky is all."

"I don't believe that. You're a natural survivor, Tryke. The fact that we're here in New Orleans is proof of it."

"We've been running. This is different. This is actively pursuing someone, and there's a lot involved."

"I know. That's why I wanted to be with you. So you could show me, teach me. We could look after one another." She leaned in close and waved her blue eyes and long lashes toward me. She was taunting me with her weapon of feminine seduction, and it was working. "I want you to take care of me, and I want to take care of you."

"I will," I said. "Yes. I mean, you're right. I should have let you go with me, but I promise it was just observation. I needed to make sure everything was right and safe before we engaged. The boring part." Usually boring anyhow. She didn't need to know the details of my risky close encounters. And I didn't need her to have more firepower against me.

"Please let me in, Tryke. I'll be fine. I promise."

"I know," I said. "We'll hunt him together, even tonight if you want."

"Thank you," she said, earnestly. She was letting me off the hook, though I wasn't buying her sentiment toward me on this matter. She may have wanted to be with me last night, but the real craving was for the release. I still couldn't believe I had agreed to this. We were actually going to do this together. It was sort of… exciting.

"I think you'll be interested to know what I discovered about the guy. Though I have to warn you, it's pretty disturbing. It should get you nice and riled up."

After relaying to Lesley the details about the guide's atrocities, I had never seen her so livid. Her eyes were red with anger, a dark crimson riddled with disgust. It was as if I had turned on a cellar light, deep in the recesses of her mind. I had a feeling this was the suppressed hatred that had been building inside of her since hearing of her grandmother's murder. Would she be able to control it once we had this guy on the table? She had already shown her composure and self-control when she found me in my lab, but she hadn't watched the actual release. She had only seen the aftermath.

• • •

After the café, we made our way over to the graveyard just in time for the next tour. I had to make sure the guide was back to his normal routine and had not gone into hiding after my near run-in with him. Of course, I didn't tell Lesley that he may have seen me. The purpose of the outing was more to check his continuity. It would finish smoothing over my absence last night, and allow her time to take everything in.

We found a spot not far from the graveyard, and watched as the guide strolled around, leading tourists as if his ritual the previous night was routine. I didn't know how frequently he conducted those rituals, but judging by his actions, it was likely often. Was it a weekly occurrence? Or was it more of a seasonal thing, as in Mardi Gras, when the young ones come out to play? They arrived primed and ready, sedated with alcohol and easily snared by a local story and some cheap parlor tricks. His makeshift creep shop down a dark alley didn't have to be shrouded in candy to attract the teenage Hansel and Gretel. It could be poorly lit, dingy, and even scream murderous dungeon, and they would still come seeking adventure. Obviously, those typical teenage horror films were onto something.

Once we spotted the guide, Lesley expressed her eagerness to head back to the hotel and begin the planning stage. I agreed, but we stayed a little longer to help her develop some patience. A hurried release makes for a messy release I told her, and she nodded in agreement, letting her eagerness simmer in the cool afternoon breeze.

• • •

Back at the hotel, we ordered room service. Lesley didn't touch any of the food on her plate, blaming her nerves. I thought of my own first release, but didn't recall being nervous. It was more excitement than anything. I didn't have someone mentoring me or comforting my moves. I just winged it, hoping I wouldn't make any major mistakes. And I didn't. Things fell into place with Ms. Dundee, almost as if it were meant to happen that way. After all, how much of a challenger would I be if I were captured during my first battle?

An hour before twilight we began our preparation, which included going over a few of the items in my backpack. Thanks to foresight and a little paranoia, I'd had a stash of my supplies hidden in my lab, which I shoved into a bag before fleeing Dallas. Given Lesley's medical background, I didn't have to explain the details behind the IV kits and syringes, but I did give her a rundown on the other things she could use in a pinch, especially if I were to become incapacitated for any reason. She tried stopping me, explaining with the palm of her hand that she didn't want to face that possibility. I gave her the abridged edition anyway.

I figured an hour would be plenty of time to prep, but once again I overlooked the fact that Lesley was a woman and needed more time. Thankfully it wasn't much more time, because we were already in disguise and had limited apparel. She changed only once. She did remind me about my own attire, wondering why I hadn't chosen the navy overalls she'd caught me wearing in my lab. I shrugged it off with a laugh, and without explaining that I wore the overalls in order to reveal my work uniform underneath at the ideal moment during the release. I wanted the releases to be official, and for the scum to know I'd witnessed their evil firsthand on the streets after they called me for help. But things had obviously changed now.

Our plan was pretty straightforward. Considering that the guide was in his shop and alone, we would conduct the release there and leave his suit right where it lay. It would likely be a while before anyone came looking for him. I relayed to Lesley that this was part of the beauty of releasing the dregs of society. She agreed, expressing her relief at not having to dispose of anything. She also delicately reminded me of my words: that she was only 'observing' the release.

Before I allowed Lesley to enter the poorly lit alley, I did a quick search to make sure there weren't any surprise guests. It was empty, and spooky, as Lesley put it.

"Are you ready?" I asked.

"I think so," she said, cupping her gloved hands over her mouth while blowing warm air into them. "I mean, yes. I'm ready."

"I can do this alone if you want to turn back," I offered.

She tilted her head and sighed, and nudged me forward. "Let's go. It's cold out here."

"All right," I said, stifling a smile.

We scurried along the edges of the brick wall like a couple of rats, stopping when we got to the lone dumpster in the alley. I admit to being a little theatrical, but it was to remind her to slow down, despite the cold, and remember her surroundings, especially the potential dangers lurking all around us.

"This is almost too cliché for a murderer's hideout," Lesley said, kneeling behind me. She jerked her head around as a few leaves shuffled along the corners of the alley.

"Okay, it's still clear," I said, waving a hand for her to follow me.

"How did you ever find this place?" She realized how close we were to the door and lowered her voice to a whisper. "There aren't any signs. Didn't you say this was a voodoo shop?"

"Yeah," I said, "but not a legit one. There was a broken wooden sign leaned up against the wall with 'Voodoo Shop' painted in sloppy letters. He obviously put it out only when he was expecting company."

"How could anyone fall for that?" she asked.

I shrugged and motioned for her to stay against the wall while I tried the door. It was locked this time. I pulled a multi-tool from my pocket and started working the lock. A few seconds later, I slowly cracked open the door.

"How did you do that?" Lesley asked. I didn't answer. I peered into the dark entrance, blocking her with my free arm. "I don't know why I'm surprised," she muttered. We crept into the open room. Lesley hung on the door, keeping it partially open with her left foot, and lingering as if not wanting to completely close herself inside the unfamiliar dwelling. The incense wasn't there, but the familiar smell I couldn't quite place the first time — the metallic scent of blood — still hung in the air. I pulled her forward by the hand, and after a forceful jerk, she released her stubborn foot from the door.

"What is that smell?" she asked. "I mean, besides the old building mildew smell."

"That would be blood," I said, stopping at the next door.

I felt her body stiffen as she leaned up against me. "What are we doing?" Her words were riddled with anxiety after hearing the word *blood*.

"Listening."

"For?"

"Relax, we have to do this right. We need the element of surprise."

"Right… you're right," she said. "I'll be quiet now."

We both flinched when a door suddenly slammed shut. It sounded like it had come from the rear of the building. This was good, because at least he was there. I knelt down beside the open door, pulling Lesley down with me, and removed a syringe from my front pocket, readying it in my right hand. We watched the door intently, waiting for the guide to emerge. I began blinking my eyes rapidly, attempting to speed up the process of adjusting to the darkness, but it was no use. They would adjust at their own rate.

No one came bursting through the door, but I wasn't budging until the person who had entered became preoccupied with some sort of task. That would mean they weren't headed in our direction. I had no intention of an awkward bump in the dark. I couldn't see Lesley, but I could feel her hanging onto my shirt with a death grip. I wanted to tell her it was going to be okay, but this was all part of the experience. She needed to be scared and get the adrenaline flowing — feel the blood pumping, let the air fill her lungs, allow herself to focus.

A few moments later, I relaxed slightly when a small object hit the floor a few rooms back. This guy was nothing if he wasn't clumsy and loud. We pushed forward slowly toward the sporadic sounds. Something I hadn't considered — likely due to the fact that I'd been thrown off my game by Lesley's presence — was the possibility that he was performing another ritual. The missing Voodoo Shop sign was a good indicator that he wasn't. Then again, maybe he had a stash of victims locked away in a room I hadn't seen. I wouldn't put anything past this demented bastard.

Lesley was on my heels, still tugging on my shirt as if we were inching along in a haunted house at the fair. When we reached the door to his ritual room, it was cracked open, just as it had been the last time, and the large mirror on the wall reflected another dimly lit space flickering with candle light. I nudged Lesley back a few feet to my side, just in case the guy came barging through the door.

I could hear the guide shuffling around, although I couldn't see him through the small opening. I took a deep breath, hoping there wasn't another group of dead swinging from the ceiling, before pushing farther through the door. Moving as slowly as I could, I tried to make as little noise as possible. No visible victims yet, only residual splatters of blood on the wall and floor. The bowls that held the blood of the three teenagers were still there, but now appeared empty, save for the clotted stains. What did he do with the remaining blood after painting his face? Drink it, perhaps?

He came into view a few seconds later from across the room, still wearing his guide garb. In each hand, he carried a dead chicken by its neck. Had he switched to animals? Or did he use them when he couldn't find a human victim? I watched as he snatched up one of the bowls and, with his back toward me, knelt down. Then I heard drips of what I assumed was chicken blood draining into the bowls. I slid back out of view and faced Lesley.

"What's he doing?" she asked.

"Looks like he's preparing for another ritual."

"There are people in there? Alive?" she whispered too loudly.

"No, chickens, and they're dead already."

She sighed. "Chickens I can handle."

"Remember what we discussed," I said. "Our plan?" She sighed again, this one sounding more like dread. "Lesley."

"Okay, I got it," she said. "Just tell me when."

"I'm ready. Head that way. You remember how to get back, right?"

"Yes."

She left before I could reassure her. I knew she probably needed to hear something optimistic, but she decided to just 'rip it off like a bandaid' as she had told me during our planning stage.

I made my way one doorway back and propped myself against the wall. In a few seconds, I should have heard Lesley's knock, and a minute later he should have passed by me, where I would subdue him. At least that was the plan. We had to have a distraction, something to grab his attention, and Lesley had agreed to serve that purpose, although reluctantly. She needed a lot of assurance that I could take this guy down.

A minute went by and I hadn't heard the knock. Considering how nervous she had seemed, I decided to give her a little more time. Another two minutes passed and still no knock. I could feel that something was wrong. My imagination cranked to high and many horrible scenarios quickly filled the eager space in my mind. The only one that didn't end in disaster was the one in which she decided that all of this was too much, and she walked back to the hotel. But even that had its dangers.

I got up from my crouching position and made my way toward the entrance. Halfway there, I heard a male's voice coming from Lesley's direction. Though it was only a murmur, I could tell that it wasn't friendly. My instinct was to run toward her, save her if necessary, at all cost. But I also had to consider the guide. Making rash decisions was not conducive to our success, or even our survival. I slipped behind the door of the room I had moved into, giving me cover from both directions.

The echoes of their voices were clearer and moving closer. Through the door I could hear Lesley's angry, tremulous voice. "All right, I'm going."

Next, the man spoke. "Are you here by yourself? And you better not lie to me. This will be much more painful if you lie."

"I'm alone, I swear," Lesley said. "Let go of me, you jerk. You're hurting me. I said I'm going."

"Why are you here?" the man demanded.

It took every ounce of willpower not to barge forward and put an end to him, but I had to be smart and strike at the right moment. I could see a flashlight waving along the wall and two shadows entering the room. I could make out Lesley's hair. She was in front, and being jostled forward.

"This was the address I was told to come to. The guide from the cemetery tour told me to meet him here." Lesley was improvising nicely, warming me with pride. Good girl.

"Well, why didn't you say so?" His demeanor suddenly changed, jumping into character. "Harvey be my cousin." He switched on the same fake accent as the guide. "Harvey! Why didn't you tell me that you had a guest coming over tonight, mon?"

"Shit," I whispered to myself. "This isn't good. If the guide comes out to meet him —"

I could see the whites of Lesley's eyes from the flashlight waving across the room. They were watering. She appeared to be tearing up, but she was holding firm.

"Guest!?" the guide yelled from the other direction.

I remained steady as Lesley crossed the threshold of the door I was behind. The unknown man entered next. He appeared to be short and thick from what I could make out from his shadow. I had one shot at this, and if I missed… well, it could get messy.

Chapter 8

I grabbed Lesley's right arm and yanked her toward me, quickly lifting my hand to her mouth. She yelped and let herself fall once she realized it was me.

"What are you doing, clumsy girl?" the man said as he rounded the door and fumbled with his flashlight. "Come on, Harvey is waiting."

I kept Lesley behind the door and I stepped a few feet along the wall in the shadows, my gloved right hand at the ready. I motioned for Lesley to hit the door with her elbow in order to distract him toward her direction and away from me.

I heard the thump, and then saw the flashlight jerk down toward her, illuminating her fearful cower. "What are you doing behind the — " the man said, and then fell silent. Somehow I managed to find my mark in the minimal light. I slowly lowered him to the floor, nearly dropping him when the acrid smell of sweat and fish hit my nose.

"Where the hell has this guy been?" I said, shoving him off my foot and quickly swiping my nose with my hand.

Lesley hadn't spoken, or moved. I reached down and helped her up from the floor by her hand. "Are you okay?"

She leaned over and grabbed her knees, "Yeah… I just wasn't expecting to run into anyone."

"A little unforeseen action. It happens. Now, come on let's move into position. He'll come looking for his cousin, if that's really who he is, once he realizes he's not coming. And with an unexpected guest arriving, it shouldn't take him long."

We moved against the far wall of the room, away from the foul smelling cousin. I positioned Lesley safely in the corner, hopefully giving her time to recover, while I waited by the door way. I wanted to ask her if she was still okay, and inquire as to whether she had changed her mind about this endeavor. She was probably regretting her decision to come now that she had a few minutes to reflect, but she knew as well as I that once she had stepped foot inside this place, there was no turning back.

"What's taking you so long, cousin? Where be this guest?" the guide yelled, his voice moving toward us. A few seconds later he continued, this time with twinges of anxiety riddling his voice. "Cal, come on man. No time for jokes. You better be bringing me a lady." He began to hum an unknown tune, attempting to shroud his growing fear.

When he crossed the threshold of the door, I saw the reflective shine of a blade in his left hand. I motioned for Lesley to stay put. I quietly stood up and cautiously followed behind him as he made his way toward the next room, his hum now fixed to a single note of uncertain trepidation.

I don't know what I stepped on, but the popping sound was loud enough for the guide to turn around and swing the blade in his left hand toward me, catching my right forearm. I winced in pain, but thankfully didn't drop my syringe.

"You're not Cal," the guide said, raising his knife, ready

to hack anything in his path. "Who da hell are you?" After a brief hesitation, he began marching toward me, knife still raised. "You better answer me or I'm gonna cut you. No more warnings."

I stayed silent, defensively moving back to the room where Lesley was. A quiet, unseen foe is much more terrifying, I have found, especially when the prey is already drenched with uncertainty. His faint shadow followed mine, dancing in preparation for battle.

He attempted once again to gain a response from me. "You gonna regret not speaking after I cut your throat."

I had a syringe and needle, while he had a huge knife. My actions needed to be quick and precise. A light above us suddenly flipped on, illuminating in bright detail the skirmish taking place. Our squinted eyes met, and for a brief moment he seemed to recognize me. He looked dumbfounded.

Lesley started to scream, but quickly stifled it as she moved to the other side of the room, next to the slumbering cousin.

The guide glanced over at her, and then toward his cousin, who lay motionless on the floor. Before he had a chance to process the situation, I made my move. He swung his knife in the air aimlessly, but it was too late. I had him around the neck. Moments later, his arms went limp and the weapon clanged to the floor.

"It's all I could think to do," Lesley said, scooting away from the two men.

I smiled and breathed a sigh of relief. "It worked perfectly."

She smiled, and then wrapped her arms around me tightly.

• • •

Lesley and I agreed that the dank, creepy lair the guide used for his victims was more than a suitable place for him and his cousin to be released. He had enough rope lying around to secure them both, along with a convenient, though shoddy, pulley system. It was a good thing Lesley and I were both up to date on our tetanus shots. After securing their feet together, I pulled out two IV catheters and a bag of fluid from the small pack I had strapped to my back. Lesley watched silently, mesmerized by my routine, as I finished setting up for the release.

I thought about what it must look like from her perspective, seeing her boyfriend unfold his secrets one by one before her eyes. How would I have responded if Lesley had done the same? I probably would have goggled at her in astonishment, followed by praises of admiration and a longing to be apprenticed. But I didn't get that vibe from her. I got more of a mixture of curiosity and anxiety.

Once I'd completed my initial steps, I sat down beside Lesley among the flickering votive candles. I remained quiet, allowing her thoughts time to breathe as they continued processing the situation that was about to take place.

After a few minutes, she cleared her throat and spoke. "So we wait for them to wake up?"

"Yep."

"Then do you just give them a dose of whatever and watch? Do you talk with them?"

"We have a little chat usually, yes, and then I basically tell them their makers are waiting for them on the other side."

It would have been a perfect time to introduce the Gamemakers, how I was weaved in an eternal battle with them, constantly searching for the players they place on the battlefield, but I had yet to determine if she was an actual player herself. If I were to prematurely engage her in such a conversation, the consequences would likely be detrimental to us.

"Do you ever ask them if they're sorry for what they did?

If they have any remorse?"

"On occasion, if they feel chatty."

"So there are times you don't talk to them at all? It's all over that quick?"

"Lesley, you have to realize these are nasty minions killing innocent people."

"Minions?"

"You know what I mean. They're scum, scavengers preying on the vulnerable."

"What about this other guy here?" she said. "How do we know he killed anyone? What if he's innocent?"

I took a second to contemplate her question. "If it makes you feel better, we'll get him to confess before we release him."

She seemed to like the idea, nodding with contentment. But I knew the other guy also played a role in the murderous scam. If not the trigger man, he was definitely part of the killing. Had I screwed up and been captured, Lesley would have been sacrificed, or had something even more sinister done to her by these two. There was no doubt in my mind.

A few minutes of silence passed before Lesley spoke again. I knew it was coming. On our way down to New Orleans, we'd briefly talked about the subject, but I never elaborated. I acted as if I may have had a brief glimpse, which wasn't entirely false. I *have* had glimpses, but there were many, and they have become more frequent since the first one. And not just visuals either. I have had nearly all of my senses tested since I set out on my quest to find the elusive entity.

"What if we see the soul?" she asked. "What do we do?"

"Count it as a double success, of course. We stopped two scum from killing more innocent people, *and* we got to see a soul. What more could you ask for?"

She mulled over the idea, but it didn't seem to satisfy her, so I decided to remind her about her vendetta. "Your grandma was murdered by trash like these. She was a vulnerable prey, a soft target easily disposed of."

After a brief pause, she spoke with vigor, her words intensifying with each syllable. "Yes, she was a very gentle woman who would help anyone in need." Her tears simmered under her lids, ready for eruption. "Okay." She nodded, her face stern.

"Okay," I said, walking over to the guide and removing a piece of cloth from his shirt. I then tied it around the head of the cousin, like a bandana, to cover his eyes. "So he can't identify us."

"Thank you," Lesley said. "I just want us to be sure."

Before I sat back down, the guide started to wake up, struggling with the ropes bound around his wrists. Startled, Lesley got to her feet and moved behind me so as not in direct sight of the man. He jerked his head around, attempting to make sense of his dire predicament. When he finally looked our way, staring me up and down and then pausing briefly toward Lesley behind me, he grunted and attempted to spit at me. I stepped back a few feet, dodging his poor attempt at bargaining, and broke out into a wry grin.

"Any more of that and I'll end this now, without a chance of redemption," I said.

"What da hell is this, mon? What do ya want?"

"You can stop with the fake accent. We're not on one of your tours."

"I remember you two," he said angrily. "From the graveyard."

"Then you'll remember the three teenagers who were on that tour also."

He rolled his eyes toward the ceiling as if to recall them while shaking his head from side to side. "I see a lot of teenagers on the tour."

I glanced down at the three bowls on the floor and then back up at him. He knew I'd been there the other night.

While in his murderous trance, he had seen me in the reflection behind the whites of his eyes. "I suppose this is a harmless place of peaceful worship, and the pulleys you and your friend are hoisted from are for … ?"

"Voodoo, mon. I hang chickens from them, drain their blood in the bowls. Rituals, that's all. I'll show you if you like."

"Don't try to beguile me, as you do your victims. This isn't voodoo you're practicing. Voodoo doesn't involve murdering the innocent." I was irritated by his persistent denials, feeling a bolus of rage sneak up my back and along my neck. I took a deep breath and turned toward Lesley. Her eyes darted toward the cousin, who was now shuffling around.

"Where the hell am I?! Harvey, are you there?" the cousin said.

"Be quiet, mon. Yes, I'm here," the guide said.

"Why am I blindfolded and tied? What's happening?"

"We have guests, cousin."

"The girl? She did this to us? How — "

"Yes, we did," I said, interrupting.

"Who are you? And why am I tied up? Harvey, are you tied too?" The cousin's voice trembled.

"Yes, now be quiet and let our captors tell us what they want."

"Thank you, Harvey," I said, "Your cousin … "

"Cal," the guide said.

"Don't tell him my name," Cal pleaded.

"Cal, I already knew your name," I said. "Now, let me ask you a question and we can move on. I need your cooperation or these bowls will be full once again." I had the three bowls at their feet.

Cal gulped loudly and said, "I'll tell you whatever you want." Sweat was beading down his face below the blindfold.

"Thank you," I said. "I only have one question for the

two of you, but I want Cal to answer me first. Do both of you understand?" They both nodded. "Great. Where do you dispose of the bodies?"

Cal didn't answer immediately. He looked toward his cousin as if the blindfold wasn't there. That was enough for me to conclude his involvement, but Lesley would need more.

"I ... I don't know what ya mean by bodies," Cal responded.

"Okay, I see this is going to take some persuasion. I don't have time for games from you two."

I grabbed the guide's IV line and gave him a mild dose, just enough to sedate him. "Wait! Don't ..." the guide started. A few seconds later his eyes were glazed over and he was mumbling incoherently. I stuffed a wad of cloth into his mouth.

"Harvey! What did you do to him!? Harvey!"

I whispered in Lesley's ear to get me a container of water from the sink in the restroom. She didn't ask why, only hurried to retrieve it. She returned thirty seconds later and handed me a glass of dirty water.

"Cal, I'm going to ask you one more time. Where do y'all dispose of the bodies?"

"Harvey, what do I tell him?" Cal called out to his incapacitated cousin, while attempting to loosen his restraints. "Harvey, come on man, answer me." I picked up the bowl and tapped it on the floor so he would recognize the sound. "What are you doing? Harvey, what is he doing?" Cal's voice was quivering.

I picked up the knife the guide had been wielding earlier, making sure to clang it on the ground, and picked up the glass of water in my other hand. I began pouring it into the bowl from a few feet above.

"Cal, I assume that sound is familiar to you?" I asked in a serious tone.

"Harvey!"

I shoved the cool steel of the blade against Cal's neck from behind him and whispered, "Your cousin is no longer with us. If you don't want to join him, I suggest you answer my question. Where do you dispose of the bodies? You already know I'm not a man of patience, so be quick."

"In the graveyard," he blurted out. "Under the tombs. But I was just following orders. Harvey does all of the killings. He makes me watch sometimes, but I never hurt anyone. I swear."

"Why didn't you stop him?"

"He would have killed me. He threatened me all the time."

"Why not just leave," I asked. "Tell the police?"

"He raised me. He's the only family I have left."

I don't know why, but I believed him. He was raised by his cousin to be a lookout man and help with disposal. Nothing more. I knew what it was like to have no one, no family to confide in. My uncle was all I had left in this world, but I certainly couldn't confide in a homicide detective.

"I believe you, Cal," I said, lowering the blade from his neck.

He sighed heavily. "Thank you."

I grabbed the syringe and whispered to Lesley, "I'm only going to put him to sleep." She nodded in agreement. A few seconds later he was snoring loudly.

"Okay, are you ready to do this?" I asked.

"I think so. Yes. But I'm not pushing the meds."

"Are you sure?" I said, tempting her toward her destiny.

"I'm sure."

I knew her likely response even before she said it. The dubious look on her face when I offered her the syringe revealed enough. I reminded her that the soul was fickle and didn't always show up for the party. I also didn't reveal that the Gamemakers had all the control and that they decided, as part of their game, whether to allow us players to perceive the soul in whatever form they chose. It was all part of their deception, a way to tweak the game by messing with the mind.

Lesley didn't seem to care if the soul showed up or not. She was likely preoccupied with seeing death in its raw form. I knew she had seen many lives end in the emergency room, but not the last remaining breath, not the moment the soul escapes its prison. This would be a new experience for her, and I was more than curious how she would respond, how it would all affect her.

I grabbed another full syringe from my pack and attached it to the guide's IV line. I glanced back at Lesley. She was staring at him, transfixed. I emptied the syringe into his IV and then stood back beside her. We both watched, motionless, as if we were enjoying the climax to a riveting horror movie. Justice was finally being served to the callous killer.

Usually my attention would be on the heart monitor, preparing myself for the moment of release, but I had no equipment this time, so that wasn't possible. I watched Lesley instead, imagining what was going through her head at that very moment. Was she picturing herself releasing her grandma's murderer? Was she filled with relief that justice was finally being served before her very eyes? Was she waiting for the soul to poke its head out and scream?

The flickering shadows behind Lesley were interrupted by a larger shadow. I immediately switched my attention back to the guide.

"Did you see that?" I whispered.

"Where?" she asked, turning toward me for direction, her eyes wide with alarm.

The room suddenly dimmed. A handful of the candles had blown out. I turned toward the exit, to the room beside the huge mirror. Lesley's eyes followed mine, her face now rigid. I felt bumps raise along my neck and arms as a chill hit the air. I let out a heavy breath, attempting to visualize the warm air from my lungs meeting the sudden cool air. Just as I inhaled, a dark figure appeared above Cal, enveloping him in complete darkness. And then the figure vanished just as quickly as it had arrived, like a tornado sucked back into the ominous sky above — or below in his case.

"He's gone," I said.

"How do you know?" Lesley asked, jerking her head around the room. "What did you see?"

"He moved along the wall and then briefly hovered above his cousin."

"Wait, what, how did I miss that? I didn't see anything," she said, disappointed.

"They never hang around for long. Sorry. Did you at least feel the room get colder?"

"Maybe a little. I can't be sure. But I did notice that a few of the candles blew out."

"I guess I'm just more sensitive to it all by now," I said.

Of course I was. This is what I was meant to do. It was all part of their plan: revealing certain truths and keeping me alert and hunting. The satisfaction of finding and beating their players was my reward.

Was it the guide I had seen? Or some other entity that had been lingering here? I wasn't sure this time. In my own lab, I knew everyone who had been released, but not this unfamiliar place. I had no idea how many innocent victims had seen this death chamber. And I wasn't sure if the innocent would go running from their suits, as the dirty ones did. They could be the blurs and shadows I see portions of lately. I knew it was all part of my progression. With each release comes new challenges, and more deceit.

Chapter 9

We removed Cal from the pulley system, rebinding his hands and feet with some leftover rope, and attached a note to his chest: *If you attempt to find me or go to the police, you will face the same fate as your cousin's victims. Remember, I know everything about you and the graves. Leave town. P.S. There is a knife in your cousin's back pocket. Your pal, Me.*

Lesley pointed out that the cousin had seen her and heard her voice, but I quickly reminded her of the poor lighting in the room, as well as his skittish behavior. He wouldn't hang around for long without his cousin there to guide him. Besides, I wasn't planning on us staying in New Orleans for much longer. We had been in one location for too long already. Our next place of residence was always on my mind. A boat to the islands — the Caribbean, perhaps? I recalled how peaceful and calm my thoughts were when Dave, I, Lesley, and her friend Angie traveled to the Gulf Coast for a brief vacation. The warm blue water, the suntan lotion and salt water filling my senses, vacationers minding their own business and happy to be away from their mundane smog-filled lives. A jocular palm tree swaying, atmosphere interrupted by the occasional hurricane and seasonal tropical rain.

I snapped back and reminded myself, quite angrily I might add, that Dr. Randal was a bigger priority than finding a secluded tropical setting. Not to mention the dilemma of how I was going to continue my battle on a small island. Anonymity in a vast pool of souls was paramount to my mission, especially if this ended up being an ongoing team effort.

Lesley was pumped, as my old medic partner Dave liked to say. She didn't fall asleep until early the next morning. Unfortunately for me, I had yet to sleep more than an hour, thanks to the array of complications sprouting new tendrils with each thought. I had to take back control, form a plan, and now that Lesley seemed to be taking on the role of partner, I needed her input. It was vital that I know her true intentions. Was she serious about this work, and could she handle a life of releasing dirty souls?

For about fifteen minutes after the release, things were a bit rocky and could have gone either way. She sat in the corner of the room for a long while by herself, not saying a word, and I wasn't going to interrupt whatever process she was employing to deal with what had just happened. I began cleaning up my supplies, periodically glancing back toward her just in case she needed me. When she finally spoke, she was still seated. She had a befuddled look on her face. At least that was how I interpreted it at the time. It turned out to be a look of concern for me.

"You've been holding this in for how long?" she asked. "That must have been torture."

I don't know what I was expecting her to say, but I just smiled and replied, "I have to admit, it feels good to get it off my chest."

She stood up and walked toward me with open arms, wrapping them around my waist. I held her back, unsure what to do next. I had in my mind that this was about her discovering herself, and then she made it about me. What did it mean? Was she a player? Or was she just accompanying me, along for the ride?

It was ten thirty before Lesley woke. She looked more rested than I had seen her since we arrived in New Orleans. The sun was annoyingly bright, attempting to tweak my circadian rhythm in its rightful place. The moon had attempted the same feat the night before and was much less successful. Insomnia stretched his legs out and relaxed, feet propped up on the counter, head tilted back, giggling like a mischievous child.

As I sat sipping my third cup of coffee on the balcony, I considered Lesley's idea of visiting an urgent care facility and pleading for some sleeping pills. The headaches from sleep deprivation were surpassing annoyance level, and Ibuprofen and Tylenol weren't working anymore. I quickly put on one of my varnished smiles when Lesley lolled over to me from behind the sheer curtain. Her smile was completely genuine.

"Good morning," she said.

"Hey." I put down my coffee and scooted the chair next to me a little closer.

"Did you sleep?" she asked, kissing my cheek and running her hand through my hair before taking the chair.

"Not enough, but I'm okay. It looks like you slept well."

"Too well. Probably the adrenaline high from last night. I crashed pretty hard once I fell asleep."

"Yeah, you were out. I put on a movie and the volume kept fluctuating up and down, but you didn't budge."

"I've been thinking about last night and I have a few ideas," she said, spryly.

What was this? She was taking initiative in our endeavor? This could be good. She was committing.

"Okay," I said.

"Let's go out today and people watch. I want you to

teach me what to look for. You know, how you read people and stuff like that."

"Doesn't sound like a terrible idea." It was a good first step, allowing me to see her potential. See if she possessed some intuition of her own.

"Then it's settled." She got up from the table and leaned over to kiss me. "I'll be ready faster than usual."

"Wait a second," I said, motioning for her to sit back down. She quickly settled back into the chair, placing her hands playfully under her chin. "We need to agree on one thing before we go out today."

"What is it?" she asked.

"I think we've been here too long. It's time to start thinking about where to go next."

For a second she looked as if I had stolen her new puppy right out of her hands, but she quickly bounced back and said, "I know, I was thinking the same thing."

"We don't have to leave right this second. But we need to be thinking about it."

She smiled, rose from her chair, and plopped down onto my knee.

"I'm with you for as long as you want me." She hugged me around the neck.

The word she used at the graveyard played over and over in my head: *married*. Somehow, her statement "as long as you want me" was another hint for me to get on with it already and ask the question. Maybe she thought her commitment should be matched by a commitment of my own… Whoa. I was beginning to scare myself a little. I think I found the hidden message embedded in her words. If I was right, I was getting way too good at this little game of relationships — something I had been horrible at my entire life.

"Thank you," was all I could think to say.

She got up from my knee with a smile and left to get ready.

I wanted her to tell me her thoughts about where she might want to go, but her silence meant she intended for me to mull over her last words. She knew exactly what she was doing. Of course it had worked, but only briefly. I had to come up with a plan to get us back to Dallas, safely, so I could avenge my mom. My involving Lesley in the decision-making was strategic. I needed to subtly introduce the prospect of releasing Dr. Randal, and have *her* bring up the idea of returning to Dallas. I also needed her sympathy, her permission to allow us to surpass logic and plummet ourselves back into the hunting den.

My first priority was keeping us safe. The second was plotting my revenge on Dr. Randal. We certainly couldn't stay in this place. New Orleans had more than enough dirty souls meandering its streets, but we needed to keep moving. And roaming the world as the Ambiguous Releasing Duo wasn't exactly practical either.

Our faces weren't plastered on the billboards yet. However, I was sure that was coming, once my uncle became frustrated. I suspected that he wanted to arrest me personally, so he was giving me a chance to turn myself in. But eventually he would surrender to his detective roots and use his resources. He always got his man, family connection or not. *By any means necessary* — a phrase I had heard him use on more than one occasion.

Chapter 10

I have never considered myself much of a people person, at least socially, but observing them is another thing entirely. Watching doesn't involve awkward handshakes, forced smiles, or the male cliché greeting, "What's up?" followed by a fist bump. Over time, watching became my sanctuary, a place where I felt comfortable, a place where I now overshadow the rest, thanks to the Gamemakers. Though they have granted me the ability to spot their minions, I have yet to acquire much more skill in the social arena, especially when it comes to the opposite sex. Deciphering just a few of Lesley's riddles has taken me many long nights, with many mistakes along the way, including some that have nearly ended our relationship. It is Lesley's pity toward my cluelessness that has allowed us to survive as a couple.

Our first people-watching session would take place at the French Quarter, more specifically Jackson Square, sitting on a park bench near St. Louis Cathedral. Though the morning was still quite cool, we found a quaint spot, and I welcomed the morning rays for the first time since arriving in the city. Wearing sunglasses, holding paper coffee cups, and sporting typical tourist attire, we appeared to be a bright-eyed, zestful couple waiting for the attractions to open.

"I like that we're among the first ones out here," Lesley said. "It's so pleasant without all the crowds."

I smiled beneath my sunglasses and took a sip of coffee.

"I thought it would give us time to talk, while enjoying a great view." I glanced over at her as I spoke. "It's intriguing how the sight of something beautiful can warm the senses, and elevate a conversation." She blushed, but didn't dare assume I meant her, though I most certainly did. Coy modesty was one of her many lovable traits. "Anyway, the crowds will be here soon enough to screw it up, and then we can begin our lesson."

"I'm ready to learn," she said eagerly. "So, what did you want to talk about? Anything specific?" She cupped her coffee with both hands, gingerly sipping the warm liquid.

"We never finished our conversation about our next stop," I said.

She stared forward and sighed, seeming to lose her recent burst of energy. "It's time, I suppose," she said absently. "Just when things were getting good."

"I know and I'm sorry, but I promise we'll continue where we left off, wherever we decide to go. By the way, do you have any suggestions?"

She continued to stare forward and said, "I have a few, yes." She looked over at me, her eyes fixed on mine. "But first, don't you think we should talk about what's going on? Or not going on, I should say."

"Huh?"

"The fact that your face isn't plastered all over the news, for one thing. Or mine. I mean, it's been weeks. You'd think there would be something by now." She sounded irritated, as if I should have brought it up earlier. I realized it was just the uncertainty getting to her, not knowing what was coming next.

"I agree it's a little odd," I said. "I don't know what to say, but it doesn't mean they aren't looking for me. Or us."

"Tryke, you have to consider the possibility that your uncle may have let you go. I've been thinking about it for a while now. You must have been, too."

"I've considered it, but — " I stopped myself. I was about to tell her my theory, but why interrupt her path of getting us back home? If she thought my uncle was still pursuing us, either alone or working with other undercover agencies, it could dissuade her from returning.

"Okay. Let's say you're right, and he *has* let us go. What does it mean? You want us to stop running?"

"Well, first off, it means we might actually be able to have a somewhat normal life. Whatever that may be..." she trailed off.

"I haven't actually considered living a normal life since we left," I said. "But I suppose it could eventually work out that way."

"It's all I've thought about, Tryke. A life as close as we can get to normal. I know, we're anything but normal, and normal is boring, but I just want us to be together and safe — not running for our lives."

I sighed. "No, you're right. Me too, but... I don't know. I guess I've been too preoccupied with our situation to even consider a normal life."

"Our situation, as in the guide? Or is there something else I don't know about?" she asked, studying me suspiciously.

She came dangerously close to placing her hands on her hips, but I thwarted it by answering quickly. "You know about it. I mentioned it on the way down here." She looked out the corner of her eye, attempting to recall the information. "My mom, and how she was treated," I said, trying to prompt her memory.

"You mean the stuff about the psychiatrist?"

I nodded. "Dr. Randal, yes."

"That was a horrible thing he did to your mom." I lowered my head and clasped my hands together, still nodding. "Have you thought about… you know, getting rid of him?" she said carefully.

"I would be lying if I said no. I've never stopped thinking of him, the way he twisted her thoughts. How vulnerable and sad she was, right up until her last breath." Lesley set her coffee down at her feet and placed her hands on top of mine.

"Let's go home, Tryke. We can work on a plan to avenge your mom on the way. And we can check on Dave. I know he'd like to hear your voice."

"You mean *your* voice," I said. "He's always liked you better."

She ignored my comment.

"And we'll stay as far away from your uncle as possible. I need to know you want the same thing. I don't want to be the only one making the decision, in case we do happen to get caught."

I looked at her. "Avenging my mom would be nice."

"So it's settled," she said with a half smile. "We'll plan our trip home tonight over dinner." Lesley's energy returned instantly, as if it had been hiding and just itching to pounce once a direction had been reached. If she was happy, I was happy. After all, we'd both get what we wanted by returning to Dallas. But what was happening to me? I was falling prey to the 'happy wife, happy life' crowd, only worse. I was just a visitor, a mere tourist, not yet ready to take the plunge into holy matrimony.

Not wanting to ruin Lesley's mood change, I didn't bring up the fact that I wasn't looking to move back to Dallas. This was temporary. Still, she must have known we couldn't work and live in that city permanently. My uncle wasn't going anywhere. And even if he did pretend to let me go, which was unlikely, it would be *game on* the first time he caught a glimpse of me. The best scenario I could foresee was him deciding not to involve Lesley. At least then she could finish medical school. I would live close by in the shadows until she was finished, doing odd jobs for cash. For now, my plan was to weave this sensitive bit of information into our discussions during the trip back.

A few tourists had showed up in our vicinity. They were dawdling around, brandishing maps and fanny packs. I settled back onto the bench and placed my arm around Lesley. We both enjoyed the feeling of relaxation, however brief.

"Let's see what you got," I said.

She removed her sunglasses and began scanning the thin crowd. A chipper air surrounded her, now that we had set a plan into motion. Things seemed right with the world.

"Rookie mistake," I said, without looking at her. Always keep your sunglasses on, so when you spot one, they won't suspect you. Eye contact is never good in the preliminary stage." She quickly placed her sunglasses back over her eyes. I stifled a grin.

"So what should I be looking for?" she asked.

"I want you to use your instincts. Find someone, anyone, and tell me what you think."

After a few minutes, she focused her gaze on a man wearing suit pants and a crisp white shirt and tie, with no jacket. He was on his phone, pacing between a couple with two kids and an older man dressed in ragged attire and sitting alone in the grass.

"Why did you pick the man on the phone instead of the guy seated on the ground?"

"Cell phones seem to be a decent distraction," she said. "He may be drawing attention to himself by using it, but he's also quickly dismissed as nothing more than annoying. The man in the grass appears way too inconspicuous, meaning people will naturally avoid him because they think he'll ask for a handout."

"Hmmm, not bad," I said. "It would be easy these days to dismiss a common annoyance, such as a loud person sharing a private phone conversation. Believe me, I have wanted to release some of them on many occasions. But there needs to be more. Was there anything else about him that made you suspicious?"

"No, not really. Only that he seemed out of place in his attire. What about you? Did you spot anyone?"

"I was paying attention to the couple with the two kids."

She seemed surprised by my choice. "Really? Why?"

"The husband has been disciplining the children the entire time, while the mom is staring at the couple beside them. She isn't simply ignoring her family while on a cell phone or some other device or book. There's no annoyance or frustration on her face. She appears to be desensitized to her husband and children, somehow pushed past the point of caring, to a more sinister place."

"Do you think she's going to kill someone?" Lesley asked, now glancing toward the woman with grave concern. "Her family?"

She turned back toward me and I shrugged. "Relax," I said. "She just grabbed my attention for a moment. She's intriguing. Maybe she's staring at the other couple and wishing she could go back to when she and her husband were alone, without the kids. Or maybe she's thinking about leaving everything behind and running. Or planning her suicide. Or a rendezvous with a lover. The point is, to me, she's the odd one in this particular group."

"Interesting. So should we pursue her?"

"No. First, we would have to know more about her. Follow her. Engage with her. Find out if she has ever killed anyone. Besides, we're here to observe only. Okay, enough about her. Who else?" I quickly changed the subject. I had to make sure Lesley understood that I never released an innocent.

"But, what about the kids? What if she really is going to hurt them, or their father? Don't you have an obligation to —?"

"Wait, wait a second," I said. "I think you have this all wrong. I haven't had to search for these people before. They've come to me, on calls. I sought out the guide for you, but I don't usually do things that way. Yes, I feel a certain... compulsion to help people in potential danger. But I can't just go release someone based on a hunch. And I certainly can't pursue everyone who appears odd. If I did, I'd never get a break."

"I'm trying to understand," she said, "but you won't let me."

"What do you mean?"

"You say you don't help everyone, or release everyone you suspect. So what are your rules? Who gets saved?"

"It's complicated, but the truth is, I don't have many rules. Only that the ones I release harm the innocent. And now that I can't work as a paramedic, I suppose I'll have to alter my tactics." But I didn't have to change anything. They had shown their tenacity for the game, and I knew they would follow me wherever I decided to go. I never had to become a paramedic, and I never had to build a lab — that was only the first arena. They had many more in store for me. I was sure about that.

"You mean *we'll* have to alter *our* tactics," she said.

"Of course," I said, smiling like a proud father.

As the morning grew warmer, the crowds began to fill the area around us. We sat on the bench and watched for a few more hours, and by the end Lesley, seemed to be getting the hang of spotting the less overtly shady individuals. She was taking this a lot farther than I ever anticipated. But what if she didn't turn out to be a fellow player? What would they do with her if she continued assisting me? Would they consider it an unfair advantage, and get rid of her? Or would they simply look at it as a challenge, and make their opposing players even craftier and more insidious?

• • •

The closer it got to lunch, the more distracted Lesley became, questioning my suggestions for food type and restaurant choices. She ultimately talked herself into a place that advertised shrimp po'boys, claiming to serve the best in New Orleans. No matter the claim, I had no real interest in food at that moment. My head was pounding, and the headache was causing bouts of nausea. The pain became so intense on the way to the restaurant that I lost any ability to focus, unable to answer any of the questions Lesley was firing at me concerning our morning activities.

A few steps from the restaurant, I felt myself stumble. Insomnia had finally managed to break me physically, knocking me to the ground and rendering me helpless.

When I opened my eyes, Lesley was standing over me, along with a man with an impressive beard and a dirt-stained face. I immediately scooted backward on the sidewalk, like a scared dog, unable to comprehend my surroundings or circumstances. Lesley attempted to comfort me, while the man repeated, "Sir, you're okay. Sir, you're okay."

Who was this bearded stranger, and why was he so confident in my safety? For that matter, why was he so close to Lesley? I quickly got to my feet and leaned against the brick facade of the restaurant. I was still dizzy, but I regained my focus, enough to realize the man with the dirty face was merely a concerned bystander. Not surprisingly, he was the only other person bothering to help me. An individual passed out on the streets of New Orleans was not a rare sight, especially when Mardi Gras was close enough that you could smell the stench of debauchery emanating from the streets like a morning mist. I took in the man's appearance. Stained clothing and a tattered tan backpack.

Beside him, wheel cocked toward the building, was a dilapidated bike pulling a two-wheeled carrying basket that I assumed represented all of his worldly possessions.

The resilience of the soul — its ability to rebound after a lifetime of constant pelting — has always fascinated me. How this apparently homeless man empathized with my situation and immediately offered a hand and words of calming encouragement. Of course, my instincts told me that he was too close to Lesley, especially considering that we had no idea who he was. I pulled Lesley next to me and straightened myself up. I could see in his eyes that this was a common reaction people had toward him, but he seemed to accept it as a fact of life. He had built a defense, and could safely interact and assist from the other side of it. I quickly thanked him for his concern and shook his hand. I offered him money for a meal, but he politely refused.

"No thank you, sir. I'm just glad you're okay." He offered us directions to a nearby medical center, which Lesley gladly accepted and jotted down.

"I'll get a po'boy later," she said. "Right now, you're going to the hospital." She thanked the bearded man, offering him one more gesture of money for a meal. The man again politely declined with a wave of his hand.

I really couldn't argue too much on the subject. I needed sleep, and it was obvious that I wasn't going to get it without medication.

Chapter 11

I couldn't stop my right foot from tapping on the linoleum floor. I was nervous, but why? Medical facilities were certainly not a new setting for me.

Lesley had been insisting for a while that I go to the emergency room, so she was pleased with my eventual decision to see a physician. The urgent care center across the street from the public LSU hospital wasn't especially crowded for noon, and the nurse told us that we would likely be seen within the hour — from what I knew, it was an unprecedented feat to be given a timeframe in a no-appointment facility. But at that point, I couldn't have cared less if I had to wait twelve or more hours. I didn't want to admit it to myself at the time, but a part of me was glad I was seeking help to finally get some sleep. Of course, my friend would also be missed, as he offered me rare glimpses into the dusty articles hidden deep within my mind's veiled basement. Such opportunities always helped to shed new light onto complicated and vexing conundrums.

The likely culprit behind my repetitive tapping was the idea of bringing attention to myself in such a vulnerable manner. I would be singled out and analyzed from head to toe in a small private room. If there were ever a chance of being spotted, it was then and there. So of course we took precautions by forming a simple story and sticking with it: we had been mugged the previous night, our wallets were stolen, and a trip to the police station would be futile because it was dark and the assailant was wearing a mask. We were a pair of frustrated, naive tourists aimlessly wandering the streets of New Orleans, out of luck and in need of assistance.

Thankfully, the nausea had subsided, though the pounding in my head was still there, which only served to intensify the haze that surrounded me. Lesley, seeing the annoyance on my face, had stopped trying to comfort me and was quietly reading her magazine. I even had trouble tolerating the rare silence of a medical facility waiting room.

I attempted to close my eyes, leaning my head back against the wall, but a couple across from us began arguing about the wait time while their child, a boy around eight years old, sat beside them reading a paperback book that I would consider a long read. I turned my attention to an elderly man in the corner. He was fixated on the blank wall in front of him. Beside him sat an aluminum walker with taped handles. He was wearing a pair of khaki pants, slightly too short, exposing a pair of easy-slip-on velcro shoes — a tradition adopted by seniors to eradicate the tedious day to day tying of shoelaces. His light blue button-up shirt was ironed, creased, and tucked in. He appeared to be alone, waiting patiently for his name to be called. I don't know why, but I suddenly had a sinking feeling in my gut as I began reflecting on my own future life.

I pictured the elderly Tryke, seated alone and staring at inanimate objects in a public arena — in a restaurant or on a park bench. I was retired, but never quite. The Gamemakers had unleashed another of their tricks by bestowing upon me an eidetic memory with a lifetime guarantee, allowing me to recall every battle, every misfortune, every painful moment in my life, over and over. But that wasn't the worst of it. Not only would I have a perfect memory, but I would be granted exceptional longevity. I would be the most sane man on earth, living well past the shelf-life of my physical body. My internal screaming would attempt to drive sanity away, but a looming darkness placed deep within would put it back in its place. Pitiful and miserable, I would spend eternity desperately longing for a blissfully ignorant mind. Lesley would have passed before me, her life snuffed out early, probably because of her unfortunate choice of me as her partner. I would be left to ponder the great unknowns alone, guilt-ridden for bringing a unique and beautiful soul such as Lesley to a dark and dreadful place. This was my battle to endure and she should not have to be part of it. She should never have come with me.

I snapped back to reality when the elderly man's name was called.

"Mr. Harrison," the nurse said. The elderly man got to his feet slowly, using his walker for balance. He pulled his pants up, straightened his belt, and proceeded toward the waiting nurse. He stopped a few feet from the door and turned around to face in my direction. I turned around to see what he was looking at. Apparently, it was me. He struggled to let out a tired smile — the wrinkles on his face stretched awkwardly as if they had not been used in that way for a long time. While he smiled, a shadowy figure emerged from his back, as if trying to escape. But then, as if burned by the air, it quickly forced its way back inside. I shook my head and blinked, and then he was once again moving away from me. I glanced over at Lesley, but her eyes were still plastered to the magazine pages. No one else in the room seemed to see what I had seen.

"Sorry," the man said. "I'm going as fast as these old legs will allow." The nurse revealed a tired, contrived smile and continued to hold the door open with her outstretched foot.

Since I'd left Dallas, the figures were revealing themselves more frequently, and in more shapely forms. For some reason, the Gamemakers must have thought I needed a push.

• • •

The doctor was an attractive, dark-haired petite female wearing a short white coat pulled snugly around a navy colored knee-length skirt. She poked her head into the waiting room and called my name. She mentioned briefly that the nurse had taken off to grab lunch, and that I would be her last patient that day in Urgent Care. Apparently she had to help a colleague out for half a shift, and would be heading back to the emergency room across the street, where she was permanently staffed. She seemed pleasant enough, offering us a seat in the small examining room. Unlike the nurse, if she was burned out from treating coughs and colds, it was not obvious.

Lesley insisted on being in the room, whispering to me on the way in, "It's not because she's gorgeous. I just want to make sure you tell her everything."

"Sure," I whispered back sarcastically.

I took a seat on the elevated examining table, crumpling the thin white paper covering the vinyl. The first thing I noticed about the room was that there were no windows. One way in, one way out. Once Lesley took her seat, the physician shut the heavy door, echoing the sealed sound resonating in my head. Because of the variety of violent patients I have had to deal with over the years as a paramedic, I usually made it a point to be near the exit of a room. But this time it was slightly different: we were fugitives on the run. And even if my uncle hadn't yet plastered our faces all over the news feeds, he could still be working behind the scenes with hospitals, especially emergency rooms. They would be a priority for notification.

The physician sat down and jotted something on her clipboard, likely a date and time. Lesley looked up at me and mouthed, "Are you okay?" My paranoia took a front seat and sweat began to bead on my forehead. I nodded and quickly wiped the sweat away with my right hand before the doctor looked up.

"So what can we do for you today, Mr. Trapper?" the physician said. She placed the clipboard on her lap and faced me.

"Michael," I said.

"Michael, how can I help you?"

I began describing my symptoms — at least most of them, keeping the more intimate ones to myself. I hoped she would simply check off the boxes on her T-Sheet and write me a prescription for Ambien, but no such luck. Once Lesley butted in and mentioned the constant headaches and my fainting spell, she delved deeper with more probing questions, just as any good physician would.

"Michael, can you lie back and remove your hat please?" My hat was part of my disguise, but I figured if she was going to recognize me, she would have already done so. She would have slyly slipped out of the room with some random medical excuse pulled from a database compiled from many long nights spent in the emergency room. I obediently removed my hat and lay back on the small table, leaving myself the most vulnerable I had been since arriving in New Orleans.

She did a quick head-to-toe examination, including an eye test and a thorough neurological check. She then sat back in her chair and began checking boxes and jotting down short sentences. The room was completely silent and the smell of saturated alcohol pads was pressing hard against my nostrils. The fear that had been building inside me began to emanate from my pores. If something did not happen soon, I was going to burst through the door like a madman ravenous for fresh air. Lesley must have spotted the angst on my face, and attempted to gain my attention. I began focusing on the floor at her feet, trying to ignore the brimming anxiety, now starting to boil.

A few grueling minutes later, the physician finally spoke. "Michael, you appear to be overall healthy, but I do have a few concerns. Stress seems to be playing a large part in your life." If she even knew half of what was going on in my life… "You definitely need rest, and I will be happy to write you a prescription for a week's worth of sleeping pills to get you back on the right track. But first I would like to get a CAT scan of your brain."

"Okay," I said. "Wait, what? I'm just exhausted is all, Doc. I don't think a CAT scan will show anything."

"I'm not totally disagreeing with you, but it would make me feel better. And I'm sure your wife will agree with me." Lesley nodded, not offering to correct the implied marital status. "Look, I am heading back over to the emergency room after I finish your paperwork. I'll write the order and call to tell them you are on the way. The read won't take long and then I'll write your prescription. Do we have a deal, Mr. Trapper?"

"Yes," Lesley quickly answered for me, staring at me with wide eyes and attempting to compel me to nod along with her answer.

After a few seconds I nodded and said, "Okay." I didn't see any other way to get the sleeping pills I so desperately needed. But it was definitely riskier to be seen in the emergency room — a place I had wanted to avoid at all costs. "I like your bargaining technique, Doc."

"It didn't take much," she said, smiling. "Convince the wife and the stubborn husband will usually follow suit. It's one of our old tactics, tried and true." I didn't think she was referring to her tactics as a physician, but rather as a woman. I was beginning to believe I had been set up the moment I stepped through the door, and had obviously missed their psychic connection to band together for one purpose.

Chapter 12

I had never been on the opposite side of the window before. It was a humbling experience, as my head was presented in slices on a screen. I felt unveiled and naked to the world as I lay motionless on the table, radiation and paired eyeballs penetrating my skeletal shield and staring upon the only place of solace I had on earth. It was the most exposed I had felt in my life, as the outhouse door was kicked open for all to see.

What lies hidden in the deepest recesses of our brains, invisible to the naked eye? What crawls under the stairs that we cannot unwrap using a machine? Some things were never meant to be found, and if perhaps we stumbled upon them, would we have the ability to comprehend? Infinite pieces of a perpetual puzzle we're not supposed to solve — a machine programmed with sporadic coding, to be filled in with this life, tinges of hope floating off in the distance, seen but never really touched. Are they even tangible?

I opened my eyes when the amplified voice from the

speaker in the room revealed that the test was complete. A young male tech lowered the bed out from the donut-shaped CT machine.

"How are you feeling, sir?" the tech asked

"Better," I said, sitting up when the bed halted. Thankfully the dizziness had subsided, but much to my annoyance, the headache was still simmering. I got to my feet and thanked him for his assistance. When I first entered into the room, I'd had a sudden bout of extreme dizziness and nearly fell down. He caught my arm just in time, and prevented me from plunging my head into the corner of the counter. After I regained my balance, we both joked that at least I was in the right place if I had cracked my skull open.

The physician had written me the script for sleeping pills and handed it to Lesley in the radiology waiting room, thanking us once again for humoring her. I had no intention of waiting around for the results, since I already had what I came for. But at the same time, I was curious and wanted a glimpse of the scan. I had noticed on entering the room that I could see the screen from a reflection near the door to the control area, but I needed to be closer to get the view I needed. So I did what so many of my patients in the past have done: I faked a dizzy spell, using drama skills I learned from the streets of Dallas.

While the tech had his back turned, and the female tech at the computer in the control room was looking down, I quickly made my way into position on the other side of the machine near the glass. I needed just a moment or two and the correct angle. I craned my neck, but before I had a chance to scan the entire screen, the male tech turned around.

"Sir, are you okay?" he asked.

With my arm extended on the counter, I clutched my head with my free hand and weakened my knees. With my head tilted down I said, "I just need a second."

The door opened from the control room. "Brian," the

female tech said.

"Yes?" the male tech responded.

I looked up through the glass and saw that she was once again seated at her computer terminal with the phone against her ear.

"Can you come in here for a second, please?" she said with uncertainty in her voice. If she was trying to hide something from me, she was not doing it well.

"One second. Let me make sure he's okay first," Brian responded. "Sir, are you sure you're okay?"

"Sorry," I said, "I just need another minute to get my bearings. The dizziness is subsiding. I'm fine, seriously, go see what your partner needs."

"Okay, I'll just be a second," he said.

Why all of the antics? Why not just ask the guy if I could have a quick peek at my scan? Because we didn't need any extra attention, and techs weren't supposed to give results. Only the physician was allowed to deliver the news.

I repositioned myself and saw the screen that the two techs were now hovering over. I quickly analyzed the reflection before the tech returned. As my eyes ran along the entire screen, I felt my insides seize in a knot and then plummet to the floor. I looked away and back again to make sure I was seeing it right. I watched as the female tech began slowly fingering the wheel of the mouse, scanning through the entire study. She halted on the image that made it as obvious as it could be.

The female tech appeared to whisper something to the male tech and then looked up from her screen toward me. I continued to stare through her, my mind attempting to process the new information. The male had not yet looked up from the screen. He was seemingly captivated by the scan of my brain. When I finally focused on her, she was looking back at me with a lamenting stare.

I took a deep breath and amazingly, in a bout of instant recovery, I shook my head and exited the room, thanking the tech once again for his assistance. He left the room and met me by the door, repeatedly asking if I was okay and if I needed assistance. I politely declined his offer, and made my way down the short hall to the waiting area.

"Mr. Trapper," the female tech said as I reached for the door.

Holding onto the handle, I turned and said, "Yes?"

"Dr. McCrey wants you to see her in the emergency room before you leave."

"Okay," I said. "I'll head that way now. Thank you." I didn't look back, but I was sure if I had, I would have seen another set of mournful eyes, filled with pity.

It was obviously Dr. McCrey whom the female tech was on the phone with. She had alerted her about the scan, and now the doctor wanted to see me in order to present the bad news herself. I was sort of shocked, but pleasantly so, that they didn't insist I go by wheelchair to the emergency room. And I was not waiting around to see if they changed their minds.

Lesley was waiting patiently, watching the small TV set high on the wall in the waiting room, a magazine flipped over in her lap. I quickly changed my demeanor from self-pity to hurried paranoia.

"Let's go," I said with a look that made it clear I wasn't open to discussion. She abruptly stood, gathering her purse. I lightly grabbed her from behind her right arm.

"Don't look back," I whispered, "just walk. We only have a few minutes."

• • •

Once we made it outside and around the corner from the hospital entrance, I immediately tried to hail a cab.

"Are you going to tell me what's going on, Tryke?" Lesley sounded rattled. "What happened in there?"

"They were asking too many questions. Something was off," I said, moving to the edge of the walkway and peering down the street as if to will a cab to appear. "Where are all of the damn taxi cabs?"

"What do you mean? Questions about us? Did they threaten to call the police?"

"No. I mean… I don't think so, but if I had stayed for much longer, they might have gotten suspicious. They asked a few questions about you and where we lived. I didn't answer. Instead I faked another bout of dizziness. I don't know, maybe I was just being a little paranoid. But better safe than not."

Lesley looked somewhat relieved, but still on edge. She quickly changed the conversation back to the reason we were there in the first place.

"Did you at least finish the scan?"

"Yes, and I was able to get a pretty good view of the computer screen when it was complete." I finally spotted a cab and held out my arm, but considering its speed it did not appear to be stopping. What the hell was going on? Then I spotted a couple in the back seat as it sailed past us.

"And?"

"Huh?" I asked, scanning the street for another cab. The road was eerily empty. I started pacing and was just about to suggest we begin walking when a horse and carriage suddenly rounded the corner. By then I was willing to take what I could get. "What do you say, shall we take a ride in a carriage?"

"Tryke, what did the scan show?" she demanded, her voice riddled with irritation.

I decided to lighten the mood with a little dark humor. "It was empty, save for the huge bleed surrounding my occipital lobe." I remained expressionless until I noticed her forlorn look. "I'm kidding." I quickly spouted out, with a nervous smirk, "It was as normal as I assumed my brain would be."

"Don't scare me like that, you jerk." She slugged my right arm hard with her fist. "First you tell me we may have been spotted, and then you tell me you have an aneurysm? What is wrong with you?"

"Sorry, I was just trying to be funny," I said, waving the carriage driver toward us. "Come on, let's take a ride so you can relax and stop hitting me."

The driver seemed more than happy to have customers and offered us a jovial greeting. "Hi there, young couple. Where can I carry you two on this cool afternoon? Perhaps a tour of our lovely city, or maybe a quiet ride to your destination? What'll it be?"

I shrugged and looked at Lesley for an answer.

"Just a ride to our hotel," she said. "But maybe take it a little slower than you normally would."

The carriage driver smiled broadly, tipping the brim of his black top hat.

"Yes, ma'am."

Almost immediately after I helped Lesley into the back of the carriage, she leaned her head on my shoulder, wrapping her arm around mine. I rested my own head against the seat, leaning back and enjoying the repetitious sound of horseshoes drumming the pavement. I wanted to close my eyes and think of nothing, but the image of my brain on the screen kept flashing in my mind, bringing with it an instant feeling of hopelessness and dread. A small white mass was visible in the rear of my brain, and from its appearance — from what little I knew of CT images — the symmetrical round shape usually meant it was benign. But there was no way of telling from just the scan. I would have to go in for further testing, which was not going to happen anytime soon.

As if things in our lives were not already in a terminal descent, this recent news exacerbated things drastically — that is, if I allowed it to. Instead of the situation bringing me to my knees, I decided to use it to fuel my agenda. As long as I was able to function somewhat normally I would finish what I started, and that began with a plan. Lesley could never find out about my ailment. If she ever discovered it, I didn't think her willpower would allow her to continue our endeavor; she would insist I be further examined and treated, if possible. Her morale would slowly wither. As for my own morale, I had to erase any pessimism or doubt.

While resting my eyes during the remainder of the short trip, I began mentally planning our next steps in order. It seemed to help me settle my thoughts. I started feeling better as the distraction took over, letting the immediacy of the recent event and news drift away with the cool wind. Though temporary, these calm thoughts were a welcome treat.

The carriage ride was not intended to be therapeutic, but a convenient getaway from uncomfortable circumstances. By the end of the ride it seemed to bring solace to Lesley, as well. When we exited the carriage, a relaxed shine emanated from her, as if she had just stepped out from an hour-long massage. I envied her, knowing that nothing short of going back in time could soothe my worries. When I left the vehicle, all I got was a cool slap of bitterly cold wind, followed by the inevitable flood of plaguing thoughts. They were anxiously waiting for the gate to open.

Chapter 13

After the carriage ride, Lesley finally got her shrimp po'boy, though it wasn't from the same restaurant that claimed to be the best in New Orleans. Because of the late hour, we had to settle for a seedy little place close to the hotel that didn't offer the best of anything, except maybe creepy patrons. As we entered the front door, I decided on a plain burger and fries. I advised Lesley that I thought it the safest choice.

We spent hours sipping on coffee and going over in detail our plan for the next few weeks, easing the anxiety that ambivalence had smeared all over our faces. By the end, we both seemed content with the plan, not to mention a little excited about heading home. However, our enthusiasm arose from different places: I had unfinished business to attend to, while Lesley wanted to see her family. But we agreed that seeing Dave was our top priority. Dave was our friend — one of my only friends — and he was alone in a cold hospital, left to face the mind's darkest corners with no assistance or comfort from the outside world. He deserved better, and he deserved better from me.

Lesley was leaning on the edge of the toilet the next morning, regretting her food choice, while I stood at the doorway without any gastrointestinal distress whatsoever. I offered her a cold wet rag for her forehead, which she accepted before shooing me away as another bolus of stomach acid threatened to make its way up her exhausted esophagus.

"Tryke, I don't want you to see me like this. Please shut the door."

"Okay," I said. "I was just trying to help. I feel bad for you, honestly." I slowly closed the door, not shutting it all the way.

"Sure, go ahead and gloat some more about how you were right, and how I should have listened to your instincts... blah, blah, blah."

"I'm not —" She started to gag again, gripping the side of the bowl. I admit I was slightly humored, but only because of her stubborn insistence to get her po'boy, despite my warning.

"You— really— want to help..." she struggled, "then please go get me something... for this horrible nausea."

"Nausea medication and clear soda. I'm on it. Anything else? Are you sure you don't need me to stay and help?"

"I'm sure," she spat out, pushing the door the rest of the way closed with her foot.

I left before she decided to grab the small pair of complimentary shampoo and conditioner bottles resting on the edge of the bath tub and hurl them at my head.

I felt rested, spry even. I had caught up on my sleep, thanks to the sleeping pills that I had downed the night before — after finishing a glass of Scotch. I slipped on my coat and exited the hotel lobby with an energy and clarity I had not felt in a long time. We were finally going to get out of this city and I was going to get my chance to get even with Dr. Randal. Ever since reading the notes in his storage, I had been seething with anger over his use of my mom's mind for his bidding. Being sheltered in an asylum was not punishment enough for manipulating vulnerable and innocent minds, and causing them to be drenched in a never-ending pain. This man deserved a special kind of release: one for the books.

After gathering the items that Lesley had requested from the corner drugstore next to the hotel, I grabbed a cup of coffee from a cafe a few stores down. I needed a moment to myself, some time to allow my thoughts a nice stretch. I wasn't planning on staying long. Besides, Lesley seemed to need some alone-time of her own.

I sat outside on the patio under the awning and people watched — one of my favorite mindless entertainment activities — while sipping on my strong, hot brew. The crowds were thickening even more now that Mardi Gras had arrived, which allowed an endless variety of characters roaming about: thinly veiled, easily accessible, long sleeved shirts on young and old women, men with colossal stacks of cheap beads slung around their necks, eager to give away their purchased trophies to the highest bidder. Plastic beads became a currency this time of year for the open brothel on the streets of New Orleans. Flashing of the breasts usually rendered a simple set of single beads, whereas two females engaging in any sexual act will result in a barrage of extravagant beads and a lightning storm of camera flashes.

As I stared out into the crowds and watched the couples, the singles, the elder drunks, and the street performing entrepreneurs, I pondered what life-changing secrets each of them held in the safety deposit boxes of their brains. I'm not talking about a secret fling from their dating years or an extra credit card or bank account, or the prepaid phone they purchased for their secret rendezvous. No, I am talking about medical conditions. How many cancer diagnoses are hidden to save the significant others from heartache and financial complications? How would the unknowing partners receive the news if they were to suddenly learn about it? How many would leave, unable to deal with the countdown to death? How many would stay and stretch out their eager hands toward the flakes of hope drifting from above?

I was holding on to hope myself, acting as if I could diagnose the tumor in my brain as benign. The truth was, I had no idea. I have taken care of many patients with cancer and tumors, some benign, others malignant, and nearly all told me the same thing: the diagnosis drained their souls almost immediately and they wished they had never known. There were always the exceptions, though, the few who refused to let it dampen their lives and accepted the challenge. No matter how many times the cancer came back, they maintained their resolve to not allow a complete surrender of their lives. Maybe they had never been challenged before, and this was a way to prove something to themselves.

I considered how the world would change if we no longer had death sentences. Without ailments in the world, how could each of us live our lives? Too well, perhaps? And then the Gamemakers would become bored and create some other challenge. A new torture to replace the old.

I suppose the point to this life for most is to savor each rare moment of peaceful bliss, to decipher what each of us considers worthy, and hold onto that for as long as we can. Maybe this is what we humans have rationalized as a way to remain sane. It is our only means of control in this never-ending twirl of life. And just as we settle into blissful ignorance, it can be yanked out from under us, a new sense of hope flashed in front of our eyes to change the rules.

Lesley deserved what I could offer her, for as long as I was able. With this potentially growing mass dwelling in my head, the unforeseen future seemed that much more obscure. I didn't have the luxury to wait for things to happen, or to completely understand them before I acted. I had to plunge into the dark waters that define most relationships, and take the next step.

• • •

The jewelry store was fairly empty, leaving me an easy target for a guileful salesman, or in this case, saleswoman. I can only imagine how vulnerable I appeared: a lone male stepping inside the deep underbelly of ostentatious bling. I had no visual credentials that qualified me to be in there. I was blingless, except for my watch.

I obviously needed help, but I wanted to peruse a little on my own in order to get a handle on this environment in which I was not comfortable. The place had a neatness about it, and a kind of symmetry — a cool smell of metal and money. It screamed costly commitment the moment I stepped inside. No matter the persona I attempted to simulate, I was out of my element on this one. I decided that I might as well give in and accept the advice treading my way, perched on a pair of navy-colored heels.

When the saleswoman reached me, I was staring vacantly toward a glass case of brooches, attempting to prepare myself for the impending exchange. I knew what I had come for and the only thing I had to do was choose one. For obvious reasons, I did not want to linger in the spotlight. I always prefer to escape uneasy situations as quickly as possible. So the answer was simple. Get in and get out. The hard part was the next step.

"Hello, sir, can I help you with one of our lovely brooches? As you can see, we have a wide variety."

I fumbled my words but quickly gained traction, just not in the direction I wanted. "I… I was — uh… just admiring these pins."

"Did you have a particular one in mind that I could show you?"

I looked up from the glass case toward the woman I had seen from a distance. She was a middle-aged lady with mousy brown hair and a fistful of diamonds. She wore suit pants and a blouse revealing a modest amount of cleavage — the diamonds on her fingers were the show, not her. But there was a sincerity in her eyes that immediately dissolved my initial assessment of her as a shifty salesperson.

I smirked and said, "I'm sorry, I'm just a bit nervous is all. I'm actually in the wrong area."

She smiled broadly and said, "I had a hunch. So what area were you searching for?"

"I'm looking for a ring for my girlfriend."

Her smile did not wane, but seemed to stretch even farther as if I had told a horribly funny joke and she had just gotten the punch line. "Okay, so the next question is, how serious is the ring?"

"I am going to ask her to marry me."

"Follow me," she said, beaming.

I followed her across the store, feeling the nerves building momentum once again. I was being led to the section where many men had dwelled before me. Surely all had stared down through the glass, past the gleam of the overly polished diamonds, and focused on the numbers written neatly on the tags. These numbers represented years of payments, along with years of commitment. Which would last longer is a question many have asked themselves as their significant other became lost in the hypnotic trance of sparkling bliss. Seeing the glass cleaner and rag behind the counter — anxiously awaiting the next pair of sweaty palms — made me shove my own hands into the front pockets of my jeans.

"Before we begin the search for the perfect ring, I need to know what price range you were looking to be in," she said.

And here was my new dilemma. How much of our precious cash could I spare for this endeavor? Credit cards were not an option for obvious reasons, which also meant I could not open a new one. Credit check, ID's and signatures were not a good idea in our current situation. It was cash or nothing.

I sighed while staring down through the case, choosing my words carefully so as not to arouse her suspicion. I wanted only to seem like a hopeful romantic down on his luck.

"You see… the thing is… I'm not really in a position to be buying anything extravagant. I am already over my head with the girl I am proposing to. She's pretty much out of my league. I'm basically leaning on the romance of the city to help me through this."

I did not have to look up to see the emotion I had triggered. Her voice was full of sappy romantic sympathy.

"She is very lucky to have such a handsome, sensitive man fawning over her."

"Thank you. But I'm the lucky one, I assure you."

The saleswoman stepped behind the glass case and I followed her one case over from the five and six figure rocks to the section for the more frugal gentleman. She began spouting esoteric jargon about grade and clarity of diamonds and the wide variety of cuts. None of that mattered to me. I wanted to know what I could afford, and hopefully it was more than a gold band.

She was determined to educate me no matter how spaced out I appeared. Eventually she stopped and asked me to choose one that caught my eye, analogizing the way Lesley caught mine. It was cheesy but it worked, though it was not Lesley's appearance — not *only* her appearance — that wooed me. It was the comment she made at that moment when we first met that had yanked me from my neatly wound life. Not to mention that her giggle reminded me of my dead sister.

I pointed toward a modest single diamond with a silver band. The saleswoman advised me that it was a marquise cut, and a decent clarity. She might as well have been speaking to me in tongues. The only thing I cared about was what Lesley would think of the ring, and whether I could afford it. My hands were still in my pockets, not yet ready to be disappointed by the price.

She noticed my apprehension and said, "Don't pay attention to the price on the tag. I just want to know if it feels right to you."

"Okay," I said carefully. I pulled my hands from my pockets and took the ring from her. It was all I had in me to resist flipping the price tag over, but I restrained myself and held the ring on my right index finger. I stared at it for a few seconds, humoring her. It did have a certain appeal: it was simple and sparkly. I handed it back to her.

"So, what did you think?" she asked, taking the ring back and wiping the diamond with the rag in her hand.

"I like it," I said. "But the question is, can I afford it?"

"I think you will be pleasantly surprised. How about three hundred? Does that sound okay?"

"Seriously?" She nodded. "Then I'll take it." Taking a quick glance at the other diamonds in the adjoining case, as well as the ones in my case, I deduced that she had given me a hell of a deal. Even if she did not take a commission, there was way more left over that she would have to account for.

"Your girlfriend will be head over heels, I just know it." She was beaming at me again as she searched for the ring's box in a drawer behind the case. "One last thing. I was so excited for you that I forgot to ask her ring size." She saw that she had me completely flummoxed. "Just tell me her build and I can take a pretty good guess. And if for some reason it still doesn't fit, bring her and the ring in and we'll size it for her. I would love to meet the future bride."

"Sounds good," I said, matching her smile.

Deciding to buy a ring was, needless to say, a very difficult decision, especially considering the new-found friend perched in my brain. How long did I have left? I had heard of people living a decent life with a tumor if all of the numerous negative possibilities did not occur. Was it malignant? Would it grow? If it did, would I slowly lose my dignity or would it kill me quickly?

What in this life has a guarantee? Nothing. From our anatomy to our meager time on this earth. We could die any minute, any second. I had known this my entire life. So why was this tumor erasing all of my common sense? I don't think it was, at all. I think it was simply reminding me of my fragility, making me hurry my life forward toward my goals, pretty much as I have always done. Yes, a reminder. That was what I decided the tumor would be known as, from then on.

Would it be fair to Lesley to marry her if I were going to die soon after? There I was again, asking the questions as if I knew the answers. A reminder. Come on, I told myself. We cannot stop living our lives, ever. The Gamemakers would not allow such an abrupt ending to their game, would they? Could this be their doing? A trap meant to cripple me mentally? Were they trying to let hopelessness flood in until I began to drown in my own self-pity? I refused to let it happen that way, at least while I still had some control.

Chapter 14

After leaving the jewelry store, I felt good on the walk back to the hotel. Things finally seemed like they were going in the right direction, and not only because of the ring and the future it held. The little bit of rest I received had brushed away the lingering haze. I knew it was only temporary, but I was content.

I had a direction, and a beautiful woman I was about to propose to. Though I had not yet figured out how I was going to ask her, or when, it was obviously not going to be anything elaborate. We couldn't afford to draw unnecessary attention to ourselves. Maybe I'd do it during a quiet evening stroll by the river, or just wait until we got back to Dallas. I knew more secluded places, and that would probably mean more to her. In fact, the Italian restaurant where we had our first date — under the gazebo where I spilled my wine after she kissed me for the first time — would be ideal. I can vividly recall the moment, the feeling of kissing a woman without being drenched in pure lust. At the time I had no idea what was happening to me, but as I began to understand, I slowly changed with it. I have since lowered my guard completely with her, and am comprehending love more than I ever have. I even tell her often, a great feat for me, considering my past.

I would go so far as to say I felt happy, and that even the Gamemakers would have had a tough time dampening my spirit. No matter how long I lived or what the new friend in my brain did to impair me, right then, in that moment, I felt alive and untouchable. I had a companion in this dreadful world who would fight beside me until the end. She'd love me through any convoluted traps that were placed in our way. Still, I knew better than to totally drop my guard — crack the seal, but don't open the door completely.

When I got back to the room Lesley was lying on the bed, fully dressed and staring up at the ceiling. Maybe she was feeling better? She never looked over at me when the heavy door to the room closed shut. She seemed to be deep in thought about something. Either that or she was focused hard on counting the bumps on the popcorn ceiling. Maybe she was concentrating on not vomiting. I remained standing to avoid shaking the bed and risk rousing her nausea.

"Are you okay?" I asked, softly. She didn't look over, but continued her upward gaze. I gave her a few seconds to respond. I wasn't sure if I had upset her, but something was obviously off. I had my hand in my pocket, and when I felt the box I searched the room for my suitcase. It was on the other side of the bed where she was lying. I needed to get it in there without her noticing the square object outlined in my front pocket. I could slide it in the top compartment of my open suitcase while I put her medication on the bedside table.

"I got the medicine you asked for, and a few other things I thought you might want."

I carried the bag with me to the other side of the bed and

placed it on the nightstand next to her. Just as I knelt by my suitcase, she spoke, interrupting my attempt to remove the box from my pocket. I could feel her eyes on the back of my head as she spoke.

"Can I ask you a question?" she asked, morosely.

"Of course," I said, turning around and meeting her eyes. I noticed her eyes were puffy and pink, as though she had been crying moments before I came in. My lively mood felt a dark presence begin to hover and move in.

"What do you really get out of releasing the bad guys? Is it vigilante justice, your personal battle with the dredges of society? Or is it something else?"

What was this, and where was it coming from? And what did she mean by something else? I inched closer to her in the space on the bed. "What is this about? I thought we went over all of this and you were okay with everything. I mean, we just went over this yesterday. You even have your own personal vendetta you wanted to handle."

"I know, but I've been thinking." She paused and sighed heavily, again turning her stare toward the ceiling. "What happens when you finish with Dr. Randal? Then what? Do we keep searching for more? Are we going to be in potential danger for the rest of our lives?"

"I don't know," I said. "I mean, I guess. I just don't understand what made you change your mind so quickly. And what did you mean by *something else*?" I felt the tension rising in my throat as the words exited.

"You said you see the soul sometimes, or blurry things. But I never saw anything when I went with you."

"Are you saying I'm lying to you?" I got up from the bed and turned toward the window, taking a deep breath, attempting to soothe the anger that was building inside.

"No, I'm just asking you to consider everything that has happened in your life. Your mom was sick and your sister. Isn't it possible that you could also be... you know — "

"You think I'm sick, that nothing I see is real. And me,

what about me? Am I real? Lesley, I can't believe this crap. After I confided in you, after I opened up my very closed life to you. This is how you repay me!? By accusing me of being sick and lying!?"

"I don't think you were lying." Her voice was soft, unhindered by the conversation, as if she knew this was how I would react. "I think you believe you saw things."

"What?"

"Your mind saw them — "

"What the hell is the difference!? You know as well as I that that's a bullshit argument. There are no absolutes in this world. It's fluid, always changing, and we don't understand a damn thing that's happening around us. What we thought we knew hundreds of years ago is now completely false. We're tiny complex specks, placed in an unimaginably huge space. It's ridiculous that I have to explain this to you, of all people." I took a deep breath and after a few seconds continued in a calmer voice.

"Lesley, don't fall prey to the mindless norm. You're better than that. Smarter."

"People get sick, Tryke. It's nothing to be ashamed of."

I ignored her comment and remained focused on my argument. "We've talked about this countless times. Atoms were once thought to be the smallest particles in the universe. Geocentricity, dark matter. Come on, think of the possibilities if humans prove the existence of other dimensions. Remember the cramps in our brains after we discussed these things? Open your mind. Lesley. It's all there for us to explore."

She knew what I was talking about, but for some reason didn't want to acknowledge it. Something had changed her. She rolled on her side and turned toward me, staring at me pitifully, like I was a clueless animal unable to see my own reflection.

"Okay," she said, "I'm sorry. You're right, I shouldn't question your sanity. I just want you to think about things, namely us. Whatever you see, it doesn't really matter. We matter." She reached her hand out, gesturing me to sit. "I want us to have a long and healthy relationship together. I don't want to spend my life searching for people. I'm done with searching. I have you."

I regained my composure after a few minutes, not making eye contact with her, and thought about her words. She seemed to be asking me to stop my battle, stop who I am. She wanted us to start over, and only remember us. But that was not an option. I could not ignore who I was and who I had become. My last ditch effort was to tell her about the Gamemakers, but that was also not an option after what I had just heard. Even if I told her about the Gamemakers, it wouldn't have done any good. She was not a player sent to do battle. At the very most she was sent as a distraction, in which case I could handle it.

"What are you asking me to do?" I said, allowing her to clarify her point.

She sat up, leaned her back against the headboard, and held out her hand again to pull me back onto the bed. Reluctantly and still simmering mad, I sat down beside her. Her makeup was smeared along her cheeks, tears now filling her lower lids. "I want you — I mean us — to go back home and live our lives together. Forget about everything and start over."

This was the part that I had not discussed with her, the part I was supposed to explain slowly on the trip back. "You have to know we cannot live there like we were before. I can't go back and work there as a paramedic."

"Then we'll move close enough so I can visit my family occasionally. How about Tyler, or Houston?"

Not a horrible choice, but I was thinking a little farther away from Dallas. "Do you expect me to stop being who I am?" First things had to come first. There was no point in discussing a place if she wanted me to change.

She swallowed and cleared her throat and said, "I would,

yes."

"And forget about Dr. Randal? After what he did to my mom?"

"Forget about him, move on. He's already in an asylum, for goodness sake. Tryke, you can't bring your mom back by killing him."

The words stung like a thousand hornets. The woman I trusted, fallen in love with, had changed, and not in a good way. She wasn't the same woman who was in the car with me on the trip down here. She had once considered avenging her own grandmother by releasing her murderer. She had gone with me on a release. This was worse than I suspected. I never really thought she would pan out to be a player, but at the very least I thought she would support me from a safe distance, occasionally wanting details for entertainment. Wanting to know all about me and then asking me to stop *being* me, now that was a twist I never saw coming.

"It's not about bringing her back," I said. "I know she's dead. Everyone in my family is dead. I get it. That's not my mission."

"Mission? Then what's your mission? Kill every bad guy in the world? There are too many. Look at me, Tryke." I stared into her blue, tear-stricken eyes and saw my reflection. My eyes were still dry. "I'm here, now, for you. I just want us to be normal. Is that too much to ask? Stop your anger toward the world and just be with me, dammit."

But that was not me. I wanted to be with her, I had made that clear, but I could not avert my eyes as the players on the battlefield ravaged the innocent. Not while I lived a peaceful life in the suburbs.

"I can't stop."

"Why the hell not? Is it an addiction? Do you *enjoy* killing people?" And I thought my uncle would be tough on me.

"No, it's more complicated than that," I said. "It isn't fun for me, I can assure you." But just as I said the words, a sinister laugh slid along my insides and echoed inside my head. I turned toward the window again. "I was chosen to do this."

"Chosen by who?"

"Just forget about it. You've obviously made up your mind. If I don't change, you don't want me. Am I right?"

She didn't argue, but got up from the bed. I heard the bathroom door open. She returned a few seconds later and set something on the nightstand. Still seething mad, I continued to stare out the window, not acknowledging the object she had placed. A minute later I heard the door to the room open and she said, "I only want you to change if you want to change." And then the door shut behind her.

The thing was, I couldn't change, no matter how much I pleaded with myself or how much I cared for Lesley. Since the moment I set foot on the battlefield, I knew that it would be a lifetime war. There was no escape for me. I was too good a player for them to just throw away after one use. I saw it for what it was, and offered a challenge. Each trap that was set, each dilemma placed to solve, I acknowledged them and set out to overcome them.

When I finally turned around, my pride safely beside me, I saw the item that Lesley had left on the nightstand. At first I didn't understand. Probably out of pure shock, and not wanting to admit the obvious truth, I picked up the object and dropped to the bed. I stared at it for over an hour, thinking how my life had become a tempest, violently raging forward in a never ending spiral of contention. Now I was here, in this small hotel room in New Orleans. How could it come to this?

Chapter 15

Positive.

A word in my vocabulary, but used scarcely. And for good reason. It could only mean more mayhem was around the corner. But this time it was different. This time it involved a new entity in my life. A part of me was growing inside of Lesley.

Though the information did not necessarily cause me grief, I still went through the five stages while sitting on the edge of the bed and holding the small test in the palm of my hand. Home tests can sometimes give a false positive, right? Why the hell now, when everything was crumbling in my life? I'll do better with Lesley, I thought, if I can just have a little more time to put things back together, more time to convince her I can work alone and we can be together. How were we going to raise a child on the run with limited money and no job? I didn't know, but it was going to happen no matter what, so I might as well face it and find her.

She was probably in the lobby, waiting for me to come to

my senses and discuss this new addition to our lives. I grabbed my keys and made my way to the elevator, going over in my head what I was going to say. The short trip had sparked no new information or insight. When the elevator opened I exited, turned toward the lobby, and made my way down the hallway. I scanned the entire lobby, but she was nowhere to be seen. Maybe she'd walked to a cafe or just took a stroll around the block to cool off and let me mull over the new information she had sprung on me. She would be back in a few minutes, after she had time to think. I decided to wait where I was and confront her on her way back in. No matter what I thought of her and her of me, this changed things a little. How much? I wasn't sure yet.

After waiting about ten minutes, a female from behind the desk called out to me.

"Sir, are you Michael?" She held an envelope in her hand.

I looked around at the few people in line with luggage in their hands and a couple on a couch adjacent from me. I suddenly remembered Michael was my alias when Lesley and I went to urgent care. "Yes…" I said, cautiously.

"I have an envelope that was left here for you."

I strode up to the counter and slowly reached out to grab the envelope as if I were sticking my hand through a dark hole filled with poisonous snakes. I methodically slid the letter opener along the edges and handed the opener back to the lady. I made my way back to the same chair and pulled out the folded pieces of paper.

Tryke,

First, let me start out by telling you that I love you and nothing in this world will ever change that. I am sorry for not following through with my part. When we left Dallas I was filled with apprehension and excitement, among other feelings. We were finally together, just you and me. No matter the circumstances surrounding us it felt good to know you were beside me and we were going to handle things as a couple. I was only playing honeymoon, well, because you know, denial. I thought that if I wanted something bad enough, things would just fall into place. I should have known better, but I don't have any regrets. I have learned more about the man I love, the good and the bad (bad being your stubbornness). You have definitely helped me see the world more clearly, and yet it seems more obscure. How you did that, I haven't yet figured out. Our view of the world isn't that different, which I guess is what brought us together in the first place. I just handle it differently. You feel you have an obligation to change the world. I just want to live in it while I'm here.

Neither of us is wrong, but now that we have a baby coming, one of us has to be. We cannot raise a child in that environment, never feeling safe, never settling down. I don't want to change you. I never did. I only wanted what was best for us, and that happens to be a somewhat normal and safe life.

I know your decision will not be immediate, so I have decided to leave and make my way back to Dallas. I didn't do it out of spite or malice, but rather so you can have time to think things through and finish what you have left to resolve in your life. I know you worry, but I'll be fine. You have taught me how to take care of myself and how to spot the bad guys. I took a bus back and left the car for you if you happen to need it, because I know what you think of public transportation. I'll check in on Dave when I get back, and I'll tell him you will be by soon.

You don't owe the world anything. You've done more than enough. Focus on your life, us, and our child.

I love you,
Lesley.

I wiped my eyes and then looked around the room to see if anyone had noticed. Everyone seemed to be minding their own business and not giving me a second thought. But what was this? Tears? This was getting out of hand, and I was allowing my emotions to take over. I could not allow such an infestation to occur, without warning, without my permission. I needed my wits if I was going to figure this one out. And then on top of everything else, as if things weren't already screwed up enough, we'd involved an innocent child.

• • •

I was still sitting in the same spot in the lobby a few hours later. The hotel clerk who had given me the letter had been replaced by another female — shift change had taken place and I was still brooding over Lesley's note. Using my thumb, I had been mindlessly spinning the engagement ring on my right index finger, as my mood shifted from frustration to feverish anger. I was no closer to rationalizing my situation, or Lesley's decision to leave.

What the hell happened? And in such a short span of time. First, she comes with me to New Orleans because she supposedly loves me, reveals a past of her own about her grandma being murdered, followed by a request to see a release, wishes for marriage in the middle of a graveyard, and then suddenly changes her mind and wants me to change. Then, she writes me a letter and leaves, telling me she still loves me and wants a normal life. All for what? Because she's pregnant? It didn't make sense. She must have thought about the possibility before she made the decision to come with me, right? Did she do it all on a whim? Was she just bored? Did she think she could change me once she discovered my lab and decided I'd be a good challenge to take on? Or was this all planned out from the moment she met me? *Woman seeking man — looking to mold the perfect mate.*

How could I have been so naive to think she could handle the truth? When they say love is blind, is this what they mean? If so, I should start listening to more cliches. And what about the supposed reason, which I didn't buy by the way, using pregnancy as an excuse to leave? I didn't think she faked the pregnancy. I believed it was an excuse to get out of the situation — the very one she *asked* to be involved in, and which I had tried to shield her from.

I couldn't be the man she wanted me to be, nor could I provide her with the life she desired. This was always a fear of mine: getting too close to someone, allowing them into my life and a peek through the window of my thoughts. She pushed past my comfort level when she decided to come with me. She knew the risks in every way. For my part, I knew things would never be normal, but she made me believe in us. I was swindled by her beauty and persistence. She caused me to feel something for her that I had never felt before with anyone else. And look where it got me. Alone, in a puddle of emotions.

Now that she had made her decision and asked something of me that was impossible, what would the rest of my life look like? Lesley had filled a void that I never knew was there. I wanted to snap my fingers and revert to that time of blissful ignorance. If only it were that easy. It would take some time to reconstruct the wall. I had come to many conclusions since my journey began, confident how the rest of my life was going to pan out. I was in control of at least part of it, my choices, no matter what obstacles or impressions the Gamemakers placed. I had overcome, and adapted. But here I was again, stripped of everything, left to decipher an array of confusing emotions. I had foolishly dropped my guard and allowed things to enter my life that I had always opposed or ignored.

I had been given hope. I had come to understand love. I was made to believe there was such a thing as loyalty. Now I had to get behind the shield once again, insulate myself from love, and see the world for what it was: a few good people on a hilltop, unaware of the river of filthy sinister souls creeping slowly toward them in the murky water. The infested beings crawled with deceit and trickery, always inching closer and trying to lure the good past the barrier of righteousness in order to yank them through to the other side.

Lesley thought my battle was a choice, but as I told her, I never chose it — it chose me. It twisted its gnarled roots around my spirit and became part of me. If she could not live with that, then she would have to live without me.

The rain had started with a few drops sliding along the huge panels of windows in the lobby, and then swiftly turned into a deluge, mimicking my mood's latest transition and intensity. I was becoming more restless with each twirl of the ring, feeling the pressure building inside. I needed to twist the relief valve on my thoughts, and a walk in the rain was just the right size wrench to do it. Thankfully it wasn't long before the sheets of rain slowed enough for an umbrella. The windblown drops helped to cool my heated thoughts.

Just as I was about to get up and embark on my stroll, a couple with their three children at the check-in counter caught my attention. The wife had her wallet splayed open on the counter and was conversing with the attendant. Meanwhile, the husband tended to the three children — two girls around the age of five and seven, and a boy no older than three. They gave off the persona of a typical middle-class family on vacation: an array of luggage, restless children, and constant idle threats followed by appeasing treats.

I considered my unborn child and how it would change everything if that path were my destiny. How could I, Tryke Harper, be a dad? And what kind of dad would I be? What kind of role model would I be — hunting and releasing the scum of the world — if my son or daughter ever found out what I did? It sounds good, ridding the world of society's dregs, but it was hardly glorious. And it always brought with it the possibility of my not coming home. I had never been a simple vigilante, one who assisted the cops on occasion. I was in a much bigger game, and it involved ancient evil.

No matter what happened to me, my child must never

know of my battles. That had to be kept secret. If they found out, they might feel obligated to continue my work, or worse, they could be clouded by the Gamemakers and see me as a threat. They might even turn me into the authorities, or — my worst fear of all — attempt to release me themselves. No outcome that I could imagine was a good one.

The happy family I had been watching suddenly took a dark spiral down when the husband reached back with his right hand and struck the little boy's head from the rear, knocking him to the linoleum floor. I turned in my chair and looked around the lobby, but no one else seemed to notice.

Oddly, the boy didn't make a scene, but quickly got to his feet and stood there, stoic, apparently battle-hardened from a short life of abuse. He didn't shed a single tear, even as his sisters poked fun at him for getting into trouble. Then he looked toward me, ignoring their taunts, and met my eyes. His pain was palpable and it slid along my spine, leaving me shuddering inside. The man didn't stop the girls from teasing the little boy, but reinforced his terror by threatening him once again with a raised hand — simply for staring at me. Only this time he did not follow through, but instead turned the boy's head around. The husband himself never made eye contact with me. If he had, he would have seen the face of the man who would soon be hunting him.

It was as if the Gamemakers had reached out and slapped *me*, and then pushed me in the direction I was supposed to be in. I felt the energy pulsing through my core and to my extremities as the battlefield unfolded in front of me — the research, the hunt, the release. I wasn't yet sure that I would release the man, but at the very least he would know that someone had noticed how he'd been treating his son.

I followed the family out of the lobby and to the floor

where they were staying. Lesley had left me. This potential specimen was a good distraction, giving me time to think, clear the mental clutter, and plan out my rendezvous with Dr. Randal. Yes, I was still returning to Dallas, though I had no idea where I would go from there. And my plan would have to be slightly altered, leaving Lesley out of the scenario. At least I wouldn't have to worry about her safety.

It felt good to be needed again. Undercover gratitude was back.

Chapter 16

I followed the family for the day, watching as the husband continually disciplined the little boy with his quick-tempered hand, and allowing the two sisters to poke fun without repercussions. As the day wore on, I couldn't help but compare the little boy to an old man harpooned by a stroke, jailed in an abusive nursing home and unable to yell out for help. Inside, the little boy knew what was right, but his mind had been caged and didn't know how to release the beast growling inside.

The abuse of children and the elderly has always sparked something inside of me that isn't easily pacified. After each strike of his hand, it took an immense amount of restraint for me not to yank the man aside and release him in a restroom or side alley. But this was all part of the process and I was not finished. I needed to converse with him first before releasing him.

I sat at the hotel restaurant bar and watched their table, sipping on my favorite Scotch — Laphroaig — on the rocks. I was exhausted from the long day of research and was ready to slowly drift off, wrapped in the tight cool sheets of my hotel bed. The stubborn complications bouncing around in the back of my head, like popcorn kernels stuck in an air popper, would fall away into the bottom until it was switched back on. Thanks to the sleeping pills I could now have a few hours of uninterrupted rest, but I had a limited quantity, so I'd have to ration them. This was a good night to use one. I would need my rest for tomorrow evening if things turned out the way I anticipated.

I was just finishing the last sip of my drink when I felt a bump against my right arm. When I turned my head to see who was next to me, I smiled inside at the fortuitous encounter. The husband was standing next to me, drumming his left hand angrily on the bar as if he was in a hurry. He ignored his own rudeness, which nearly made me drop my glass. A few seconds later, he revealed his short temper for all to see when he slammed his empty glass on the bar and hailed the barkeep for another fresh beer. When the barkeep didn't acknowledge him right away, he unleashed the cowardly beast inside one more time by pounding his glass on the bar again, spraying moisture left behind by a previous drinker.

The barkeep looked over at him and said in a calm, trained tone, "I'll be there in a second, sir."

The husband grumbled and looked over at me. I watched him through the long mirror cluttered with bottles in front of me. He seemed to be studying me for some reason. After a few seconds he said, "You alone?" It didn't sound like a pickup line, but more like basic curiosity. If I hadn't been tracking the man, his question would have definitely raised a red flag of caution. But once I noticed his glazed eyes and unsteady balance, I would have just sized him up as an annoying drunk. I forced myself to perk up, leaving the desire for sleep safely in the back of my head. I had to take advantage of this situation.

"Yeah, why?" I said, keeping my stare forward.

"You're lucky, man."

"I am?"

"Those were the days."

I glanced over at him. He seemed to be looking past the bottles and the mirror, and off into his past.

"It's not as glorious as it appears," I said. "Trust me. To be honest, it gets kind of lonely."

"But you have your freedom. No damn kids to yell at, no old lady to hound you. Fair warning, man, don't get yourself into what I did."

The bartender grabbed the man's glass, wiping the counter with his trusty white towel, and asked, "What'll it be?" His voice had no vengeful or irritated inflections. Years of serving drunks had built a tolerance for the kind of behavior that would send most people over the counter with a knife.

"Budweiser," the husband responded rudely, as if the bartender should have known his drink of choice. The bartender filled his glass without a second glance and made his way to the next waiting patron.

"What is that?" I asked.

"Huh?"

"What did you get yourself into?" I clarified.

He turned around and pointed to the table where his family was sitting. "That's what."

"Who are they?" I asked, following his finger.

"They aren't my kids, man. I banged their old lady and now I'm stuck with them. Their schmuck of a dad was too weak to hold onto his wife. And then he had to go and get himself killed by cancer. What a weasel. He let cancer kick his ass, after I did. Now I'm stuck with his damn kids all the time instead of every other weekend." He took a long angry swallow of his frosty, freshly tapped beer.

Not his own children? And the dad is dead? Beating other people's kids riled me up even more, not to mention the fact that he knowingly took another man's wife. And on top of that, he married the woman and assumed responsibility for her kids — but without the necessary feelings of love and commitment. I clenched my glass, picturing myself whacking it across his nose, and then the restaurant breaking out into laughter as the man struggled to stanch the bleeding. The Gamemakers had outdone themselves on this nasty specimen. A welcome back gig, perhaps?

I took a deep breath to stifle the building rage.

"Weak people, man," I said. "They deserve what's coming to them."

The husband nodded and chugged the rest of his beer. "I like you, man. What's your name?"

"Mike," I said, "and you?"

"Andrew," he said, patting my shoulder like we were old pals. "Hey, let me buy you a drink, Mike."

"Okay," I said, releasing another smile inside.

He hailed the bartender once again, but this time with a little less asshole in his gesture, leaving the empty glass flat on the counter. "What are you drinking, Mike?"

"Scotch," I said.

"The hard stuff. I can respect that. I'll have one too, in honor of our new friendship." How flattering. I made friends with a drunk child abuser in five minutes flat. The bartender arrived and Andrew slung his words at him. "A pair of Scotches on the rocks for me and my new friend here."

The bartender glanced at me and I shrugged with a half smirk on my face. He almost lifted the corners of his mouth but restrained himself, returning to an unamused, stoic demeanor.

If a sprightly drunk wants to pay for your drink, then smile and allow them, no strings attached. And if a scum stepdad child abuser wants to buy you a drink, smile and accept the gesture and then strike a conversation, all the while attempting to figure a way to lure him away from his so-called family. Little did this moron know, he'd stepped one foot at a time into his own grave.

Andrew lifted his glass, motioning for me to lift my own. He knocked his against mine and said, "Cheers," and took a swig of his drink, though a much smaller swig than from his previous beer. "Whoa, that's some strong shit, man."

I smiled and took a small sip. I wanted to keep my wits about me. Things were changing in my direction, which meant I might not have to wait until the next day. "Yeah," I said, "it'll sneak up on you. You gotta watch it."

"I'm counting on it. So, Mike, what is it that you do for a living?"

"I'm an accountant. Yeah, I know, pretty boring stuff."

"Maybe, but mine isn't much more exciting. I sell furniture part time, just so I don't have to hear the old lady bitch at me. She's probably staring at me right now, seconds away from coming over here to yell."

I turned around in my stool and glanced at his family and then turned back around. "Nah, she's tending to the kids."

"So what brings an accountant to New Orleans? An accountant convention?" He laughed, taking another sip of the Scotch.

"I wish my company was paying for my trip. No, I'm just here for Mardi Gras. Heard many stories about this place and had to see it for myself. Anything would do really, to get away from my mundane life for a few days."

"You said it, man. Same here. Same shit day to day. I need a break. Especially from her damn kids." He finished the rest of his drink in one gulp, shaking his head and coughing from the potent sting. "I brought an entire bag of beads with me. The good ones, you know, the ones that bring out the big tits and ass. The wife thought I was bringing them to give to the kids in case they didn't catch any at the parades. Man, she's stupid." He shook his head and took another sip.

"Nice," I said.

"Hey, Mike, I got an idea." He motioned the bartender back over. "Two more."

"I'm good at the moment," I said. "I'm already three ahead of you."

"Okay, a double for me then," he told the bartender, and then turned back toward me. "Whaddya say we bust out those beads tonight?"

"You and me? Sure, but what about your wife?" The bartender placed the drink on a napkin in front of him, not lingering, probably because of the same feelings I was having about the guy.

"I'll be right back." He took a modest sip from his drink and shook the sting off. He then strolled with false confidence over to the table where his wife and stepchildren were sitting. I turned my stool around and watched as he methodically shoved his family to the side. His wife's expression showed no disappointment or anger. It all seemed routine, as if she anticipated the inevitable. Another family member battle-hardened by a cowardly infiltrator. His interpretation of her being a nagging wife didn't fit her response or demeanor. It was obviously the way he rationalized his destructive behavior.

When he returned a few minutes later, he wore the smile of a man who had accomplished the impossible — a facade to impress his new friend. "I take it you told her what was up." I was feeding his ego.

"You bet your ass I did."

"So what's the plan?" I asked.

"Finish these drinks and then head to Bourbon Street. Search for some prime tail."

"Sounds good," I said. My plan was now much less convoluted as I had initially imagined. It seemed that all I had left was to find a suitable place to perform the release. The bar was loud and busy, and I was careful to keep my voice down as we planned the rest of the evening.

He finished his double Scotch, and what little inhibition he had was disappearing fast. He was drawing nearer to the entrance of his own cave of webs, where I was patiently waiting. He pulled his wallet out and produced his credit card, handing it to the bartender. When the bartender returned, I watched as Andrew scribbled his name on the receipt and then proceeded to cross a line through the tip section, ignoring the amount of restraint and reserve displayed by the patient man who had served him.

"I'll meet you in front of the hotel in a few minutes," I told him. "I gotta piss real quick."

"Sure, man. I need a smoke anyway."

I watched for a minute as he stumbled out of the bar and into the lobby toward the entrance. I handed the bartender some cash to make up for Andrew's lack of respect. My intention for staying behind was not to use the restroom. It was to distance myself from Andrew. I wanted to leave the bartender with the impression that the man had been nothing more than an annoying drunk stranger who was looking for someone to lean on. And I didn't want anyone to see us leave together. When the wife began to search for him in a day or so, I didn't want to be the last one he was seen with.

I sat alone and finished my drink before making my way to the elevator. I exited through the side entrance to the restaurant, emerging to a sidewalk that was obscured from the front door where Andrew waited, exhaling plumes of smoke.

Chapter 17

Andrew wasn't much of a conversationalist, but he was — I had to admit to myself — entertaining. This was in no way a redeeming quality. It was simply the alcohol, allowing him to switch over to humor in order to hide his true self. But no matter how hard he tried, nothing could overshadow the darkness inside of him. It itched to find another opportunity to hurt the young boy. The callouses and scars built up along the boy's impressionable brain were never going to be enough for Andrew. His mission in this life, his purpose, was to torture the innocent, and it was my mission to release him from this place. He would never stop on his own.

The small amount of Scotch that I did consume was now wearing off as we made our way toward Bourbon Street. What little warmth it provided was no match for the bitter cold wind that had just increased in intensity. One would think brutally cold wind gusts with a high likelihood for precipitation would thin the streets of New Orleans, but they would be wrong. The crowds were just as thick as on a warm, cloudless afternoon.

When we made the turn onto Bourbon Street the crowds went from dense to a congested traffic jam of screaming, highly-intoxicated individuals. There was no way in hell I was going to proceed any farther. I knew there would be crowds, but I had no idea it would be shoulder to shoulder the entire length and width of the street. It would take us hours to cross through to where we were going, and that was if I didn't lose him in the crowd. I had to think, and fast.

"Andrew. Hey, man," I said. He was already making his way toward the center of the street, just about to group up behind a line of middle-aged ladies. "Andrew," I yelled. He didn't turn around, unable to hear over the deafening crowd. I hurried toward him and snagged the back of his shirt seconds before he melded into the swiftly moving horde.

"Mike, what the hell? Come on, let's go, man. Titties are waiting." Then it came to me. He had forgotten the bag of beads that he had been bragging about in the bar.

"Your beads," I said in a hurried voice. "Where are they?"

"Shit! Holy shit, how in the hell did I forget the beads!?" He patted himself down as if they were hiding in his pockets. "We have to go back for them. We have to get them or this whole night is shit."

I nodded, and pulled him to the side, away from the conveyor belt of people flooding forward. Once the crowd's gravity yanked you into orbit, there was no getting loose until you reached the next street.

"I got an idea," I said. "I know a place a lot closer than the hotel where we can get some killer beads for cheap."

It was like I had handed him the key to a warm hotel room filled with willing, large-breasted women. "Shit, yeah," he said, "let's go."

• • •

Luring Andrew where I wanted him was not as difficult as I had once thought. Whatever minuscule amount of discretion he owned, there was not much left to challenge my direction, especially given the bait that I had offered. Obviously I had no intention of buying beads, nor did I know of a place that sold extravagant ones for cheap. But I did know of a little secluded shop nearby that was perfect for his release party.

Once we made the turn into the alley, his ranting about his plans for the beads switched to questions about our location.

"Are you sure there's a shop down this alley?" Andrew said. "It looks pretty dead, man."

"Trust me, I know. I ran into this place after getting lost. It looks sketchy, but it's a local hangout."

"Fine, whatever. Let's just hurry up and get the beads. It's cold and I'm losing my buzz."

"We're here." We were standing under the flickering red light, next to the entrance.

"Where? Here?" Andrew peered through the dirt-encrusted glass door. "There aren't any lights on."

"They keep the front entrance dark, to cloak it," I said. "I told you, man, this place is for locals only."

"How'd you get in then?"

"The guy liked me for some reason. I don't know. I was nice."

Andrew laughed at my explanation. "Okay, is there some secret knock or password that we need to enter?" he said, sarcastically.

"Not that I'm aware of," I said.

"Wait a second. Is this one of those voodoo shops I heard about, where they sacrifice shit, like goats? If so, I'm not going in there. That shit scares the hell out of me."

"No," I said laughing, "nothing like that. They just sell cool stuff for locals, at good prices. And they don't like the punk, drunk tourist teenagers rampaging through their store. Just let me do the talking, all right?" I turned the doorknob. It was unlocked, thankfully. Having to break in would have thrown off the entire plan. I guess Cal wasn't concerned with locking up his cousin's death chamber before leaving town. Now that I thought about it, it would have certainly put a wrench in my brash plan if Cal had decided not to heed my warning. I remained cautious, just in case.

"Sure," he said, a small amount apprehension in his voice. If it weren't for the alcohol, I felt confident he wouldn't have entered. I couldn't blame the guy. The place gave off an ominous vibe, and for good reason. His instincts were spot on, just misdirected.

I moved quickly ahead of him before his eyes had time to adjust to the darkness. Lucky for me, I was an opportunist and had planned ahead. I had enough supplies inside my inner jacket pocket. I also had the place mapped out in my head. I moved to the far wall on the right and waited for him to catch up.

"This place is musty as hell," Andrew said. "Where the hell are the lights?"

"Follow my voice. The door is on your right. Just use your hands and follow the wall."

"I have to admit, Mike, this place is pretty lame," Andrew grumbled, as his fingers slid quickly along the wall. "They could at least light a damn candle or something."

A few seconds later, he was next to me. He ran into my shoulder with his hand. "There you are," he said.

"Here," I said, "I'll guide you the rest of the way. It'll be easier."

"Thanks."

I grabbed his left shoulder with my left hand. A few seconds later, I was lowering him to the floor, allowing a mild thump as punishment for his not tipping the bartender.

• • •

Most things in the guide's death room were as I had left them. Just a few items had been removed, likely by Cal for sentimental reasons. Thankfully he was nowhere to be seen. If he were smart, he would be several states away and starting his life over — not many get a chance at a fresh start.

Andrew was not a particularly heavy man, but dragging him through a few rooms in the dark was a pain in the ass. After attaching him to the pulley system, I sat in the familiar chamber and rested until Andrew decided he was ready to wake up. With the alcohol in his system, he may have taken a bit longer, but I didn't care. I had no place to be and no one waiting on me. I could spend all night working, and all day sleeping if I wanted. I was a free man once again — lucky, as Andrew had put it.

I sure didn't feel lucky or free, though. In fact, I had never felt completely free, unfettered, or liberated. There had always been a tugging, a weight pulling on my soul ever since I can remember. I'm not really sure there is such a thing as free in this life, other than a false perception from our ever-acclimating brains. But I had to remind myself that none of it mattered at the moment. I had a job to complete and I knew better than to let my mind wander off into the depths of hopelessness. I have always managed to find a way out, and I wasn't going to let despair stop me this time.

I must have drifted off for a while, because when I woke up Andrew was silently staring at me, stuck somewhere between disbelief and denial. I had removed everything from his pockets, including a lighter, which I'd used to light the array of candles that were left over from the tour guide's many death rituals, and which were now scattered around the room. I was sure to shed enough light around the chamber so he could build a horrible scenario in his mind. He needed to see the blood stains along the walls and floor, the small animal bones lying in bowls, and the writing in blood on the huge mirror — thanks to yours truly — that read 'See you soon.'

I remained motionless for a few minutes, letting his mind drift off into whatever nightmarishly dark realm he could imagine. I wanted him to get a taste of the terror he'd continually bestowed upon the young boy. How long must one terrorize a child before he becomes as numb as Andrew had? I would assume a long time, which is why this filth was in front of me. He deserved to have the same done to him, but I didn't want to be in the presence of this piece of garbage long enough to return the favor. Besides, the faster I released him the quicker the little boy could return to childhood. Sure, there would be scar tissue on his tiny soul, but hopefully we'd met in time, while at least a shred of innocence remained.

"Andrew," I started. I sat in the corner of the room, my face obscured slightly by shadows and flickering candle light. "This may come as a shock to you, this environment, your inability to protect yourself, hands bound, but it shouldn't if you believe in justice. Do you, Andrew? Believe in the right of the innocent to be avenged?"

He remained silent and still, but when I stepped from the shadows his dumbfounded look was replaced by scrunched brows and anger. "What the fuck, Mike? I thought we were friends. What the hell is all of this? Why am I tied up?"

"Friends," I said, laughing. "*Mike* isn't even my real name. But enough about me. This is really about you. Your mission here. I have to say, you don't hide it very well."

"Hide what? What mission are you talking about?"

"Don't be coy, Andrew. You boasted the minute I met you, revealing the nastiness for everyone to see. You reeked of false sorrows and deceit, so arrogant in your moves that you performed in front of a live audience in the lobby. I suppose no one has challenged your parenting techniques until now. Am I right?"

"You don't know what you're talking about!" he spat. "So what if I discipline them. I'm the only father they have left. They need it. Come on, man. They wear on you. They need a good spanking to put them back in line. Aren't you going to have kids one day?"

"Not yet."

"You'll know what I mean soon enough."

Why was I letting this man speak to me as if he had anything of value or interest to say? Maybe it was because I actually *did* have a child on the way, and I desperately wanted advice. But advice from this guy?

"Don't lecture me," I said. "Those aren't even your kids. And you push around and beat that little boy like you were a bully on the playground. That's his life you're screwing with! You're creating scars that he can't erase!"

"Fuck you, man. Now let me outta here before I fuck you up like I did the boy." His demeanor suddenly switched, as if his mission statement was being etched on his brain with a soldering gun. "You think this shit scares me? Who the hell do you think you are?" He was trying another technique I had seen many times — intimidation.

"Just the one who is about to release you."

"Now you're making sense," he said, smiling a little in relief. "Just let me go and we'll forget the whole thing."

"I think you're misinterpreting my use of the word *release*," I said.

I got up from the chair and walked toward him. I wanted him to flinch, to feel the angst before the first blow landed. I wanted to keep striking him over and over as he did the boy, until his reflexes numbed. But what good would it do? All I needed was one good vulnerable flinch. That would suffice.

"Your time is up, Andrew. You've had your fun, and likely made them proud, but I have found you. And *this* is my mission."

"You're fucking crazy, dude. There aren't any missions." I walked swiftly toward him. He clenched his teeth, squinting his eyes in preparation for the pain he was sure was about to come. I stepped behind him and tied a piece of cloth around his mouth. He struggled and attempted to kick me, but only managed to topple a bowl, spilling fragments of animal bones onto the floor.

"I will not be punching or slapping you," I said. "Nor am I here to torture you until you reveal a particular truth. I am here to simply stop you from damaging any more lives." I grabbed his arm and pulled the syringe from my pocket. Until that point, he hadn't noticed the IV in his left arm. He attempted to pull away from me, but his action was futile.

As I was about to inject the substance into his IV line, I glanced at the mirror across the room and noticed the full shadow of a man hovering next to me. I jerked my head around toward him, but the image was gone. What the hell was this? Was his soul attempting to escape before I even had a chance to release it? There was no chill in the air that I could feel or sense. The candles were unmoving, not flickering as they would normally be in the presence of the soul. I glanced back toward the mirror, but the shadow was not there anymore. I turned him toward me and stared deep into his dark eyes. They were fearful, and full of anger, but I sensed the soul was still hovering anxiously inside.

"You aren't leaving on your own!" I screamed. "This is my part to fulfill!"

His eyes widened. He started mumbling something behind the cloth that I was pretty sure was some vulgar threat. I snatched his arm, pulling it toward me and quickly finished my mission before there were any more escape attempts. What the hell was happening? Things were changing rapidly now that I was back releasing on my own. Ever since arriving in New Orleans, the game had seemed to be taking another direction — full forms, partial forms emerging, surrounding the room, trying to escape before I intervened. What did this mean for me? Did I have to be quicker? Were the specimens becoming wise to me? What about the possibility of the souls escaping before I was finished with my part? Could they find another body to occupy, evicting the previous tenants?

I sat down on the cold floor and tugged on my hair as my head pounded with pain and confusion. I was distracted and flummoxed by his escape attempt. The possibility of a dirty soul taking over the body of an innocent was highly clever, but also disturbing. This new twist brought with it all kinds of potential challenges.

I had no idea how to manage this latest piece of information, so I placed it in the back of my head for later. I would have plenty of time on the drive back to Dallas to decipher its meaning.

Chapter 18

On the afternoon after the release, I was sitting on the balcony of my hotel room watching the crowds file down the street. My phone was on the small table beside me, and it seemed to be taunting me to call Lesley. For the past thirty minutes, pride had me locked in a full nelson wrestling hold, restraining me from picking up the phone and dialing her number. She should have been home by then. I thought she would have given me updates on her trip back — at least a text message. I had been checking my phone regularly, but there was nothing. No text or voice messages.

I knew she kept her prepaid phone on her, especially since she took the bus. She was already gambling with her safety by traveling alone, and now she was also risking the welfare of our unborn child. I only wanted to make sure they were both safe, but I felt so betrayed that I couldn't even muster the will to text her. Our horns had clashed and were interlocked. Neither was budging.

So why was this so hard? Why couldn't I just drop my

crippling pride? I was in a skirmish with my subconscious, which was making sure she had ample time to mull over her decision to leave. As I struggled to make sense of the situation, my little friend growing on my brain extended one of its slimy tendrils and knocked, reminding me of his presence. How many breaths did I really have left to allow pride to intervene in my decisions? What worried me even more than breathing was the shrouded length of time until my mind was completely incapacitated, leaving me unable to make a decision. I had been in too many nursing homes and seen more than my share of neutralized minds to let things dawdle. Which also meant I couldn't let the unknown stifle my plans. So what should I do?

I would give her more time so, because I didn't want to seem overly eager and desperate. Once she was home and settled, she would text me. For now, I was going to focus on Dr. Randal.

From the moment I decided that Dr. Randal deserved a much worse fate than rotting in an asylum, I had struggled with the possibility of having to harm an innocent to get to him. My only way inside the secure facility, other than breaking in, was with the help of Dr. Fortune — a psychiatrist who had shared an office space with Randal back before he went on a killing spree. Dr. Fortune was the one who had written a note permitting me to gain entry and visit with him. From our last interaction, I didn't anticipate Fortune having any issues with access, but I wasn't going to let anything stand in the way of avenging my mom.

My plan, once I had gained entrance to the asylum, was to help him escape — I would figure out the details on the trip back. Once out, I would hunt him just like he made his patients hunt their victims. He would feel the terror that his victims suffered through. Once I captured him, we would have a rational conversation — as rational as possible — and I'd make him relive every agonizing moment he placed in my mom's vulnerable mind. He would see himself for what he truly was, and then and only then would he be released.

I was not hunting him to cure an ailment. This was simple, age-old revenge. I had to watch my mom wither away as she struggled with the thoughts placed there by him. Day after day she sat staring into space, suffering. His release would not be short, or pleasant.

I found Dr. Fortune's office number online. I dialed the number and after a few rings a female answered the phone with no discernible accent.

"Dr. Fortune's office. How may I assist you?"

"Yes, ma'am, I was wondering if it might be possible to speak with Dr. Fortune?"

"May I ask who is calling," she said, "and is he expecting your call?"

"No, ma'am, he is not. My name is Tryke Harper. He had helped me once before and I am once again needing his assistance."

"Yes, sir, Mr. Harper," she answered quickly. "Give me a second and I will transfer you."

"Thank you," I said, pleasantly surprised. I didn't remember her voice as the lady who had helped me the first time I visited his office — there was much less abhorrence and bitterness in this woman's voice. No interrogation or scolding about how valuable his time was. Maybe I had made an impression on the good doctor the last time we spoke. Still, I thought it was a bit odd, but I didn't linger on it long. I had managed to get through to him and that was all that mattered at the moment.

A minute later the phone clicked and a man said, "Hello, Tryke, good to hear from you. I was a little surprised when my secretary said it was you calling, pleasantly surprised that is. What can I do for you?"

He was certainly perkier than the last time we had met. "Do you remember granting me access to the asylum to visit with Dr. Randal?"

"Of course I remember."

"Well, he told me a few things that were quite disturbing about my family and —"

"I was afraid he would do that. Your story about your dad's journals and the determined look on your face reminded me of my own past. So what did he tell you?"

Dr. Fortune seemed truly interested. I wasn't expecting to have a lengthy conversation on the phone, but if it would get him to write me another note to see Randal without conflict, then so be it. "Did you know he was hypnotizing his patients and making them do things for him?"

There was a pause and when he spoke again, his voice had a more serious tone. "I'm not going to lie, my old colleague has held many secrets for a long time, which I have learned more about since he has been in the asylum. After you visited with him, he confided in me a few weeks later about his hidden storage unit. Whatever you two talked about must have sparked something for him to get in touch with me."

"So you know about his crazy plot involving his patients?"

"Unfortunately, yes. But only what little he told me. I never visited the storage unit for obvious reason — evidence and what not. He swore that no one knew about it, but I wasn't taking any chances."

"Why did he want you to see it?"

"Guilt, I suppose. He didn't really elaborate much about the storage. He briefly mentioned his patients and then his thoughts quickly shifted back to his wife and daughter."

"Did you tell the police about the storage unit?"

I needed to know if the unit was still available. It would serve as the perfect setting for his release. Since Fortune knew now, I would most certainly be implicated in Randal's escape and death, but it no longer mattered. I was already wanted, and by the time they found him I would be far away.

"No," he said, "I figured he was suffering enough, having to live with the fact that he'd killed his wife and kid. His reputation was already ruined, not to mention he has a life sentence in an asylum. Why make things worse? Besides, I was the one who testified to his insanity."

I suppose I should thank him for getting Randal placed in an asylum. It would have been a far greater task to get him out of jail.

"Good point." I had to agree and stay neutral. If he were to suspect I meant Randal harm, he might not write me the note.

"So what can I do for you, Tryke?" he asked again. "I take it he told you about the storage unit, and now you have questions regarding what you found. Is that the case?"

"Yes." Wait, I thought. I'd never mentioned that Randal told me about the storage unit. But what did it matter? He hadn't told the police. "I have some more questions after reading my mom's file. I called you because you helped me last time, and I thought that if you didn't mind, you could write me another pass to visit with Dr. Randal. So I can get some final closure."

"I have a better idea, Tryke, if you would be open to hear me out."

"Okay..." I said, unsure of the sudden turn in the conversation.

"In my professional opinion, I think talking with an outside acquaintance first would be helpful. It would organize your thoughts and you could make a list of the questions you want answered. How about we have a session before you go see him? Allow your thoughts some room to stretch their legs. I won't charge you a thing. Also, I wouldn't mind a little insight into what you found in the storage. I have some appointments open this week."

"I appreciate the offer Doctor," I said, "but this is sort of personal. I don't think I'm comfortable talking about it just yet."

"Tryke, I'm a trained psychiatrist who already knows a little about your situation. You can trust I will keep the session confidential. And if for some reason I am unable to satisfy your thoughts, or you feel uncomfortable at any time, we'll stop immediately and I will write you as many passes as your heart desires to visit with Dr. Randal."

I needed his help, but I did not want to discuss anything with this man. He was nice enough, but he would never understand my side. Nor could I take the chance of him finding out about me and my battle. Not that I didn't trust myself, but what if he somehow tricked me into hypnosis?

"I'm not one for office visits," I said "Nothing against you, but they make me uncomfortable."

He laughed. "I completely understand. Then how about we meet for coffee somewhere? You name the place."

I considered the request. A public place. What could it hurt? And besides, he was offering a free pass without conflict with an innocent.

"Okay," I said, "but it will be a few days. I'm not in the area at the moment."

"What do you say we meet a week from today, then?"

"That should be okay, but I'd rather call you when I get back into town to set a time and place."

"Sounds good. Just call my office and Patty will patch you through to me."

After hanging up the phone with Dr. Fortune, I felt a wave of unease wash over me. What if Fortune was cooperating with the police? I quickly pushed the thought aside. My paranoia was kicking in after realizing I was about to make my way back to Dallas. *Risky* wasn't a strong enough description of my next venture. It was borderline insane, a preposterous act that tempted fate — that was, if one truly believed in fate — an action that would inevitably precipitate my capture. I wasn't one to tremble in place until something bad happened, and I was always up for pushing the fence open just a little bit farther to catch a glimpse of what was waiting on the other side.

Chapter 19

I thought about the conversation I'd had with Dr. Fortune for the better part of the next morning, not only due to its strangeness, but also because it reminded me of the trip I had to make back home. I'd known since arriving in New Orleans that I would eventually have to return to Dallas and settle a debt with Dr. Randal. But I thought I would have Lesley with me to lean on and help with the planning. I had never before relied on anyone but myself when it came to organizing one of my missions, but I had to admit that the longer we were together, the more comfortable I felt having her beside me. It was nice to have another brain to bounce ideas off of and to argue back with me about a point. Even more than that, it was nice having someone who understood me.

But that was before the betrayal. Now that I knew she was not a player on the battlefield and her commitment was never what I thought it was, I could move on with my goal as if it had never been interrupted.

My thoughts weren't just focused on Randal. I had to

make it back to Dallas in the first place. I had to be as inconspicuous as I could and hope that there wasn't an APB out on Lesley's car. The make and model would place a target on me and warrant a closer inspection by law enforcement. Hopefully, the tinted windows and a change of license plate would be enough to deter a closer inspection.

It was late afternoon and I was making my way to the place where I had stashed Lesley's vehicle when we first arrived — under a bridge among a forgotten graveyard of waterlogged cars and trucks marinating in the filth left over from Hurricane Katrina. It was a good distance away from the hotel, but I didn't mind the walk. The cool air was a welcome relief for a brain on the brink of overheating. I had a ton to do, and all needed to be precise and without error. One slip and I was done for, locked up for good. I had to be quick but thorough, finish what I came to do and move on. If things went as planned, I would then make my way back to the coast and probably toward Florida, just as I had decided before Lesley left.

Halfway to my destination, I decided it had been long enough. The unknown was ripping me apart and distracting my thoughts, so I chose to be the one to abandon my pride. If I knew she was okay and that the police hadn't arrested her, it would make my journey that much less stressful. It would knock out at least one of the many worries clouding my thoughts. All it would take was a simple broad text to get information on her condition, and nothing more. I stopped on the sidewalk and quickly typed out two words, and pressed Send.

Okay? Safe?

I continued walking — allowing my nerves room to breathe — and holding the phone by my side. I didn't know why I was nervous. It was only a text. It didn't require reading body language or putting on a false facade. Barely a few minutes had passed when my phone let out a short vibration, although it felt like hours. I stopped again, unlocked the screen, and stared down at the short return text. The brevity of the message wasn't what frustrated or concerned me.

Yes, but…

But? What the hell did that mean? Was she joking? Not likely after our last conversation and the letter she had written me. Things would be serious from here on out until she got the answer she wanted. So what was this then? Was she considering how to respond? Or was this part of her plan, to make me suffer? I waited what I thought was an appropriate amount of time, and then texted her back. Anger, frustration, and confusion all bound and wound tightly, and didn't allow my patience room to enter.

But? What?

This time the wait was even more agonizing because of the tiny bomb of information she had planted. I paced the sidewalk in front of a bakery. From the inside, I probably looked like one of those annoying people animating their entire conversation in public: aimlessly pacing and running my restless hands through my hair, a frustrated look on my face. When she wrote back a minute later, the text had much more information. I sat down on an empty bench and began to read.

My parents aren't happy that I loaned you my car. And before you get mad at me, it was either tell them you had it or they report it stolen. I know, I know, I should not have gone home first, but I couldn't handle the bus any longer. A man stared at me all the way from Shreveport to Dallas. I felt unsafe. Not to mention, I was constantly nauseous. I had nowhere else to go. I told my parents that I needed a break from school. How are you?

Stupid! Stupid! Stupid! What was she thinking, going back to her parents' house? Now, they're involved. Has she told them that she was pregnant? Have the police been snooping around the house? Were there pictures of me on television? I assumed not, because she hadn't said so. I quickly responded, careful to avoid any angry remarks that would stifle the conversation. I needed information, not a text war.

What did you tell your parents about us? Have you checked the news feeds? Anything?

This time there was a longer pause between my text and her answer. I pictured Lesley thinking about how to phrase her next words.

I told my parents that I'm pregnant. It was all I had to keep them from asking a hundred questions. They instantly forgot about the car and college. They think you are only borrowing the car for a few days to get back and forth to work while your truck is in the shop. I haven't had a chance to check the news, but my parents didn't say anything to me about it.

I sighed out loud, inadvertently drawing attention to myself. A couple exited the bakery. I turned away from them and held the phone at arm's length, using all of my will not to slam it against the concrete. What was happening? The Lesley I knew would have avoided complicating our situation further. She was smart, but something had changed her.

She wrote back before I had chance to respond.

Have you decided anything?

I got up from the bench and started walking again toward my destination, leaving the bakery patrons to find another person to entertain them. I wanted to tell Lesley how mad I was that she had left, and how betrayed I felt. I had trusted her to be my companion, to join me in battle until the end. And to think I was going to ask her to marry me. I was stupid to believe the Gamemakers would ever allow me a companion. It was all a ploy. Her agreeing to be part of this was another of their tricks. An attempt to throw me off, a devious distraction on the field of battle. What better way to defeat your enemies than through the heart?

I will let you know as soon as I get back into town. We'll talk in person.

This had to be done face-to-face and not over the phone. The only good thing that had come out of the text exchange was that she was safe, and the fact that my picture wasn't being broadcast everywhere. She obviously hadn't changed her mind, nor did I expect her to. She had given me a choice and left me to decide our fate. But little did she know that she had already decided for both of us. As mad as I was at her for leaving, I didn't want things left undone. I would release Randal, Lesley and I would talk things over, and I'd be on my way.

Lost in thought, I hadn't realized that I'd stumbled upon the array of forgotten vehicles under the bridge, but the fetid air burning my nostrils brought me back to my surroundings. Though I had the spot pinpointed on the map, I hit the panic button on the key ring to speed up the process — nausea was quickly setting in. Once I picked my way through the substantial amount of detritus, I located the car. I snagged a license plate from one of the other vehicles and quickly fastened it in place. Then I got out of there.

● ● ●

It was dusk by the time I returned to the hotel. I stopped and fueled up the car and grabbed a few snacks for the road, including a variety of energy drinks. I decided I would check out of the hotel early in the morning. After I finished packing and setting out my clothes for the following day, I sat on the end of the bed and considered how I would spend my last night in New Orleans. With Mardi Gras in full gear, the idea of wading through more detritus on Bourbon Street didn't seem appealing. So I settled on a relaxing evening for one: a boring hearty meal and a stiff drink, followed by what I hoped was a decent night's rest. I had an eight-hour drive ahead of me. I still had some sleeping pills, but since I was alone again I didn't enjoy the luxury of completely dropping my guard. A few *night-drifts* — a name I gave unworthy naps — would have to suffice.

The restaurant I chose wasn't fancy or well-known, but a local spot that the hotel clerk said was a quiet local hangout that served a decent jambalaya. There was music on Friday and Saturday nights, usually a jazz player. She said that even though it was Mardi Gras, the tourists usually steered away from it. She didn't elaborate. I suspected the owners did a decent job of keeping the riffraff out.

The dimly-lit atmosphere of the restaurant, along with the smooth music emanating from a small stage, provided a soothing blanket on which my busy neurons could lie back and relax. I sat alone by a window facing the street, sipping on a glass of Scotch after finishing my meal. I was pleasantly full and slightly intoxicated, but not from the liquor. Sometimes food had a way of evoking that same euphoric feeling. The jambalaya had accomplished just such a feat. It contained exactly the right amount of heat and salty creole flavor, and the side of buttery garlic bread melted delicately on my palate. Seeking to minimize any stops I'd need to make, I even ordered a second plate to take with me in the morning.

My euphoria quickly evaporated when my attention was captured by a man across the street, sitting alone at a small cafe table. When I took a second glance toward him, I caught *him* staring at *me* from under a straw hat, the kind a typical tourist would wear at a beach resort. He didn't look away, or seem to care that I had caught him. I looked behind me to see if maybe there was someone else he had been looking at, but there were only busy waiters passing by on their way to the kitchen. He was obviously observing me. But why?

I wanted to keep my cool, but the longer I sat there, the more uncomfortable I became. I could feel my heart steadily picking up its pace. The delicious food I had just devoured began churning, threatening a mass exodus. Get hold of yourself, Tryke. It was only a man staring. Maybe he thought I looked familiar, and was in the process of trying to figure out who I was. Not totally farfetched, as I was doing the same thing. But as I sat there trying to think of all the reasons this man might be focused on me, I couldn't shake the gut-wrenching feeling that he was more than a curious tourist attempting to put together a puzzle of identity.

I pulled some cash from my front pocket and placed it on the table. I had noted the restaurant exits when I was first seated, and now I began recalling them, just in case. I also began mentally rehearsing my escape route out of the city — the one I had outlined on my map. I was confident that as long as I wasn't surrounded by a SWAT team, I had a pretty decent plan in place. First, I would walk briskly through the kitchen, out the back door, and into an alleyway that led to a main street where the crowds were thick. I would lose my hat and top layered shirt, dropping them into a trash receptacle. I would then look for a gaggle of drunken college kids and blend into their group.

Sipping on my drink, I tapped my right boot nervously on the linoleum and began searching up and down the street for conspicuous vehicles, namely unmarked police cars. It was all clear, except for a marked New Orleans cop car adjacent from the restaurant. I felt a little better, but there was no way I'd be dropping my guard any time soon.

When the waiter returned, I handed him the cash on the table and thanked him with a tip. I decided I would sit ten more minutes, and if the guy was still across the street and staring at me, I was going to approach him. I could have taken the more cautious route out the side door and back to my hotel, but I'm always up for inching the gate a little farther open. Besides, if anyone was going to be caught by surprise, I wanted it to be him, not me.

The man was still there, his gaze unwavering. I got up from the table and slowly made my way to the front of the restaurant, trying not to lose sight of him. If this guy *was* an undercover officer, he wasn't doing a very good job of being inconspicuous. Now that the couple seated behind him was gone, he was the only patron seated outside, as obvious as the red flashing light in the famous hurricane drink of New Orleans.

I crossed the street at the corner, leaving him at a diagonal from me. With my peripheral vision, I could see that he was watching me as I lolled across the street. Once on the other side, I removed my hands from my pockets and headed down the sidewalk to his table. His head was down, looking at what appeared to be a cell phone, but his body language made it clear that he was tracking me. I could hear my own footsteps, one foot in front of the other, the heels of my boots scraping along the concrete, the other sounds of the street blocked out as I approached his table. When I was only a few feet away, he looked up and smiled under his straw hat.

I didn't smile back. I couldn't. The familiar face didn't warrant a pleased expression.

Chapter 20

Dr. Fortune was in New Orleans.

"Have a seat, Tryke." His tone was less chipper than it had sounded on the phone, though not entirely unwelcoming. It was him all right — thick brown hair, a questionable wig, round spectacles, and a demeanor that matched that of an aging psychiatrist. Intrigued, not to mention baffled, I did as he asked. "I hope you don't mind," he said, "but I went ahead and ordered you a drink. Scotch, I presume?"

"Yes… thank you," I said, ignoring how he had guessed my drink of choice. There were other things on my mind at the moment. For instance, I had spoken with him within the last twenty-four hours and he didn't mention anything about being out of town. In fact, he said he had some appointments open this week. I suppose he had enough time to fly down here since we talked, but even if that added up, what were the odds of him choosing New Orleans and spotting me? Was he cooperating with the police? I was beginning to understand what bait felt like.

I searched the street once again for any sign of a police presence, attempting to do so without signaling my own suspicions.

"We're alone, I can assure you," Dr. Fortune said. "You can relax."

"Huh? What are you talking about?"

"Tryke, its okay. Your uncle doesn't know I'm here."

Wait, what? How did my uncle know Dr. Fortune? More importantly, how did *anyone* know I was here?

As I was about to begin my interrogation, the waiter interrupted, setting a glass of Scotch on the rocks in front of me.

"That will be all for now, sir, thank you." Dr. Fortune's voice was stern. The waiter shuffled away without question.

I desperately wanted to down the entire drink to calm my nerves, but until I had more information, I needed to keep my head clear.

"You mentioned my uncle," I said. "How do you know him?" I somehow managed to keep my voice and demeanor calm and cool, though my insides were kicking and screaming with guarded vigilance. I'd done pretty well over the years at training myself to remain calm under pressure. At the same time, some of it had come naturally. I suspect the Gamemakers had something to do with that.

"He came to my office a week ago, flashing his badge around and asking a ton of questions. He started talking about some journals. I assumed they were the same ones you mentioned the first time you came to see me, when you were searching for Dr. Randal. Once I assured him that I was no threat, he broke down and confided in me. He told me that he was coming to get you here in New Orleans and take you back home. He wanted me to come with him, thinking that a psychiatrist could help bring you in without conflict. I immediately declined by telling him that I didn't feel comfortable with the situation."

"So why are you here?" I asked. I tried to mask the fact

that what he'd just told me about my uncle had evoked a newly heightened level of alertness. If Fortune could hunt me down, a homicide detective certainly could. But for some reason, I couldn't quite understand how my uncle knew where I was. And after Fortune's next words, I never came back to it. My uncle probably never told him anyway.

"Before Dr. Randal died, he told me a secret about your mom that included him."

This bit of shocking information caused me to lose my cool, and confused me even further. "Wait a damn minute," I said. "Just wait! What? Before he *died*? I just talked to you on the phone a few hours ago. You said you could get me in to see him."

"I know, I know. Just hear me out. I realize all of this appears obscure to say the least, but I have my reasons." He held up a lone finger. "One second." He motioned for the waiter to bring him another drink. "Things are complicated, but I want you to know that I'm not the bad guy."

Not the bad guy? What the hell did that mean? I didn't trust this man, but he had unleashed some magical words that triggered a keen interest of mine. I picked up the drink in front of me and took a sip.

"First, tell me what happened to Dr. Randal," I said, staying vigilant and surveying the immediate area again for a quick exit.

"He had been on suicide watch since he arrived in the asylum, but somehow he managed to acquire some string. He hanged himself in his room a few days after I met with him. He had seemed disheveled and a bit vacant, but I didn't think there was anything unusual about that. When he told me about your mom, though, something inside of him seemed to spark."

"I'm listening," I said, attempting to hide my desperate yearning for this information about my mom. Dr. Fortune was up to something. I just didn't know what. Not yet.

The waiter returned, dropping Fortune's drink in front of him. He immediately took a long swig, as if his next words needed a nudge.

"He told me that his greatest regret, only after the murder of his wife and daughter, was your mom." He paused and took a deep breath. "This next part may be a little hard to hear."

As I sat waiting for the climax, I took another sip of the watered-down Scotch to quench my parched mouth again.

After I lowered my glass to the table, he continued. "Your mom may have been involved in the murder of Dr. Randal's wife and daughter."

I sat there, silent, unable to comprehend what I had just heard. I suddenly felt dizzy, like I had just gotten out of the Gravitron at the state fair. At first I thought it was anxiety, as panic and anger had begun building from his last words. Dr. Randal had done the unthinkable, taking away my mom's will, and bending her thoughts to his will. Now I find out that the son of a bitch is dead. There would be no vengeance for my mom. And on top of everything, my mom was involved in the murder of Randal's family? I didn't believe it, but now that he was dead, how would I ever know for sure?

Dr. Fortune allowed me a few more minutes to process the information, but no matter how much time I was given, I wasn't going to be able to do it there, in his presence. I needed time alone, to think, to put the pieces together.

"How... wa — sh —," I could feel my tongue swelling as I attempted to expel the words from my mouth. I knew what I wanted to say, but for some reason it wasn't coming out. My mouth felt like a fan had been blowing hot, arid wind in it for hours. I lifted the drink from the table, spilling most of it down my face and shirt. My vision was blurry, but I could still see Dr. Fortune reaching over to place my glass back on the table.

"You're going to be okay, Tryke," he said. "Take a few

deep breaths and listen to me."

The next thing I remember, we were walking out from under the covered patio and onto the street. The wind wasn't cold anymore, likely due to the numbness I felt all over my body. Dr. Fortune seemed calm and encouraging. I could hear a cacophony of intoxicated individuals and the occasional blast of horns, but I had a hard time focusing on my surroundings.

After what felt like a few blocks of walking, we came to a narrow passageway and slowed our pace considerably. It seemed as though time was lapsing, and I struggled to put things together. My thoughts were scattered, and I tried to grasp onto anything I could. Dr. Fortune had been quiet for a long while, or maybe it was the time lapse again. I couldn't be sure. I looked over at him, but he seemed to be focused on our route. I wanted to demand to know where we were going, but I still couldn't get the words out.

The passageway narrowed even more and then we stopped. I noticed a very faint light above me, and then we moved through a doorway. The darkness beyond completely enveloped me. I felt suddenly calm, not knowing or caring where he had led me. Just before I completely lost consciousness, a familiar smell hit my nose — incense and blood.

• • •

When I awoke, I felt a horrible ache thumping along the top of my head. I also felt a sharp pain running up both of my arms. I was groggy, as if I had just experienced one hell of a night on Bourbon Street. When I reached out to grab my head, I realized my wrists were bound, hence the pain shooting up my arms. My legs had given out, and I was now resting on my knees. The room was dark, save for the faint yellow glow from under what appeared to be a door. It was adjacent to me, about fifteen feet away.

Initially, I had no recollection of how I had gotten there.

It was as if the last twenty-four hours had been erased from my memory. Attempting to make sense of my situation, I let my eyes relax so I could get some kind of grip on my surroundings, and then hopefully find a way out. A few minutes later — and no closer to recalling my memory — my eyes acclimated to the darkness. The place felt oddly familiar as the shapes around the room materialized. That's when the smell hit me and I knew where I was. I squinted toward the far wall in search of the mirror. My gut contorted as my memory began to unwind.

Through the reflection, I could see a faint figure, a shadow, either kneeling or sitting. I still couldn't determine where the figure was in relation to me. I wanted to call out, but for some reason I wouldn't allow myself. Suddenly, the figure moved, startling me. I reflexively yanked my arms, but they were allowed only so much leeway. My right arm tugged and, with no other choice, the left obeyed. The shadow grew in size as it got closer. I was fixed in place, unable to move.

And then it spoke.

"You weren't out long," the familiar voice said.

My memory by now had returned as I stared up at Dr. Fortune. I tried not to look surprised by his appearance, but it was too late.

"You were suspecting your uncle, weren't you?" he asked. "You thought I was going to turn you in? Quite the contrary, son."

I cleared my throat. "Then why am I strung up like a prisoner?" I could feel the heaviness in my voice as it left my mouth. I had obviously been drugged.

"I do apologize for the manner in which I am conducting this," he said, "but as you well know, you are quite dangerous. So you will have to excuse the restraints until I have certain assurances from you."

"Assurances?"

"First things first. You must know that I am here to

protect you from the police, not turn you in. I had to get to you first, or I may have never had another chance. Especially after talking with your uncle. He really has it in for you. As much as he says he wants to handle the situation peacefully, I got the feeling that if you didn't abide by his orders, he was going to end you. From a purely professional perspective, he looked like a man on edge. I don't think he has much bargaining left in him."

"Why do you want to protect me?" I asked. My memory informed me that there was another statement on which he'd failed to elaborate. "And you said that my mom may have been involved with the murder of Dr. Randal's wife and daughter. What did you mean by *may* have?"

"Your mom had nothing to do with the deaths of his wife and daughter. And by the way, Dr. Randal is still alive, safe in the asylum."

"But why…?"

"It was a distraction, a way to trigger a response. And it worked. You drank the sedative mixture I placed in your drink. Again, I apologize for my deception, but you have to admit that you wouldn't have listened to me otherwise."

As mad as I was that I was being held captive, I was relieved to know he had lied about my mom, and about Randal. He was still alive, which meant I could have my revenge after all. That is, if I survived whatever the hell this was.

"You'd be surprised by my decorum," I said. "Though I have to admit, I *am* becoming less cooperative by the moment."

He laughed at my response, but I wasn't amused. I wanted to know what was going on, and why I was being held against my will in the very place where I had released the cemetery guide and the abusive stepdad.

He stifled another laugh. "Let's just say I have a vested interest in you. And I have for a long time."

"Can we get this over with, please, so I can feel my arms

again? Also, some water would be a nice gesture."

"Of course." He loosened the pulley above my head, providing enough slack for me to sit. He then removed the cap from a bottle of water and poured a few drops into my parched mouth. I should have hesitated to drink, but what reason would he have to sedate me again? I stuck out my tongue like an exhausted dog and scarfed down the liquid. "I suppose I should start from the beginning," he said. "How I came to be."

Chapter 21

Fortune circled the room, lighting a few of the remaining votive candles, and then pulled a chair in front of the huge mirror and faced me. Flickering candles and a creepy counselor gave off the ambiance of ghost-story time at camp. All that was left was for him to hold a flashlight up to his face as he told his tale. Unfortunately, he began without the flashlight.

"It all started when a pharmaceutical rep came to my office. I wasn't too keen on most of them, but I had been doing business with this particular company for years. Not legal business, but under-the-table drug trials for the latest psychiatric medications. It was an easy way to make a few bucks and be on the cutting edge. Most of the drugs were boring. Antidepressants and so forth. But this time my guy mentioned a hypnosis drug. I was more than intrigued, as I had recently hit a wall in my treatment plans. Are you aware of the art of suggestion, Tryke?"

I cleared my throat.

"Of course I am. It's hypnotism."

"Yes, but an art form nonetheless." He offered me more water, but I declined stubbornly. He shrugged and set the bottle back down. "I used to be horrible at it, which is probably the reason I became so infatuated. My colleague, Dr. Randal, was well known for his ability in hypnosis, so obviously I asked him for advice. For some reason I could never get a grasp on the technique, initially, until I introduced a supplement to the mix. I tried a ton of different drugs in the beginning: LSD, mescaline, MDMA or ecstasy, nitrous oxide. Even alcohol. They definitely helped, but I wanted my patients to be alert and receptive, not groggy and withdrawn."

"What were you treating?" I asked, attempting to sound more interested than I actually was. This interest seemed to please him, as his eyes lit up immediately.

"Addictions mostly, but hold on. Patience, Tryke." He held up a finger. "I'm getting to the good stuff. So, this pharmaceutical rep explains to me that there is a drug in trial that has a half-life of one to two hours and gets into the system fast. I was to be the first to use it on real subjects. Why me, you ask? They knew me already and my ability to keep my mouth shut, and well, I had made it abundantly clear to them that if they ever had trials for a 'suggestion drug,' I wanted in." He pulled his chair closer, a huge smile from ear to ear beaming in the candlelight. "I started right away, testing it on a few of my long-term patients who had failed my hypnosis. It worked immediately, and beautifully I might add, with hardly any side effects. And like a kid with too many gifts to open on Christmas, I began treating as many of my patients as I could. But it wasn't enough just to treat their ailments. I wanted to explore the drug's limits. I came up with a hell of a trial. I named it Project Gamemaker."

I felt a twinge of anger rise up in my throat, fall to my stomach, and begin to twist in tangled knots. "Why are you telling me all of this? I already know about the war plan."

"Come on, give me a minute," he said. "I'm getting there. Yes, you know about what you read in Dr. Randal's storage unit, but what you don't know is that it was actually my plan. I planted it in his head. He was the leader of my project, my first-in-command. Only he never knew it. He thought it was all his idea, which was actually key to my project. And before you judge me too harshly for deceiving a colleague, know that I never planned for it to go as far as it did." He paused and crossed his legs. I assumed he was allowing me time to process his words.

Fortune was behind it all? Where did my mom fit into all of this? Was Randal really innocent? Fortune had already lied to me once, so how could I be sure he was telling me the truth? My first instinct was rage and anger. I wanted to rip through the restraints and then him as I considered the implications. But I needed more information before I completely lost my temper and did something stupid. Besides, a little patience went a long way with a narcissist like Fortune. All I had to do was stay calm, keep my tone innocuous, and entertain his ego — a feat easier said than done in the situation I was in. He seemed more than happy to boast about his so-called accomplishments, and for some reason he seemed to want me on his side. I gritted my teeth and nodded toward him to continue.

"The original plan was just to see if the subjects would take the medication. The story: The Gamemakers were the cause of their afflictions — auditory or visual hallucinations — and the pill, if taken during session, would stop them. I was testing their loyalty; basically, how well the pill performed."

"How did you get Dr. Randal to take the medication?"

"Easy, we had coffee every morning and discussed the project — I made the coffee," he said, winking. "He thought he was giving his patients sugar pills, a placebo effect, and they were to stop all of their medication and only receive hypnotherapy, which he had a talent for anyway. As far as he knew, I was writing a paper on hypnotherapy for a magazine and he was helping me out." As I predicted, his passion inflamed with each of my questions. His voice gave way to a hunger to reveal the information that had been patiently brewing for an audience.

"So what the hell actually happened? What went wrong?"

"I had a camera set up in Randal's office — not known to him of course — and watched the sessions. The first month went well, things were on track and the pass rate for most of the recruits was high. Very few were kicked out of the program. The next month I started seeing a few patients argue with Dr. Randal during session. Still, not a bad ratio for a new drug. All I had to do was supplement the memory of those who failed out so it never came back to me. Randal sent them to me for one session and then they were released back to their medications. Things were fine until one of the recruits who had failed out came back to my office irate and demanding answers. What he was saying was nonsense but it still made me apprehensive. I was about to nix the entire program and forget about the one rogue patient and let him go, but he kept coming back. So I had to get rid of him before he went to the police and I was investigated. One session later and he was gone."

"He never came back? What did you tell him?" I knew the answer but I was acting bemused. I still needed more answers. The more detail he gave the better. I was still attempting to put the jumbled mess of information between him and Randal together.

"The story I gave him was sloppy, but it worked all the same. He took his own life. The next day, I read about the man in the paper, and realizing I had been the cause of his death, something was unleashed in me." His fervent voice amplified the room as he continued, not blinking about the man's suicide. "Beyond adrenaline, this was something more. Bloodlust began pooling in my veins. In fact, it fueled the new story I had fabricated. The story needed to be complex enough for a group, discipline oriented, and more deliberate — a direction. I told them that the battle had changed and the pill was no longer good enough. The Gamemakers were angry and were sending their minions disguised as everyday people — basically whomever I decided needed to be killed — and those minions were the cause of their afflictions. The mission was simple: kill the minions, kill the affliction. Dr. Randal did as he was told, relaying the story flawlessly to his patients. And your mom was his right hand."

"What?!" I blurted out, briefly losing control of my temper, which had been hanging by a thread. "How was she involved? Tell me!" Remembering my goal, I took a few deep breaths to regain my composure the best I could.

"Calm down a second and let me explain. They had a thing, not sexual of course, but a close relationship. And I simply helped bring it closer. I needed her. She was third in charge and was responsible for keeping the recruits in line, and foremost keeping Randal firmly in place — he listened to her. I had sessions with her occasionally and planted just the right information so she and Randal could experience an epiphany together and strengthen the bond."

So, according to Fortune, Randal was also a victim, along with my mom. If he was indeed telling me the truth, I was close to releasing the wrong man, and an innocent one on top of that. I wasn't sure what Fortune had in store for me, but I had a strange feeling that he was on the verge of losing it. He seemed to be putting together what he had done by explaining it to me. His teetering sanity was becoming unsettling, and I couldn't wait around any longer in victim status for him to erupt. Once I had him in a vulnerable position, I would allow him to reveal what he meant by a 'vested' interest in me. To do so, I needed to be in charge of the conversation.

It was time to rile him, and that involved my becoming overtly angry, which wasn't hard for me to do at the moment. I also had to remain in control of my actions and not let go. His ego was large enough that anything that threatened it would evoke a strong need to lash out, or in this case prove his superiority.

"You piece of crap! All along I thought it was Dr. Randal who was responsible for playing with my mom's exposed mind. It was you!"

"Yes, Tryke, I'm the mastermind behind the curtain," he said proudly.

"Like a chicken shit tyrant, not getting your hands dirty directly."

"Cursing is unbecoming of you, but you're right. Except for being a coward, or chicken shit, as you put it. Unlike you, Tryke, I prefer to be a voyeur of the act. I set things in motion and watch the results. We aren't much different, you and me. We just take on different roles — you are a performer and I am a director. I know what you do and I have felt what you felt — the dark rush filling your insides." He stood and faced the mirror, elevating his voice as the words left his mouth. "It sinks its warm teeth in me and feels me with exhilaration."

"I don't share a damn thing with you!" I needed him near me so I could grab him, not knowing if he had a weapon other than the sedatives he had slipped in my drink. Once in range, I could perform my wrist trick to get loose — my wrists were slightly disproportionate to my hands. Once he did bite, I would have to do this the old-fashioned way. I didn't have any of my usual tools with me. My back pack was in my hotel room.

"More than you think," he said turning back toward me.

"I don't believe a damn word that spews out of your mouth! Dr. Randal was the real master — "

He violently kicked the chair in front of him, landing it a few feet to my side. He had been hiding behind cowardly pills so long he wasn't used to anyone questioning his words. He walked toward me and grabbed my hair, tugging it hard in his hand, and whispered, "I created you, and I can end you just as easily."

• • •

"Thank you," I whispered, and then slipped my right wrist from the restraint. I clutched his head with my free hand, pulling it closer to mine, and then yanked him to the ground. He was a tall man, but not much for brawn. I reached up with my free hand and started unbinding my left. I looked back and he was on his knees, recovering quickly. In his right hand he wielded what appeared to be a syringe with a needle exposed — I could see the sharp tip glinting in the candlelight.

My left hand was still caught up as he began a lunge toward me. Thankfully he had allowed some leeway in the pulley system earlier, and I sidestepped his clumsy move. My left hand was freed but my legs were still wobbly and numb from being stagnant. I rolled toward the mirror, searching for anything I could use as a weapon. All I found was the chair he had been sitting in and a few melted candles.

He grunted toward me again, syringe still in hand. I lifted the light metal chair and held it in front of me like a trainer holding off a lion, or in this case a spindly giraffe, until my legs had rebooted.

"Let's — not — do — this," he spouted out between breaths.

I was close to the door, but I wasn't going to run. Nope, we were going to finish this here. My legs finally regained their blood flow. While he was still out of breath, I lifted the chair to chest height and dashed toward him. He tried blocking with his left arm but to no avail. Outmatching his strength, I thrust him back against the far wall, simultaneously watching in slow motion as the syringe in his right hand came within inches of my neck.

I dropped the chair and rammed my fist down on his right forearm, making him drop the syringe. I then kicked it across the room with my boot. He swung but missed. He leapt to the ground, his eye only on the syringe. He fell short and began flailing his arms like a drowning man unable to swim. I stepped toward him, and as I did, he turned over and swept my feet from under me.

He tried again for the syringe, but this time I was quicker. I grabbed him in a choke hold, squeezing with all of my residual anger until he went limp.

I didn't want him dead… yet.

Chapter 22

While Fortune snoozed, I searched the rooms of the building for a sturdy table, finally finding one propped against a wall in a closet. I reworked the pulley system in the room in conjunction with the table, and that was where he lay, facing the huge mirror, with one candle lit at his feet so he could see himself for what he was. I should have thought of that a long time ago in my lab, using a mirror, before and after the release.

Instead of mulling over the tangled mess of a story he had told me, I had been deciding on the manner in which to release him, which included making him talk beforehand — I knew that once I had him in a vulnerable state he would clarify his intent. Since I did not have my bag with me, I had to rely on other means. I didn't want to risk leaving him alone for the length of time it would take me to retrieve my tools from the hotel. Besides, I was pretty sure Fortune had a stash on him somewhere. I searched his pockets and found it neatly packaged in a small container that fit in the inside pocket of his jacket. I still wasn't sure that a nice and easy sedated release was sufficient for the man who had tortured and maimed my mom's conscience, and stole her innocence.

He interrupted my thoughts when he sighed loudly, almost sounding as though he knew this would happen.

"By your weary sigh, I take it you're not surprised by your predicament?" I said, sitting in the shadows of the room so he could not immediately see me. He had attempted to put on a show for me but was unsuccessful. It was my turn now to return the favor.

"I'm surprised to see you stuck around," he said deviously. "I must have intrigued you." He attempted to yank his head up from the table that he was bound to, but he stopped quickly after realizing it was futile.

"I have to admit, you *did* intrigue me. And I apologize for the manner in which I am conducting this, but as you know, you are a dangerous man." I got up from my chair and emerged from the shadows and faced him in the dying candlelight wearing a smirk on my face. I offered him the same gesture he did for me: a sip of water, which he gladly accepted. He thanked me with an ill-tempered nod. "Your level of cooperation and accuracy of events will decide your fate," I said. "So choose your words wisely."

"The only lie I told you was at the cafe. Everything after that was a fact."

"You can understand my suspicion, but let's say I believe that you weren't lying about the rest. How about we trace events, so I can keep up?" I pulled the chair next to him and sat. I crossed my legs, ready to hear the climax to his elaborate scheme. "Let's begin where you left off, after you told me you were the mastermind, and before the crazy rant about how much you enjoyed killing."

"I'm not sure what you want to know, Tryke. Are you looking for details of the killings?"

"Don't be coy," I said. "You know the information I want." He legitimately looked bewildered by my accusation. "You mentioned that you had a vested interest in me. What did you mean?"

For a few moments, he appeared to be collecting his thoughts. When he began to speak, he had more precision in his words, and less passion than before. "You probably don't remember, but I first met you when you were pretty young, around five I believe."

"No, I don't," I said, keeping my answers short so he could maintain his train of thought.

"I thought not. Anyway, you often sat in the waiting room. The front desk secretary would keep an eye on you while your mom was in session with Dr. Randal. One day curiosity, like it does to all young boys, got the better of you, and you wandered into my office. We had our first conversation then. Do you know what your first words to me were?" I shrugged, not having a clue. "'Do you want to talk?' you asked me with a sincere, sort of sullen look on your face. Of course I invited you to have a seat on my couch. I was intrigued by this little guy needing some dialogue. We didn't talk about much, as I recall, but your demeanor fascinated the hell out of me; it was like *you* were analyzing me. From that moment on, whenever you came in with your mom, you visited with me. We had ourselves some pretty nifty conversations for a boy your age. In fact, your perception was way beyond where it should have been. Your mannerisms were also developed, along with your organizational thought. Once I started project Gamemakers, you were an obvious choice as a sort of side project. I had to. It was just too good to pass up. Especially since your mom and sister had hallucinations, concluding the eventual high probability of your acquiring the gene. The narrative would fit nicely if you ever developed the symptoms."

I remained oddly calm, desperately attempting to recall my childhood at that time. I pressed on, as only pieces of memories flashed through my mind. "Wait, so you're telling me I was one of your recruits?"

"Your mind was so fertile I only had to treat you for a few sessions."

"Treat me? How? Did you feed me that experimental pill?"

"I had to, it was part of the test. And boy did you pass. After the session with the pill, I never had another session with you one-on-one again. I never had to. Tryke, I have followed you, anxiously waiting for that day when and if the symptoms manifested themselves. Then you did it, you built yourself an office to kill the minions placed here by the Gamemakers. I never got to hear of your symptoms first hand, but I assumed they started sometime in your late teenage years."

"But... I never had any — ." I never had any auditory hallucinations. The blurs I saw were souls of the ones I released... My sister... I saw her soul hovering above the swimming pool after she drowned. I know it was her... it had to be. That was my beginning, not this way. Not Fortune and his twisted story. No, he couldn't have... I mean, if I was a mere product of brainwashing, then every soul I released was in vain. The room spun as my mind fell deeper and deeper into the ravenous belly of reality. My entire life was a lie?

"I know this is a lot to take in at once. If it makes you feel any better I only guided you a small fraction. You developed the rest of the story yourself. As you can imagine, I have been waiting a long time to talk with you. I wanted desperately to be there for you, to guide you, but I had to keep my distance and let everything unfold naturally."

"Don't act like you gave a shit about me," I said. "And naturally, really? There's nothing natural about feeding a child mind-altering medications for the fun of it."

He ignored my words and continued his train of thought. "I have so many questions. For example, what premise did you use to choose the minions? I never told you that part."

I attempted to gain traction, my mind's claws reaching out for anything to grip other than his words. I was becoming angry, and not because he was pushing my buttons, but because he was making sense. "First of all I am not afflicted with any type of ailment, so right there is a flaw in your story. And as for the rest —" I didn't have an answer. I knew he was right about implanting the information in my head. Denial has always been there when I needed him, patting me on the back, telling me everything was going to be okay. But he knew he had done everything he could for me and was slowly backing away with raised hands and finally sneaking out of the room.

"I never wanted to control you, Tryke, I wanted to unleash you."

I needed to keep talking and asking questions to avoid losing all control. "To what means? Why mess with my mind? Just to make a little cash on the side?"

"I'm not that shallow," he said. "Sure, it was an experiment for money in the beginning, but once I got a taste for blood, it became part of me. The hunger grew inside and released a euphoric darkness. Each death made it grow. A piece of them attached to me."

His poisonous words dug deep into my subconscious like sharp canines tearing through meat.

"Enough! You want to know how I chose the ones I did? They were never a part of me. I never had blood lust running through *any* vein in my body. I chose them because they hurt the innocent. They preyed on the weak and then had the audacity to call 911 to help the ones they injured. So you see, we're nothing alike. I released pernicious souls from their restricting suits. I made the world a safer place. You are nothing but a leech, preying on the vulnerable."

"Genius! You used your resources and surroundings to complete your mission," he said, again ignoring my words. "Tryke, we are a good team. See how we contrast one another, your conscience and cunning, and my coerciveness? Besides, we're practically family you and me. I mean... your sister *is* a part of me."

● ● ●

"What the hell did you say!?" I snapped.

"Your sister... you never knew. I'm sorry that your father never told you. Probably for the best. Who knows how things would have turned out."

I wanted to end this now, but the conversation had just taken a turn down a dark alley and I needed to know what was at the other end. Either he had gone completely mad or he was about to unveil another missing puzzle piece to my life.

"Never told me what? My sister drowned after falling out of our tree house. What else could there be?"

"You might as well know everything, so we can have a fresh start. Then you can begin to trust me again, as you did when we first met." It wasn't going to happen. I was a little more aware than I had been back then. I remained expressionless as he continued. "First you have to know the reason the project fell off track and Randal ended up in the asylum. I told you about the camera I placed in Randal's office. Well, one day your mom had some concerns about the pill and voiced it to him, and Fortune being the good friend to her that he was, somehow found a way to surpass the orders I gave him and sympathize with your mom. She didn't want to take the pill anymore and Randal allowed it. After a few sessions with your mom not taking the pill, Randal came into my office asking questions about the story line. I knew then that I had to do something about them both. My top two recruits had fallen, and everything I had built was about to crumble. So, I had no choice but to implement the Sacrifice command on them both."

"What are you saying?" I could feel the acid shooting its way up my esophagus.

"Tryke, come on, you know what happened to Randal. It

was the only way for me to survive. If they were to find out the truth, I would have gone to jail. Or worse."

"Why not just get Dr. Randal to commit suicide? Why have him kill his family?"

"Dr. Randal was my friend, and your mother meant a lot to him. I didn't want to hurt them — directly." I had ignored my mom's role for some reason, and in a few seconds I was about to realize why. "Your mom I handled much the same as I did Randal. I told her that her daughter was one of the Gamemakers' minions. She handled the rest."

"That's… impossible. I was there the morning my sister died. I was only gone for a few…" I pictured my sister's sapphire eyes and long auburn hair, and the giggle that still echoed in my ears whenever her memory surfaced. My head began pounding furiously and dizziness and nausea took over, clouding my mind as I struggled to remain standing. I tried to control my breathing but the short breaths kept repeating, enhancing the dizziness. I sat down on the floor and lowered my head to my knees in an attempt to regain control.

"Enough time for your mom to drown your sister and slip back into the house."

His words were cold, as if part of a movie script without consequences. They scraped along the inside of my skull like a barber's straight blade being sharpened on a strop. "Why," I mumbled. "Why take my family from me for no reason? Why murder an innocent child?" I lifted my head. A sudden rage took over and quickly pushed aside the anxiety, grabbing hold of my ear and yanking me to my feet. He was telling the truth and I knew it. I went to his jacket and quickly removed the syringe from his inside pocket. He was staring up at the ceiling, ignoring me. I gripped his hair, and as I suspected, it was a toupee. I threw it to the floor, and then grabbed the thin strands remaining underneath. I shoved the syringe into his neck, not plunging the substance in just yet. I had one last thing to tell him. With my face inches from his — the candlelight revealing his cold remorseless eyes and a stoic resilient face — I began my final words to him, "I —"

"You're still going to kill me after all I've done for you? After filling in the missing pieces from your childhood, this is how you repay me?" he said, his voice still emotionless.

"Yes," I hissed.

"Before you kill me, don't you want to know how your father plays into all of this?"

I sighed, keeping the needle securely in his jugular vein. "Speak, and fast, your toxic words have caused enough damage to me and this world."

"I needed Randal and your mom away, never to return — both in an asylum was my choice. Dr. Randal was easy. I called the police anonymously after he killed his family, which got him arrested. The insanity plea was simple for him. I helped it along in court when I was called to testify. When it came to your mom, I made the mistake of telling your father — anonymous phone call to his work, not telling the police. He was supposed to call the police and have her committed."

My dad wanted her to be protected. I was sure of it. He was protecting us both. Maybe he knew he was sick back then and wanted to keep me out of foster homes. The three journals were for my mom, possibly a reminder of her voices. He likely changed them to what he wanted to put in them — obviously nothing incriminating about her, if they were ever found.

He continued, "I kept an eye on your family after that for years, watching your mom slip into a depression after your father passed. I suppose it wasn't a total failure, she never made any waves or returned to my office. Your dad kept the secret to himself all the way to the grave — an honorable man to say the least. More so than I. I probably would have killed my wife if she harmed my child — that is, if I had a wife or child."

"Good thing you didn't breed," I said, somehow restraining my thumb from pressing down the plunger.

He ignored my comment and continued. "So you see, I have been the father you never got to know. I've been here the entire time watching and waiting until you needed me. That's why I came as fast as I could when I heard you were in trouble. How could you kill me, a father coming to help his son?"

"You are nothing to me, but a murderer of the innocent. You came here to protect yourself; to protect your damn project. How many innocent sick people have come to you for help only to be experimented on and then thrown away and murdered? How many have had to live with the struggle of knowing they took an innocent life, their memory in pieces for the rest of their lives?"

"Many. I had quite a bit of fun with the remaining patients in the trial. Suicides, family kills, even a few random slayings in public. Just because Randal was in the asylum didn't mean I couldn't continue killing. All I had to do was implant future dates to the remaining recruits and watch from a distance."

"That was meant to be rhetorical."

"Your sister was better off not suffering through decades of sickness, Tryke. It was merciful of me to end her life." I yanked the syringe from his neck. He sighed in relief and said in a short breath, "Thank you. I knew you would come to your senses and understand."

I ripped a piece of his shirt and shoved it into his mouth. "I'm not giving you the pleasure of being released by me. I'm going to let you do it yourself. I placed the syringe in his right hand and loosened the pulley system. I was doing my best to contain the simmering rage that was vibrating my hands at the mention of my sister. "Do you remember the water you drank a few minutes ago? It had your favorite mind altering pill dissolved in it. Your words have been truthful and your mind obedient."

The sweat began beading along his forehead despite the chill in the room

"Now, I need you to do me a favor." I sat back in the chair and crossed my legs, reflecting how he likely appeared to his patients. He sputtered some gibberish behind the wadded cloth as he struggled. "Dr. Fortune, the Gamemakers have infiltrated your body and you are now contaminated. For the safety of others, primarily your patients, you must terminate yourself. The syringe in your hand is the remedy to your ailment." His hand twitched, using all of his will to resist the order. He blinked rapidly, his eyes streaked red, sweat now pouring down his face. He jerked his head around and stopped when he caught a glimpse of his reflection in the mirror. He tilted his head like a flummoxed dog and furrowed his brows as he stared toward himself, unable to completely realize the situation.

He barely flinched as the needle penetrated his skin. He pushed the plunger on the syringe slowly and methodically as if giving the body time to recognize the solution. As the substance made its way through his cardiovascular system, I had one more thing to tell him.

"One hole in your story Dr. Fortune. Me. You should realize that all theories have unexpected twists along the way, especially this one. Human souls will inevitably see past the deceit being laid upon the body. When it does, one can no longer be controlled, or coerced as you put it. We are not simply a single unit, we are two: a soul and a suit. When the suit is in trouble, the soul eventually finds a way out. For example, mine has been cleansing the world of people like you, searching for the creator of the deceit. Now that I have found it, I will soon be back in control. Yours, however, has been glossed over and smeared with malevolence toward the weak and innocent, blinding it and dooming it to darkness forever."

Chapter 23

I sat for a long time in the chair facing Dr. Fortune's empty suit, going over and over in my head everything that he had said. Though my soul was now finally free, it still didn't erase the facts that Fortune had told me. My entire life was a sham, an experiment, led by a crazed murdering psychiatrist. My mom was made to kill her own daughter. My dad was made to believe his wife's sickness caused her to murder her child, never learning the truth, that her mind was tampered with and manipulated. My dad had been duped, blindfolded, while a trusted doctor took advantage of his entire family.

What was I supposed to do with all of this? The man that led the trail of destruction was now dead and could do no more harm. That should be enough to soothe the anger, but for some reason I didn't feel any better. In fact, there was still a lingering feeling of dread deep down inside that I couldn't shake. Maybe it was because a remnant of him, his experiment, me, was still left in the world. He had a point about me being his son; in a way he *had* created me. None of us had a choice to be born, just as I had no choice of him molding me when I was a child. I had to face it, I was a virus created to end life. With my maker dead, the choice was now mine to make.

I could end this before I had a chance to cause more harm to the world in the name of Dr. Fortune. There was plenty of substance left in the vial to end me. What did I have left when my entire life had been a lie? Even the things that I had built — my relationship with Lesley — was formed on a lie. My standoff nature, my fear of relationships, and my fear of the world had all been manufactured. The world would be better off without me, right? I was sick, just as my mom and sister were. Everything I had seen was simulated by me. I was designed for repetitive destruction. I was a monster.

I grabbed another needle and syringe from Fortune's neatly packaged container and filled it. I then set it on the table in front of me and stared at it while I chewed over my life.

If I were to continue on, what rules would I follow? What premise would I use to continue with my life now that I had found out the truth? If I resumed releasing souls, continuing with Fortune's narrative, what would that mean? Wouldn't it be continuing his legacy? Possibly, but I wasn't sure. Fortune had said it himself that he had only guided me a small fraction of the way and that I chose my own minions to release, meaning I chose bad guys over the innocent. That had to count for something. It meant there was still some good left in me that was not taken by Fortune. Was it enough, though, to override the poison he had planted?

· · ·

An hour later I was still in the same spot, trying to determine where I fit in the world and if I should stay in it. There were so many obstacles in my way, placed there by the death machine that was Fortune. The only glimmer of self-worth I could muster was the thought of my unborn child. I had gone back and forth over and over and I finally realized I couldn't just leave. How could I abandon my child, left alone in this world to face the horde of demons waiting with salivating tongues to taste the innocent? If I were to bring children into this world, it was my obligation to watch over, guide, and protect them.

If there is such a thing as a normal life, I would attempt a go at it. But *normal* was a word that had become so foreign and obscure to me, I didn't quite know what it meant anymore. I had acclimated to a life that was anything but normal. There was always a part of me that had longed for something, a piece that had been missing, and I had finally found it; it was the innocence that Fortune stole from me. He meant for it to be peeled away slowly over time until I became what he wanted me to be. And it had worked. He robbed me of those beginning years of purity, when one learns about the world they were sprung into. That stolen piece of innocence is what I have longed for subconsciously all of these years. It's what made me who I am. I realized then that everything I had become revolved around that longing.

I wasn't sure what would become of me and Lesley, not having figured that far into things yet. Whatever happens in my life, until the end, I will try to slowly forget the horrible pieces of my past until the last are scraped away from my subconscious completely, leaving only those of my family together. I'll survive, as hard as it may be; I only had to remind myself. I would work through the madness and search for the single fragment of sanity, waving from a distance, begging for a chase and dreaming of being captured one day.

I felt good when I finally stood, a sudden burst of energy shooting throughout my body as if I could run a mile, full sprint. I had found a missing piece of my life and released another one. My mind finally had room to breathe, a huge barrier lifted and moved to a better location so as to keep anxiety and my foolish OCD from penetrating and invading. There was a new control over my life, as if the remote had been finally found after two decades of imprisonment in a deep hole in the couch. I had just awakened from one hellish nightmare and the sweat was still fresh on the back of my neck.

I placed the syringe firmly back in its case.

As I began picking up evidence scattered around the room, I heard what sounded like a door being kicked open — the entrance door. Startled, I dropped the bag I had in my hand and immediately pulled out the syringe I had just packed away. I cautiously made my way toward the front of the building. Cal, the tour guide's cousin, immediately came to mind as the intruder. I stopped in place when a second door was kicked open. He knew this place better than me and from the sound of things he was still frightened from our last encounter, nervously smashing open doors — forced courage getting the better of him. He was moving fast, so I decided to stay behind the door in the room I was in and let him come to me.

One last release and then I was done. I let him go because I was trying to win some sympathy from Lesley, allowing her to see the merciful side of me. I could hear his heavy footsteps approaching the door I was kneeling behind. Next came the flashlight — as I suspected — projecting shadows on the walls around me. I was surprised by the deliberate moves of the light, not clumsy or shaking as I would have anticipated. He hadn't said a word when he crossed the threshold of the door; no shouts of 'I'm armed and dangerous', or 'your ass is mine.' I caught a glimpse of him through the crack of the door as he slowly passed by.

It wasn't Cal.

We all experience those moments in our lives when everything is going great and then suddenly, out of nowhere, you feel a flash of dread that reminds you danger is inching closer. Multiply that feeling by a thousand and punch it in the face over and over until the nerves are damaged and you can't even form an expression because everything is numb.

My happy ending quickly faded to black. Every sliver of relief that I had felt a few minutes before was shoved aside and replaced by fear. My heart pounded furiously against the inside of my chest, my breathing rapid. Inhaling through my nose only made it worse, and unfortunately, louder.

I was stuck, unable to move as the man aimed the light directly into my face.

• • •

Uncle Frank hovered over me, his flashlight blinding me, his gun drawn and pointed in the same direction as the light. We stared at one another, silently and for what seemed like hours, before either of us said a word. I said the first thing that came to mind.

"Fancy seeing you here." With the light blaring in my eyes, I couldn't see if he cracked a smile, but if I had to guess I would say he did not.

With his gun still raised, he said in a stern Clint Eastwood hushed tone, "Are you alone?"

"Sort of," I said. "I mean, the only one alive."

"No time for jokes, son. Who's in the other room?"

My nervous joking quickly turned to angry sarcasm. "You should know, you went to see him before coming here."

"You mean Dr. Fortune? He's in there, dead? Tell me you're lying, Tryke."

So, Fortune wasn't lying about Uncle Frank going to see him. "Before we continue this conversation," I said, "would you mind lowering your gun?"

"After you lower that syringe in your hand." I did as he

requested. "With your foot, slowly shove it to the far wall."
I sighed and kicked it as he directed me to.

"Now, your turn please," I said. He turned the gun away
from me and cautiously lowered his hands, but didn't
holster the gun, keeping it ready by his side. "Thank you.
Now look, before you start in on me, you need the facts.
Your Dr. Fortune wasn't innocent. He wasn't the man you
thought he was."

"I know more than you think, Tryke."

"Like my mom was the one sick and not your brother?"

"Yes."

What? He knew about my mom? Why didn't he tell me?
"Then why, while I was in my lab, did you mention my dad
being sick and not seeing his symptoms?"

"Dr. Fortune explained everything to me. How Dr.
Randal used your mom and formulated some elaborate
story using hypnosis. After reading the journals you left
behind, I realized how sick you had become. Like I said
before, I should have been there for you, being that I was
the only family you have left."

I was trying to keep from smirking at the idea of
Fortune's lies and my detective uncle believing him. But my
simmering anger was doing a good job of keeping it hidden.
At this point what good would it do to convince him of the
truth? Fortune was dead. It was basically his word against
mine, but I had to at least try. If only to get it off my chest.

"This is way more convoluted than you know," I said.
"What if I were to tell you Fortune was behind it all and
used my mom and Dr. Randal as his top two recruits?"

"I'm listening," he said, unconvincingly.

Pleasantly shocked by his unexpected reception, I
continued. "Fortune was paid under the table by a
pharmaceutical company to test a hypnotherapy drug. He
had Randal administer it to his patients with a story line
attached. Basically, he had them kill innocent people."

"Uh, huh," he said, sarcastically. I should have known he

wasn't actually listening to me. My next words came out in a roar.

"He had my mom kill my sister, dammit! He even screwed with *my* mind when I was a child! Bet you didn't know that!"

He remained in a silent pose, so I continued, somehow managing a much calmer tone. "My dad knew that my mom killed Katy, but he never knew she was drugged and was ordered to do it. I don't know what he thought, or how he dealt with it, but what I do know is that he never turned her in. He knew he was dying and didn't want me to be an orphan. Above all, I suspect he didn't turn her in because he loved her."

I felt my lips begin to tremble. All of my rage was compacted into a mega emotion I had not felt since losing my mom. Everything I had witnessed, everything I had done, my entire family wiped out, Lesley and our child, all pouncing down on me and tearing at my soul. I felt the deluge of raw tears flow down my face. Though I wasn't one for letting emotions infiltrate my defenses, I allowed this one room to breathe. I wanted to feel sorry for myself again and soak in my warm sorrows and let them bathe me. I wanted everything sinister inside me, out, once and for all.

I don't know how long I let myself dwell in self-pity, but by the time my uncle spoke I felt a wave of exhaustion envelop me.

"Son, if you are telling me the truth then I am truly sorry for what took place. It's an unfortunate chain of events and they never should have happened. But it's in the past now and you can't fix it by going around and killing people."

I laughed through the remaining tears still bubbling over. "I know," I whispered, giving in. "I know." I felt the energy coming back when I thought about all of the victims I have had to transport and how many predators got away. I looked up at his unwavering, rigid face and said, "So, your answer to all of this is that you wanted me to wait on the law to fix things? I would have long been dead. Fortune had fun for how long? Decades, and no one came to the rescue. No one saved my mom. No one saved Dr. Randal's wife and child. No one saved my damn sister!"

"We didn't know," he pleaded. "If we had — "

"Exactly, and how many years would it have taken to get him behind bars? How many more lives would have been lost if I hadn't stopped him?"

"I don't know, but there are rules, laws that we all have to follow. It's not a perfect system, I admit that, but it works most of the time."

"That's not good enough. Innocent people deserve better than 'most of the time'."

"What do you want me to tell you, Tryke? That I'll do better at my job and you can go on killing? Sorry, that ain't going to happen. But I will get you some help. And we will uncover the truth behind what you told me, and if they are guilty, people will go to jail."

"So you think it's fair Dr. Randal is locked away in an asylum? What about me, your family, is it fair to me too? You think an apology and your 'I'll do better' speech will bring back my sister? Or make things right?" I chose to ignore his pledge to arrest people. The damage was done.

"I'm not saying that. I will get you help, that much I can promise. Would you rather be behind actual bars?"

"No, I'd rather start this life over."

"Unfortunately that isn't an option. Bars or mental help are your only options right now."

"What choice is there to make, really? I mean if I want to live, right?"

"I can't rule out they will not go after the death penalty if you don't plead insanity, but I will do everything in my power to see you don't face that path. You definitely have an insanity plea."

"I'm not insane and you know that," I said.

"All I know is what will keep you from getting the death

penalty."

I had to face the coming wrath. I knew what was next: the court dates, shackles, stares of judgment. No one knows everything that I know and the fear was that no one ever would. No one was going to believe a sick man who has killed people, whether they deserved it or not.

"What's left then?" I said. "I mean, it's pointless to go around in circles with you. You have obviously made your mind up and that's it, no matter what I tell you." He had me. I had nowhere left to run. "So how do I do this? Do I just go with you and we make our way back to Dallas?"

He nodded. "We'll take it one step at a time, son."

Chapter 24

So here I am, captive in my uncle's police issued vehicle, on our way back to Dallas. All that I have done, worked toward, believed, has come down to this time and place. How the heck am I going to get out of this one? For now, I don't have an answer, or a plan. Even if I were able to get free, what then? How often would I get to see my child while evading the law? And that was based on the notion that I could convince Lesley to allow it. She has changed now, and I can't be sure where her loyalty lies. The best I can hope for is to put on a good behavior persona and hope for a lenient judge.

I open my eyes from the loud burst of thunder that rattles the vehicle. The rain hasn't stopped coming down for the last hour. It has been attempting to soothe my seemingly never-ending headache, and all the while irritating my traveling companion. The cause of the headache: my suspicious sinister friend, growing like a creepy shadow on my brain. What was its intention? A temporary burden or death, or both? I guess I have to wait and find out.

My uncle decides not to shackle me, thanks to the special bond we share of being the only remaining Harpers left. It's not like I had a weapon. He tossed everything I owned in an outside trash receptacle before leaving town. All I have are the clothes on my back and my prepaid phone. Once he found the sedating material in my bag he didn't bother to check me further. What was I going to do with my phone anyhow? I don't have a gang of misfits to call to break me out of the car and save me on the interstate, nor do I have the will at the moment. I am beat and have all but accepted my fate.

We cleaned up any evidence of my DNA in the building before leaving New Orleans. According to my uncle, it was part of my rehabilitation, and of course he didn't want the Louisiana authorities to trace me to the death of Fortune or the others, saying the case would be better off not crossing state lines and involving other agencies. He even shrugged off the tampering of evidence. However, I did remind him that once they discovered Fortune's body, they would find his address.

"What did it matter?" he said. "Once his practices are revealed to the world no one will care if he's dead or not, and most will chalk his death up to the dark suits of the pharmaceutical world keeping his mouth shut."

I suppose even the strictest of lawmen can step outside the law every now and then when it comes to family. I would request for him to let me go, but that's out of the question completely — his intentions are clear. He rationalized his arrest of me as a way to help me, a way to make it up to his brother and my mom. If I were a regular citizen he would have probably shot me already, not caring if my intentions were to release only the dregs of society and protect the innocent. In his eyes, only officers of the law have the right to protect the innocent and lay judgment.

We just passed the city limits of Shreveport, Louisiana,

and are about ten to fifteen minutes from the Texas border
— two and a half hours to go. He has yet to tell me where
we are going once we arrive in Dallas, though I suspect the
police station for booking. I doubt he is going to let me go
by my house and take a shower and change clothes — the
jail has plenty of jumpsuits to handout. Will I get a chance
to say goodbye to Lesley as a semi-free man? Not likely.
This is it, my last stretch of road before the beginning of the
end of Tryke Harper.

"I have to say, at least you left your mess in one place in
New Orleans," Frank says, startling me. I am in one of my
temporary drifts, neither awake nor asleep. Small talk from
Uncle Frank? Really? The weather is probably dampening
his mind as dark thoughts of his brother and my mom and
sister ache along the crevices of his conscience, leaving tiny
painful paper cuts.

"You're welcome," I say ruefully, continuing to stare out
the rain pattered window.

"I would never have guessed things would turn out like
this in our family," he says. "I really hate that I have to take
you to jail, but what choice did you give me?" I glance
forward and in my peripheral I can see him look my way,
but I continue with my vacant gaze. "You know I told your
old man I would watch over you after he passed. I really
screwed up. I failed him. And you."

Yeah, you told me. Guilty much? I know I shouldn't
project all of my anger at him but he happens to be family
and he's taking me to confinement to be rehabilitated by
the state. I merely let out a mumble of 'hmmf,' not looking
over at him.

"I don't know… with me being the detective in the
family, maybe I should have had more instinct."

I cast a furtive glance over at him and see his gun wink at
me from behind his jacket as he turns the steering wheel. I
probably have time to grab it, force him to pull over, and
let me out. He still has his radio in his car, even if I take his

phone with me. And even if I put a bullet in his police radio how far would I get on foot? I could always make him get out and then take his vehicle, but he'd just flag down a driver and then would be forced to call it in. My end would be a high-speed police chase followed by me being pumped full of police issued rounds of ammunition. I turn my attention to the mundane road ahead and let the idea fall away with the road behind us. He switches the car radio off, leaving the vehicle quiet, save for the heater humming along on low. It isn't that much of a difference. The radio is tuned to some classic country station, and barely audible. "So," he begins, "did uh… Lesley come with you, or did she merely let you borrow her vehicle?"

• • •

Not that I have completely forgotten about it, but it is in the back of my thoughts, locked away securely until needed. I had been trying to avoid the subject of Lesley, hoping beyond reason that my uncle would forget she has been part of my life. How much does he actually know about her? He obviously found her vehicle, but did he check her college to see if she's been in class?

"I hope you're not implicating her in any of this," I say, my voice amplifying at the mention of her name.

"Should I be?"

"No," I say quickly. "I didn't tell her where I was going. All she knew was that I was borrowing her car. Nothing more."

He sighs and says, "I know she was in New Orleans with you." My insides curl into a knot. "How much does she know, Tryke?"

We had cleaned up any evidence in the guide's lair if she *had* left some behind. Did he find some evidence that we missed? It had to have been something big that he knows was hers. Unlikely. No, this is a simple baiting technique to tell him more.

"What does it matter?" I ask with a flare of protective anger.

"It matters to the case. She will be interrogated once this investigation officially begins."

"By who, you?"

"No, they'll insist on an unbiased officer to conduct it. She's your girlfriend, Tryke. You had to know she would be questioned."

"We're not together anymore," I say, attempting to hide my unresolved feelings for her.

"Hmm, I assume she did not agree with… for now let's just stick with the facts and we'll work forward from there. If you're honest with me your transition will be much smoother. And hers also. I'll do my best to keep her from being questioned too harshly."

Lesley interrogated? I had not considered that angle of this mess. She would need a lawyer and… "Is it possible to leave her out of this completely? Like she was never part of my life? Or at least say she was an ex from long ago?" I hear the desperate pleading in my voice and I don't like it. I don't like being trapped and vulnerable.

"I wish I could," he says. "She's seems like a nice, smart girl. Good grades in medical school, good upbringing. A pity if things were to turn out bad for her."

What was this? A subtle threat? Was he starting my interrogation on the trip back? It shouldn't surprise me, really. What is he after?

"What do you want from me?" I growl.

"The truth."

I loosen the restraint of my guard a little more. "And if I tell you everything, will you leave Lesley out of the investigation?"

"I can't promise anything right now. For an ex-boyfriend, you're trying awfully hard to keep her out of this. Why is that, Tryke?"

"I need your word or I'm not telling you anything."

"Don't be like that, son. You know as well as I that I have enough evidence against her to place her in jail."

He wasn't bluffing. Her car was New Orleans, and she had been there also. She had seen my lab. She knew things. For all I know he caught up with her on her way back to Dallas and interrogated her already. He isn't backing down. I have one final angle to play. If it fails, then my child will be placed in state care while their parents rot in jail, or in my case, an asylum. Lesley would eventually get out, but not before the harm was done to the child and her. This is no longer about me. I am done for, and my only concern is for their safety. I have to tell him now, before we arrive back in Dallas. He needs time to mull over the possibility of his dead brother's grandchild being born in jail.

"Lesley's pregnant," I spout.

"What?"

"Lesley's pregnant," I say, continuing to gaze out the window.

"Why didn't you tell me sooner?"

"When did I have a chance?" I am trying to remain calm and cool, pushing the emotions crawling around to the side.

"So, what am I supposed to do with this information?" He is getting flustered, his hands tightly gripping the steering wheel. I have obviously put a kink in his arrest plan. But how big a kink is the question?

"You're the detective. I just thought you should know."

"Fine," he snaps, "I'll have her tested before we proceed with questioning. Not that I don't believe you or anything, but you are in a dire circumstance and my experience tells me that when people are in a dicey situation, they will sing to anything."

"I'm not just anyone. I'm your nephew, remember. And the child will be your niece or nephew," I remind him. I am playing the family card to its full potential.

He continues to stare forward through the steady moving

windshield wipers, fingers now drumming on the steering wheel. I'm not sure if my effort has changed his mind about anything, but he is at least thinking it over. In the end, it may only fuel his admonition of my receiving help, but if that's the case, then I am not going to let my child and Lesley be incarcerated without a fight.

I knew it was coming. I just didn't know when. I sit quietly, patiently waiting for the lecture to begin about how I'm not fit to be a father. That would come first before he tells me anything concerning what he is going to do about Lesley and the child. Considering the situation I am currently in I would have to agree with him. I am certainly not the ideal father: holding down a steady job and providing a warm caring home for a child to be raised in. According to society I am a vigilante, a menace, and I should be stopped at all costs. But, if I were able to explain my case to the public, I'm sure there would be many who would pull for me and would accept what I do as long as they don't have to watch or be part of it. It would be followed by a horde of appreciative nods, who would then scamper off in the opposite direction.

The expected lecture about fatherhood doesn't happen. We both just sit silently with our complicated thoughts.

Chapter 25

We are now in Dallas, about to exit I-635 onto the turnpike. Morning traffic is in full force and the wet roads aren't helping the jostling vehicles or the short tempers behind the steering wheels. I suppose that's one thing I will not have to deal with anymore.

My uncle has not spoken to me since I brought up Lesley being pregnant. Apparently he needs time to consider the possibilities of proceeding with his original plan. If silence is an indication of my plan working, then it is definitely going in my favor.

"Let's see this lab of yours," my Uncle Frank spouts out, breaking the silence of the car as if in the middle of a conversation.

Bewildered, I look over at him and say, "Really? Why? I thought you had everything you needed to put me away." What is he up to now? My mind begins foraging through possible reasons. Is he going to perform a mercy killing on me and let Lesley and our child live a normal life without me? Is it simple curiosity?

"This is for me. Yes, I need to know for the investigation, but we would eventually find your lab after analyzing the many tapes you left behind," he says haughtily.

How could I have been so stupid to leave visual evidence behind? In my defense, it wasn't as if I had left it on the kitchen table; they were in a hidden room in my house behind a sliding bookshelf — added after the house was built and after my mom died.

"For you?"

"I just want a well-rounded picture of the events that transpired... to assist with the insanity plea. I will not be the one doing the official investigation, but I can paint the picture for them if I understand a little more."

His words are not convincing. I sense he knows more than he is letting on. Even so, what could it hurt by showing him the location? He's right, they will eventually figure it all out. But why give him something if I'm not getting anything in return?

"What about your unborn niece or nephew?"

"I told you, Tryke, that I'll have Lesley tested."

"And if it's true?"

"I'll consider it then."

"Not good enough," I say, acid creeping back up my throat. "You're really going to let your blood be born in jail!? What kind — "

"I'll pass that bridge when I come to it. I already told you I would consider it."

He isn't budging. I am as close as I am going to get to a bargain with him. I still have to argue the point though. "Why should I do anything for you? What if I refuse, huh? What then? You going to bypass the asylum and push for the death penalty? So damn what. I'm dead anyway. What's the difference, die by the state's hands or drown in my own drool from the head potions in the asylum?"

"I don't think you'll do that."

"What?"

"Refuse."

"How come?"

"Because you want me to see what you have built, what you have accomplished. You're probably aching to show someone the inner workings of your workshop. Am I right?"

"Lesley — " I stifle my words immediately.

He furls his eyebrows and unleashes a dark knowing smirk. "Go on," he says.

"Fine, but I don't see the point," I say, diverting my near mistake of mentioning Lesley's visit there. I have to constantly remind myself to be receptive to his wishes. He has the upper hand and knows it, but that doesn't mean I have to reveal all of my secrets just yet. I'll keep him on a string just like he is doing to me until I have it in writing that Lesley will not be implicated in anything and my child is safe. "Head in the direction of my house and I'll guide you from there."

"Thank you," he says without expression.

I could have just told him the location — the abandoned Peter's Grocery building where my dad had been manager — but I am choosing not to at the moment. He has a point I suppose that I had not considered until now. As secretive as I was about my lab — and for good reason — I felt from the beginning that my work was unappreciated. It had to be that way, but it was still hard to accept. I had named it "undercover gratitude" to help lessen the blow, but as time passed I continued to long for some sort of recognition, if only from one person. As much as I dreaded Lesley discovering my lab, something inside sparked with pride when she saw my workspace and the results it had allowed.

Now, as I look back I don't really know how proud I am of my accomplishments. Yes, everyone else who has seen my lab has been a horrible person who deserved to be released and removed from society. But was it really me doing those things? If things had been different — my family not plagued with sickness — would I have chosen to be a paramedic? Would I have been witness to terrible acts that triggered a need to avenge the victims? Was releasing the filthy my destiny?

There is no way of finding out my real purpose in this life, no matter what piece of evidence I uncover. I may have been altered, I may have been tampered with, but if I were to believe that that was all I am, then I am no more complicated than a programmable machine. Machines don't possess a soul, nor do they have the option of free-will. Our souls influence our actions and decisions more than any outside sources possibly can. They can be damaged, and anything capable of being damaged is capable of being repaired. Was I damaged? Of course I was, but it is only a scratch.

Once we reach my neighborhood, I say, "Peter's Grocery," out of the side of my mouth, before he is able to ask for further directions.

"Your dad's old store? The abandoned one?" His apparent shock is forced.

"Yes… it's the only Peter's Grocery there was," I say.

"Hmmm, I never would have guessed. What on earth made you choose that location? Why not just use the hidden room you had constructed?"

I don't feel much like elaborating about anything at the moment. My ongoing pep-talk to myself about my destiny and soul is quickly pushed aside as I mention Peter's Grocery. Memories of my dad flood my mind from when I was a boy: hiding under his work desk, rummaging through his desk drawers intrigued by the variety of small objects, staring in awe through the windows at the shoppers below. I am suddenly sad, missing his boisterous laugh at my shenanigans. He would prop me on his knee no matter how much work he had to do, always making time for me. He could always come up with a story on the fly, an adventure that he began and I would have to continue with my own twist. When he tucked me in at night, I would relay to him my next part of the story and we would talk about it for as long as I wanted, though my part was rarely as good as his.

What would my dad think of my endeavors? How my life had turned out? Would he blame Dr. Fortune, or would he ask me to take responsibility for my actions? If the latter were the case, would he tell me to embrace my choice? Of all the stories we weaved together they all had a lesson attached in some form or manner — most ended with the protagonist accepting responsibility for their choices. Though I have to say, I don't recall mind control ever being a factor in any of the stories. I need his advice. He would believe me, and explore every option in my arsenal to resolve the problem. Of course, he would only offer the catalyst. I would have to ultimately unravel the issue and put the pieces back together.

"We're here," my uncle says.

I have my eyes shut and my head leaned back against the headrest. It has only been a few minutes, but his words snap me back to the present as the memory of my dad fades.

• • •

To my surprise, the building looks the same as it had before I left. There is no sign saying 'under contract' or 'for lease'. The last I had heard the owner of the building had defaulted and Lester Development was in the process of purchasing the property from the bank. The startled man I had run into on the outside of the building had told me they were going to tear it down and build office spaces in its place. Now a part of me wished it had been torn down, all of the evidence I left behind destroyed. But another part of me, the nostalgic side, is glad to see the dilapidated building still standing. Maybe the owner found the money he needed to keep the property.

I guide my uncle to the back entrance in order to show him my entire operation from beginning to end, leaving out of course the vetting and hunting process, for now. He wants a 'well-rounded' picture of my lab so I will give it to him. I explain where my truck is usually positioned and how I manage to get the bodies up into the room. Before entering the backdoor, he warns me about evidence tampering and then jumps to questions about the sedatives I used and from where I obtained them.

Standing at the base of the stairs, I say, "Not everything at once, uncle."

He lets out a huff and motions with his light for me to lead the way. The dark stairwell leading to my lab that I had traveled up and down countless times is now illuminated by my uncle's obnoxious flood lamp that he pulled from the trunk of his vehicle. It seems a little less vibrant traveling the stairs as a captive — much bleaker and damp than I recall. A few steps in and then suddenly the door flies open from behind us, allowing the cold February wind to rush up the stairs. When it reaches my ears a chill slides down my back, instantly bringing up the memory of Mr. Crow — my first visualization and my first breakthrough with my experiments to find the human soul.

The video of Mr. Crow revealed a shadow but it disappeared the second time I watched it, leaving me to consider the possibility my visions were false. Then, after watching the video again I realized that though the image was gone, something — Mr. Crow, I deduced — had triggered the stair alarm. I was reinvigorated at the time, my mission laid out and overtly clear once again. Now, things are quite a bit more complex and muddled. My mission, no matter the validity, is over. Whatever outcomes I had been witness to, the only result I will have to show will be my incarceration. All of my hard work will be set aside and forgotten in a dust-covered box in a secure police evidence room, all traded for a twin-bed suite at Bolin Asylum.

"Don't touch anything when we get up here, Tryke.

Everything is evidence," my uncle reiterates again, minutes after telling me at the bottom of the stairwell. He also warns against any 'funny business', which I took to mean not attempting to flee. I just nod and walk ahead of him as he directs me to.

"You do know I was the one in here, right? These are my fingerprints," I say sarcastically, nearing the top of the stairs.

"Yeah, I meant don't rearrange anything. I'm not worried about your prints."

I open the door slowly as if anticipating a group of teenagers or a homeless person to come bursting out. It had always been one of my fears, each time I returned, that someone would stumble upon my lab and call the police, or steal my equipment.

I open the door and see that it is just as I had left it — sheets covered the equipment and table, a spy hole in the blacked out window facing the space below, a few poles where I hung IV fluids, and my trusty chair where I performed my own variety of interrogation techniques.

Behind me, my uncle enters the space, and after a brief moment — from which I suspect he is clearing the room as police procedure would dictate — I hear him holster his gun. I glance back at him and he is removing his cowboy hat. He appears to be marveling over the space I created as he flashes his wide beam around the room. He stops and focuses on the table in the center of the room, a sight he likely recalls from the camera feeds. He moves around and takes a closer look. He pulls back the sheets apprehensively and studies my equipment.

"This is quite the operation you had here. Looks like your own private emergency room."

"I guess you could say that," I say, leaning against the far wall, leaving him at ease to peruse the space.

"Only you weren't saving lives, you were taking them," he says with contention.

I am ignoring his latest jab at me while staring at the spot where my dad's desk had been, picturing him walking around the room on the phone as he did often. My thoughts had mostly been on my work every time I was here, but now, since my uncle was with me, the memory of my father is everywhere around me. I always admired his authority, and the charming gentleness he exuded. People respected him because he respected them. "Sorry, dad," I mumble to myself, "for not turning out as good a man as you."

"How about you take me step by step, Tryke, on how you killed these people in here. And please, for the love of Pete don't tell me you tortured anyone. Just lie to me if you did. It will be hard to convince a jury to save you if that's the case."

"Huh —? Oh, right, yeah sorry. I was just thinking of... dad."

He lets out a deep sigh and says, "I don't think your dad would approve of using his old workspace as a murder room."

"It's a little more complicated than that."

"Is it, son? Or did you actually enjoy doing what you did?"

He glares at me with a hatred I had not seen before. What is he doing, testing me to see if I was lying about Dr. Fortune? Seeing if I am truly a sociopath? I cast a surreptitious glance at an object on the table partially covered by the sheet and then switch my gaze to the floor and focus on nothing in particular.

"You don't believe me. Why should I be surprised? By the way, if you hold so much hatred for me, why didn't you use your resources and plaster my face all over the news and let the New Orleans police take me in?"

I push off the wall with my right foot and circle the room, keeping my distance so as not to appear threatening.

"Yeah, about that..." His face turns darker in the

shadows, somehow. "I wanted you to myself."

"You wanted… wait, what?"

He sets his cowboy hat on the center table and says, "You disgust me, Tryke." His voice holds a deep-seated anger and I am caught off guard. I stop where I am, ten feet away from him. "Your family weakness, this so-called illness, it sickens me. I am so tired of hearing the excuses, the pleas of insanity." He walks around the center table and stops a few feet away from me. I am focused on his right hand, watching it closely. I am speechless, still dumbfounded by his words. "My brother would still be alive if it weren't for your mom. She and your sister stole everything from him until there was nothing left."

My voice suddenly returns with vigor, "My dad loved my mom and sister. He never considered them a burden."

"Bullshit! You never saw him like I did. You never saw the pain in his eyes when he talked about your mom."

"So, you *did* know that it was my mom who was sick."

"Of course I did. When your dad asked me to look after you and give you that letter I reluctantly agreed to it. I didn't tell him, but if I saw the sickness in you I made a pact with myself that I would stay away and not let what happened to my brother happen to me. You were not going to kill me as your mom and sister did him."

"That's why you never came around after my mom died? Because you hated us?"

"That's correct. And I still do."

"So, now you want to kill me? Staying away wasn't good enough? Why didn't you do it earlier? Why wait until now and bring me back here?"

"I never wanted to kill you, Tryke. Not in the beginning. I just wanted you away from me like I said. I didn't care if you were sick or not, I wasn't taking the chance. That was until I found your room and discovered what you had been doing. I knew I didn't have a choice then. If I turn you in, I'll be scrutinized. I'm close to retirement and I don't need anything interfering with it. Especially a sickly, cold-blooded killer."

"And killing me now is better? If they find out you killed me, what then?"

"They won't. I'm the law, Tryke. I can manipulate any evidence I choose. If you are alive I will be obligated to visit you. I will be the one they come to if you do something in the asylum, bad behavior and what not. I want to retire in peace. I don't want that in my life. I don't want you in my life."

He pulls his gun from his holster and points it towards me. He has not cocked it yet but for all I know he could have a bullet in the chamber at all times, ready to fire. I don't have anything readily available to defend myself with. I eye the loose sheet covering the table close to me. I can yank it off the table and lunge it toward him, temporarily interrupting his aim. It may just give me enough time to make a run for it. I stare toward the open door and begin calculating the distance. I am a good ten feet away and he is closer to it than me, but with the distraction it may just cancel out his advantage.

He notices me staring at the open door and says, "There's no use in running. I've been shooting my entire life. I don't miss."

I sigh and stay where I am, the temporary momentum deflating quickly. I search desperately for the words I want to say but panic spreads throughout my body. I immediately switch my gaze to the floor and try to focus. This is no time to panic. I have to control what is happening. I attempt to block out everything in the room as the tension builds inside like a pressure cooker with no relief valve. My hands start shaking uncontrollably, my mouth suddenly torrid. I attempt to hide my hands in the shadows without seeming conspicuous. I begin uncontrollably clearing my throat over and over, trying desperately to wet my parched mouth. I try to speak but only grunts of throat clearing and repetitive 'humf''s are coming out. I don't look up at my uncle. I open and close my hands to concentrate on something — anything. I try counting repetitiously in my head, but then as if anticipating it, something inside me starts chuckling, reminding me of its power. And then, as if out of nowhere like I have been given a gift, I speak in a clear concise manner. The words flow out like trapped water behind a dam that had finally broken free. It is my only immediate defense.

"You let your brother die alone. You could have been a supportive brother and assisted him, but you chose to hate. You had a choice, but my mom and sister did not. You are the one that killed your brother, not my mom and sister. It was always you. He came to you for help, vulnerable, crying, and what do you do? Nothing but hate the ones he loved." I look up and notice my words impacting him. He loosens his grip on the gun, slightly lowering it away from the center of my chest — but still very much pointed toward me — and then wipes the sweat from his brow with his left hand.

"No!"

"Yes, you even killed your own wife. You hated her burdening cancer didn't you? And now you are going to complete your path of murder by killing me, the last remaining family you have."

He slowly moves toward me, his boots dragging along the floor. He keeps the gun pointed toward me at waist level, his hand mildly shaking. I take a step back and feel the covered table behind me. I have nowhere to go. This is it, my last words have been spoken. I notice my shadow along the wall and it appears to be moving independently of me. And then I notice his. They circle one another like two gladiators moments from clashing. The arena floor will soon be saturated in blood.

He stops a few feet in front of me. His face is covered in the darkness of the room and I am unable to see his expression. I notice I am in reach of his gun. I have seconds to act but for some reason I do not. I cannot. He leans in towards me and I reach out to him and embrace him with one arm.

Suddenly a deafening sound rattles the room and I cannot hear anything but a muffled echo. A strong scent of gun powder fills my nose and then a drenching warmth fills every vessel in my body like I just slammed a double shot of whiskey into my veins.

I can't hear him, but I read his lips: "I'm sorry."

Chapter 26

Uncle Frank shuffles around on the metal table, lifting his head in short bursts. I sit silently in my trusty aluminum thinking-chair across from him. While he was resting, I spent the last few hours ruminating on how to proceed with my life.

His gun had a bullet loaded and ready to go, but lucky for me I was only grazed by it. When I reached out and embraced him, I managed to move the gun far enough for the bullet to miss the many vital organs in my midsection. The wound still hurts like a bitch, but I'll live, for now. The object that I spotted on the table before he pulled his gun on me saved my life. How could I have been so careless as to leave a full syringe behind? Whatever the reason, it has allowed me to live — a curse or a gift?

My uncle has now revealed his true face, one that had been hidden since my dad died. He never came around, and not because he thought my sickness would kill him, but because he was afraid he would reveal the darkness inside him too soon.

"Tryke," Frank grunts. "Get these restraints the hell off of me. Now!"

I switch on the two flashlights — I found another in his car — that I had pointed toward the ceiling, giving the space a more inviting ambiance for us to discuss matters at hand.

"Shouting will not help your situation," I tell him.

"I treated you fairly and this is how you repay me?" he says, still struggling to loosen the leather binding his wrists.

"You were going to kill me. You call that fair?"

"It was going to be a mercy killing. You're sick, Tryke. I was only doing what I know to do."

I shake my head at his selective amnesia. "What? Have you suddenly forgotten your words? You hate me, and my mom, and my sister. We killed your brother, according to you. This sounds strangely like revenge to me."

"Pity, not revenge." His tone has suddenly changed to survival mode from his earlier, seemingly in control, disgust for me. "I see that now. I was really only angry at your mom, not you or your sister."

"Sudden epiphany, Uncle? People in dicey situations will sing whatever tune is necessary. So your logic is that my mom had a choice and my sister and I did not?"

"Okay, look, I made a mistake. What do you want me to do? To say I'm sorry and leave you alone? Fine, I will do that. I'm sorry for everything. I don't hate any of you. We'll leave each other alone and live our lives like we were doing before."

He is my only family left. I trusted him and he betrayed me and my entire family.

"You had your chance to do that and you chose to come after me. You chose to hunt me."

"Whatever it is you have planned, I assure you that if you go through with it, you will be put to death when they catch you." His voice is riddled with fear. "And they *will* catch you, I promise." As long as I have known him, I have never heard fear in his voice. Until now.

"Don't be hasty," I say calmly, stifling the pitting anger. "All I want to do is talk for the moment, and then we'll see where it leads from there."

"What is there to talk about? I already apologized."

"I don't want an apology. I want answers."

"I'm not telling you anything until you let me out of these ridiculous restraints." He peers over at his jacket, which I placed on the table by the door.

"Don't worry, I secured your gun back in its holster and it is safely in your jacket, unloaded." He notices the ripped piece of blood-soaked sheet next to me, and my torn shirt.

"It's only a scratch. Don't get your hopes up."

"What answers do you want?" he says.

"Why do you project your hate for yourself onto your family?"

"It wasn't supposed to be like this. I never wanted to hurt you."

"You're not answering the question, just as I knew you wouldn't. It was rhetorical anyhow. I just wanted to see how dedicated you are to your narrative. It seems that you have mixed feelings about yourself. Let me tell you what I think of you. I think you like to kill. You like the thrill of the hunt. That's why you became a homicide detective. You wanted to see death, blood, and murder. You wanted ideas on how to kill people. You weren't going to incarcerate Lesley. You were going to murder her after you killed me."

He shakes his head. "Don't compare me to you. I was never going to hurt Lesley. I was only threatening jail to get you to talk. I wanted to know where this place was. That's it."

"You risked bringing me back to Dallas to know the location of my lab? Really? You could have just finished me off in New Orleans and let it look like Fortune and I killed each other. You had plenty of evidence to plant."

He turns his head away from me and doesn't answer.

Wait a second. He knew all along. When he found my hidden room, he knew then. But why did he — ? I grab one of the lights and yank the sheets off the tables one by one, searching the top first and then underneath. Nothing. I turn the light to the walls. When I reach the entrance door, I notice two brown paper grocery bags resting behind it, their tops rolled partially down. I pilfer through the contents and find a roll of plastic and a few rolls of duct tape, along with two body bags.

"Two bags? One for me and one for Lesley? You knew about this place all along, you son of a bitch!"

He lets out a heavy sigh and turns back toward me. "I figured it out after I got off the phone with you. It took me a while, but by the time I made it here, you were gone."

Of course he avoids the question about killing Lesley. I still want to know how everything connects — Fortune, how he found me in New Orleans. But I let it go, for now.

"And then you went to Fortune and came after me. How did you know to go to Fortune? Were you partners with him?"

"Hell, no," he says. "I don't want anything to do with damn head doctors. As far as I'm concerned, him and Randal were part of the problem. They encouraged the sickness, wielded it as if it could be contained. I knew Fortune was dirty, I just didn't know how dirty. Your father never trusted him, but could never tell me why. After reading your diaries along with your dad's and the storage files, I knew he was part of it somehow."

"What did you have on him?"

"Nothing. It was all about Dr. Randal, but after I showed him my badge, he sang like a canary. He told me everything, even things that weren't in the files, but blamed it all on Randal. His crime, he claimed, was not turning his colleague in earlier. Before leaving, I realized he knew too much. After I was finished with you, I was going to go after him. It was an easy murder/suicide plot, but you went and killed him first. I had no idea he would come after you himself. That was a twist I never saw coming. After that part of my plan was ruined, all I had to do was plant a note and make your death appear as a suicide. That's why there are two bags. The second one was for Fortune. Lesley was never going to enter the picture unless it was absolutely necessary. In other words, if you didn't cooperate."

I stifle my anger once again and ignore his mention of Lesley. "How did you know I was in New Orleans? And why involve Fortune in the first place if you already knew where I was?"

"After seeing the Elderly Slayer's body on your table, I searched his house. I glanced through the history on his computer and saw the travel searches for New Orleans, and took a shot in the dark that that's where you had run to. Concerning Fortune, I needed help, a partner. I only wanted information at first to help me, and when I realized he knew too much that's when I asked him to come with me. Initially he was only going to be a spotter for me, someone you wouldn't immediately flee from. Once I had you in custody, we would all travel back here to your little murder room. You'd show me, as you did, and thinking I had no idea, and then I would finish it. When he refused my request to come with me, I had to change the plan to leading him here after I was done with you. Same overall plan, only slightly altered."

"Bravo on a completely failed scheme. Your detective skills worked on capturing me, but your battle with your flawed conscience was your weakness."

"The only flaw in my life was your mom and sister and you. My brother should have never married your tainted mother, and you and your sister should never have been born."

"I see your false remorse has once again retracted itself back up your ass."

He let out a sinister laugh. "You always did have a wise

mouth, just like your old man. Only he wasn't a killer."

"I bet your brother would be proud of you," I said, "protecting his family after he died, just as you told him you would."

"The only thing I wanted to protect was me."

"Well said." I shook my head. "But why the lax police procedure? Why didn't you cuff me if you planned to kill me?"

It *was* a strange rookie mistake for him to make. My uncle wasn't one for taking unnecessary risks and he wasn't one for making mistakes, especially when it came to police procedure. He had allowed the opportunity, but why? Did he want a challenge?

He shrugs, "I don't know. Maybe I wasn't completely convinced."

"Convinced of?"

"Killing you. I knew you deserved it, but I didn't want to be the one to do it. Just like you don't have it in you to kill me. So you might as well stop this madness and let me loose."

"Did you forget, you pulled the trigger. You meant to kill me!"

"Maybe, but not without second thoughts."

"I'm glad you're proud of yourself, but not all of us are so weak in our convictions. Some of us can see things more clearly."

"Here we go," he says with disgust in his voice. "I read your diaries and know about your number system. How each victim of yours has a number that correlates with the chance to see their soul. What a bunch of hocus-pocus. This is it, you crazy shit. This, your surroundings, the physical world is everything. What you see is what you get. There's nothing more. After we die there is only darkness. Good and evil don't exist, just what we humans make up to make us feel less alone. Get over yourself already. Like it or not, Tryke, you are mentally unstable. It's as simple as that!" His eyes suddenly turn a shade redder. "You want to know if I have a soul? You want to see it leave so you can feel better about this life?! Go for it, you coward! Your sickness will fool you again."

I muster as much calmness as I can and consider my next words carefully. "Not everything is as black and white as you'd like to think. My search for the soul was only in the beginning. I know it exists. Now, I'm just playing the game the best I know how with the tools I was given."

"This isn't a game," he says. "This is life and death!"

My calm words contrast with his furious ones. "It's not the kind of game you're thinking of, Uncle. This is far greater than your tiny mind can imagine. We are little fragments in the scheme of things, but even as small and insignificant as I may be, I have to do my part. You are as blind as you are dumb, and you're controlled by your own hatred. You were not sent by them. You interfered, and look where it landed you. Your arrogance allows you to think you're in control, but you're not."

"I chose not to kill you."

"You fired your gun, remember."

"I missed on purpose. I'm not arguing with a crazy person."

I entertain his delusion. "Okay, fine, why did you miss? Why the sudden change of heart?"

"I remembered your dad and how much he cared for you. How worried he was that you'd become sick like your sister. This is real, Tryke. Here, now, us. You can tell the difference, I know you can. This isn't the way. Your dad would not have hurt anyone, especially his family."

"No," I say vacantly. "You're not going to use my dad against me. If he had known what Fortune was up to, he would have killed him himself."

"Angry, yes, but never murder. He believed in the justice system, same as me."

I let out a short laugh. "You make me laugh, you really

do. I can't afford to believe in something that fails so hard and so often, and neither would my dad. His letter would have been much different had he known. I would have had instructions, a guide on how to deal with this life and the Gamemakers." I let it slip, but what did it matter at this point?

He wrinkles his forehead and stares at me, but doesn't pause for long. "I never saw revenge in his eyes, even behind the alcohol-stained pain. He was hurting inside, deeply, beyond the cancer, but he would never have hurt anyone. Even the worst of people."

Nothing was real in my family's life. Every strand of truth was stolen from them, leading them to act and live their lives based on a lie. A spiraling downhill ride to nowhere in a narrow hole filled with jutting, jagged spikes, slicing without remorse. I will not be fooled anymore.

"Things are not as simple as we like to think. Good and evil are way more complex, and multidimensional, and we will never completely understand the concept until we move on. There are forces beyond our sight that are constantly pulling and pushing our levers, manipulating tiny infractions in the universe."

My short spiel must have triggered something inside, something itching to be revealed one more time — one last strike to satisfy his dark mind. "You want to know the truth?" he asks. "Here's the truth." He looks at me, his appearance now somehow more haggard than it was just minutes ago. His face has turned a dark crimson, matching his rising temper. "I was going to go after Lesley once I killed you. And the topping on the cake was you telling me that she's pregnant. Your sickness would finally die with you and your unborn child!"

"Thank you. You have answered the calling, as I knew you would. Yours is the worst kind of soul out there. It is filthy, saturated with so much hatred that once it is released the wails and screams it reveals will be heard throughout the underworld, and they will all know that a balance still exists. That no matter their attempts to escape, there will always be another emerging on the other side to battle them."

"You think you are the good and I'm the evil? You're not only sick, you're demented."

"I never said I was good, Uncle."

"Do you hear yourself, Tryke?" He speaks to me like I am an unruly child, sounding as though he's about to send me to my room. "This nonsense you spout doesn't change the fact that you murder people."

I could have brought up the fact that he was going to kill Lesley and an innocent child, but it does not matter anymore. There is no use in prolonging the inevitable. He will never be able to see things until he is released. He thinks his badge is a justification for what he does, but the truth is staring at him in the reflection of the polished shield. As mad as I am at him, he does not deserve to be tortured. The Gamemakers have once again urged me forward to keep the game going, all but placing the syringe in my hand. They would never allow a non-player to kill me.

Chapter 27

I have a few stops to make before leaving town. I must keep each of them brief, not knowing how much time I have left before the hounds are released. Mercy General Hospital is my first, where Dave lies comatose.

Dave was one of the most unlikely of friends for me to have. He has always been so different from me, settled comfortably in his life, knowing exactly what he believes in. He has always shown passion and intensity as a paramedic. I also revealed a passion, though mine arose from a very different place.

Remembering the name of the nurse I had spoken to on the phone, I ask for her when I get to the secured door leading to the ICU. Much to my surprise, she is working. Having never met me before, she tells me through the speaker to meet her in the small waiting room to my right in a few minutes. Small waiting rooms are seldom used for good news. The emotions in these tight spaces can become so enveloping and tense that you can almost see the souls weeping together if you pay close attention. I leave the door open, just in case.

A minute later a young female wearing white scrubs and a genuine smile walks into the room. I am alone, so I assume it is Elizabeth. She isn't at all like I had pictured her from the short time we'd spent on the phone. I imagined a middle-aged lady, maybe even older, with a shy demeanor and a homely appearance, but she is a young, comely woman with a seemingly pleasant personality.

"Freddie," I say, getting up from the chair and offering her my right hand.

Without hesitation she returns the gesture and she shakes my hand. "Elizabeth," she says smiling. "But you already know that, sorry."

I smile back at her. "I didn't know if it was visiting hours, but I had some time and was wondering if I could see Dave. I won't be long, I promise." The hours for visiting are on the wall twenty feet from where I am standing, and they are very clear. It is almost eleven a.m., and the hours are 9 a.m. to 9 p.m. I know I am well in range of the times, but it is always a nice gesture to show respect when you need something, or not, in this case, meaning I don't need unnecessary suspicions.

"He's not here anymore."

"What do you mean? Did he wake up?" She is smiling way too much for it to be the other reason he isn't in ICU anymore.

"No — I mean yes. He's on the second floor. He's awake, but he still has to go to rehab every morning. In fact, he just got transferred two days ago. I have to say, it's bittersweet for me."

If I could see my face, I'm sure I would be beaming. The news brings with it a sudden rush of relief that had been nesting in my guilty subconscious, and I can't say a word.

"I can tell that you want to see him badly. Come on, I'll take you over to him. I need to see what he wants for lunch anyway."

"Sure," I manage, and we walk toward the elevators. "So y'all have become pretty good friends, I take it."

"You could say that," she says blushing. She turns away from me and presses the elevator button. I follow her inside and we get out on the second floor. I wasn't expecting him to be conscious. My plan was to sit quietly with him for a few minutes and then leave one of the two letters I have for him that are folded in envelopes in my back pocket. Though I am ecstatic about him returning to the conscious world, what am I going to say to him? I don't have a speech ready. I am suddenly nervous and can feel my palms beginning to moisten.

"He's going to be glad to have a visitor, especially a work friend," Elizabeth says as we exit the elevator. I hold the door and let her exit first. "He loves talking about the calls you guys go on." I nod with a half-smile. We walk halfway down a hall and pass a nurses' station, and then we stop in front of a room where the door is cracked open. A television is blaring on the other side.

"He's probably watching one of his westerns," she says, as if they have been married for years.

"Yeah," I say, revealing my nervous half-smile once again.

She knocks on the door and pushes it open and says in a chipper greeting, "Dave, it's Elizabeth, and I have a visitor for you."

"Come in," a voice says, but it doesn't sound like the Dave I know. This voice is muffled, and sounds as if the person is speaking out of the side of his mouth.

I motion with my arm for Elizabeth to go in front of me and then I slowly trail behind her into the room. Once I turn the corner, everything comes to light. It is definitely Dave in the room. You can't mistake those trusty pair of horrible brown leather sandals he loves, but there is something different about him. His face immediately lights up when he sees me. I shake my head at the sandals and smile toward him, but my smile quickly fades to pity when I notice the left side of his face doesn't cooperate with the right.

"Hey, Tryke, man have I missed you, buddy."

"I missed you too," I say instinctively, trying my best not to stare toward his mouth.

"I see that you met Elizabeth,"

"Yes," I say, attempting to broaden my smile.

"Elizabeth, this is my paramedic partner and friend, Tryke Harper."

"I thought you said your name was Freddie." She looks at me with a raised eyebrow.

"Sorry," I say, shrugging. "That's my alias."

"I told you he was weird," Dave says. "He doesn't trust anyone."

That's an understatement, especially at the moment. She seems to brush off my name change when Dave does. "Tryke," she emphasizes, "I've heard a lot about you."

"From this storyteller? Doesn't surprise me."

"Well, I'll let you two catch up," Elizabeth says turning toward Dave. "What did you want me to get you for lunch?"

"How about some subs today, your choice where," Dave says, his words exiting slowly, as if he is concentrating on each one.

"Okay," she says. "Tryke, how about you?"

"I'm good, but thank you." Actually I am starving, not having eaten since my 'last night in New Orleans dinner'. I'll get something on the way to my next stop. She bends over and hugs Dave. He hugs her back with his right arm. I assume his left arm is like the left side of his face. She shuffles out of the room and leaves the door cracked open.

"Nice, huh?" Dave says, attempting to raise his eyebrows in unison like he used to when he was being his typical cheesy self.

"Yeah, nice work. You know you only got her because

you were unconscious, right? How'd you manage to keep her once you woke up?"

He smiles, shrugs his shoulders, and says, "It's good to see you, man. How's my other girlfriend doing?"

I walk to the window and stare out, "Yeah, about that."

"Don't tell me y'all broke up?" I don't answer him. "Really? What happened? You two are perfect for each other."

"Long story, but there's no hard feelings between us. I take it she hasn't been up here?"

I turn back toward him and he shakes his head. "No."

"So, she doesn't know you're awake?"

"I called both of you this morning," says Dave. "Left messages. I assumed that was why you showed up."

"We both lost our phones, but that's another long story. I would have been up here more, but Lesley didn't like seeing you like that and I…" I lower my head. I am not displaying a totally false sentiment. I was legitimately concerned for him, and still am.

He nods toward the small artificial Christmas tree that Lesley and I placed in his ICU room before we ran. "It's okay, I know y'all were at least up here once. Thanks for the tree, by the way. Lesley's idea, I imagine." He is wearing a pathetic but warranted look on his face. We visited more than his own family.

"Yes," I lie, "of course."

"So, how have things been?"

As bad as he needs a friend to converse with, I have to get on with what I came to do. I wouldn't mind a drink and a few moments of mindless words myself, but maybe sometime in the future. That is, if I have one.

"Not that good," I say, "and that's one of the reasons I'm here. I have to leave."

"Leave? What do you mean?"

"Too many bad memories here. I have to move on, get away for a while."

"Because of Lesley?"

"No, I mean… not only that. It's a little more complicated. That's part of why I came to see you. There are some things you should know, and I have a favor to ask of you. But before I tell you anything, I want to know what you remember."

"About what? How I got here?" I nod. "Not much, just what Elizabeth told me from the newspaper. That bastard nursing home slayer tried to kill me."

"Yeah, he did. And Clyde and I coded you. Sorry we didn't get there sooner," I say, nodding and staring toward his left side. I quickly look away.

"You saved my life. Thank you. A little disability – so what? But please tell me they at least got that son of a bitch."

"Yeah, they found him."

"Good."

"They found him dead at his daughter's house," I stress, searching for a response. With his belief system, I'm not sure what kind of justice he's hoping for.

"Good riddance," he says with flair. This response opens the door for me to tell him certain things.

"Both of them."

"What?"

"There are some things you need to know. I have most of it written down in a letter — I didn't know you had come out of your coma — that I am going to give you. I don't have a lot of time, so forgive me if some of the minor details are missing. Hopefully the letter will help you understand things better." He knows my serious look, and I am wearing it proudly. I have to improvise quickly and come up with a story. I also have to be very careful with the details; this is not in either of the letters, and for good reason. He pays close attention as I relay the tale.

His memory is still intact as I tell the story of Dr. Kimberly and her father, and how they used him and me to get what they wanted. I never tell Dave why they actually wanted me, but he assumes it is because Kimberly was attracted to me. I tell him the elderly slayer was after us because we interrupted one of his rituals. He is shocked to learn that Kimberly was also a killer and his sidekick. All in all, he seems to buy the story.

Next, I tell him the reason I am leaving town, but only pieces of the truth. I tell him I avenged him by releasing the elderly slayer, but not in the manner in which it was actually done. I explain how it was self-defense, and then I emphasize that no one will believe my side of the story if it were ever to come to light. The papers have still not released the official autopsy reports and the police have kept it quiet. Dave offers to help clear my name, but I am adamant about no one else knowing. I tell him to leave it alone and he reluctantly agrees, pushing aside his virtuous knightly side at my request. I also ask that he keep the information from Lesley, and he agrees, reluctantly. My hope is that they never get up the nerve to discuss things over drinks and play the truth game — that never leads to good things.

"This is not a permanent goodbye, man, so don't get all blubber-faced about it." I smile and quickly say, "No offense." I let out a shallow laugh.

He grins, but it fades fast. "I still don't know what to say, Tryke. I wish you would stay. No one will find out."

"I have to do this." I pull both envelopes from my back pocket — they are marked 1 and 2 — and place them in his right hand. "Read both of them. Read the second one at least twice and give it some serious thought before making any rash decisions. It's going to be tough to absorb, but you'll understand in time. My new number is on the bottom of the first letter." I get up from my chair while he is staring at the two envelopes with a dumbfounded look. "And one last thing." I reach out and grab his hand. "Thanks for being a good friend." I let go and leave before he drags more out of me that I don't want to say. I'm in a time crunch, and I still have two more stops.

Not knowing if he would ever wake up from his coma, I had to plan accordingly. I wrote two letters: depending on the condition in which he returned, the first letter was meant to be read to him by a nurse the moment he woke, or preferably by him if he were able. The second letter, however, was a little more sensitive and I was going to mail it to him after I vetted his awareness and abilities. Basically, I want to know if he is able to take care of himself and live a somewhat normal life on his own without constant care. It is imperative for the request I have for him.

It would have been much easier to just set the letter by the bed of an unconscious Dave, but I suppose it is a relief to fill in the empty spaces in his memory that I knew would be there if he were to wake up. I certainly couldn't leave that information in writing. The letters, and me leaving town, make more sense with a story attached to them, not to mention the gaps I left in the letters, which would now be somewhat filled in.

Chapter 28

Bolin Asylum

The three-story, gothic style building, surrounded by a rusted wrought-iron gate covered in vines, was a perfect match for the way most perceive an aging asylum — right down to the crumbling sign and tall, dark, mysterious, grimy windows. The building exuded a sinister vibe that would leave any sane person shuddering, even in the light of day. I, myself, get a tingling along my spine every time I think of the place, like a disembodied cold finger sliding along my bare neck. It wasn't that long ago that I was sure I would end up in this forsaken place, stuck in the dark recesses of my head and shackled by mind-altering medications. But, as fate would have it, this is not yet my time to waste away in such a facility.

Visiting this place is beyond my better judgment, but it is imperative. I have to speak with Dr. Jake Randal, the man I had originally thought was behind the hypnosis plot and the one I had been planning on releasing. He needed to know the truth. No, he deserved to know the truth. He has to understand that he was ordered to kill his family and that it was beyond his will. He was not a cold-blooded killer, as Fortune had wanted him to believe.

Dr. Randal and my mom held a special bond between them; a friendship. They shared a darkness that was unknowingly placed inside them both and used to control each of them. They attempted to help one another to see through the manipulation, but neither could ever quite put things together before it was too late — before they were ordered to commit the unthinkable and murder their own family.

I am in the parking lot, mulling over how I am going to handle telling Randal the truth. And more importantly, once I tell him, would he even believe me? The drugs and the torment may have already pushed his mind to accept his fate. The last time we conversed, he seemed to be partially disconnected from the world, stubbornly hanging on to a thread of sanity and swaying on the ledge.

I am hoping that, as Sylvia's son, I will have some sort of credibility with him. Also, he has already met me once before. It may take a little convincing, but if I fill in some of the details I feel certain he will be able to see the truth. If not immediately, then someday. I can only hope I am not too late. If he has already faced the five stages of grief with his dead family and is in the acceptance phase, then I will have to unlock that sensitive box and slowly raise the lid.

I decide on a short and direct explanation, and then I will stay quiet, let him process the information, and listen to what he has to say. I will answer any questions that he has, and then I will leave. I want desperately to free him from the asylum life, but this is not the time. I will return at a future date and fulfill what I believe my mom would have done given the knowledge I now possess.

Before I turn off the ignition to my truck, I notice a compact car with dark tinted windows running a few spaces over, perpendicular to me. I don't recognize it, nor does it appear to be law enforcement. I want to get out and go inside to get this over with, but for some reason this car is making me nervous. I'm not overly paranoid, yet, but merely being cautious. It's probably just the tinted windows, the unknown, that is bothering me. I turn my radio down and crack the window of my truck, just far enough to listen outside. I will give it a few minutes, and if nothing changes, will proceed with my plans.

The parking lot is not at all full. If the person in the car *is* after me, they aren't exactly being inconspicuous — the car is running and the parking lights are turned on and they are in plain view. I tell myself that they are probably just waiting for someone.

I take a deep breath, remove my keys from the ignition, and get out and lock the doors behind me. For good measure, I keep my keys at the ready in my right hand. Though it is cloudy, I keep my sunglasses on to shield my eyes from the person in the vehicle. I choose the path in front of the vehicle instead of the rear. I watch closely out of my peripheral as I attempt to walk casually toward the entrance of the asylum. I am almost directly in front of the vehicle, one row of cars between us, but I still cannot get a good look at the driver through the windshield. A few steps more and I hear a car door open and shut. I want to turn around but I don't want to seem nosey or paranoid. I keep moving forward, minding my own business, until…

"Tryke Harper," a voice says, freezing me in place.

• • •

Lesley is standing in front of the not-so-inconspicuous white car. She is expressionless. Her hair is down and dyed back to its original night black color, with a pair of sunglasses perched on her head. I don't say a word. I ignore the initial shock of her being here and just stare at her, taking in all of her beauty. I then focus my attention on her stomach where our child is growing. Lesley isn't showing yet. My anger toward her for leaving immediately fades.

We both stand there, silent, staring at one another like two gunslingers at high noon. I break the silence once I realize the awkwardness between us. "Lesley," I say stupidly. "How —?" Then I remember Dave. He must have gotten in touch with her somehow and told her I was in town. Has he read the letter yet? "Oh right, Dave."

"You should have called me and told me," she says.

"I was going to, after I finished here."

I want to run to her and tell her everything is going to be okay, but I cannot. Certain things have to be done first. She has to know where I stand.

"This isn't going to solve anything, Tryke. Let it go and come be with your family."

She doesn't know about Fortune. She still thinks I came here to get even with Dr. Randal.

"Things have changed," I say, quickly rerouting the conversation away from a reunion speech. "Randal was not behind the plot. He was part of it."

"Huh?" Her eyebrows furrow. "What are you talking about?"

I don't immediately respond. She walks ahead and stops a few feet in front of me. I remove my sunglasses and notice she has been crying.

"He was a victim, just like my mom. They were both ordered to murder their families." I try to keep my composure as I think of my little sister. "I only came here to tell him the truth, not to get even." Lesley doesn't know the details of what my mom was made to do and she still appears confused. Either that or she's suspicious — I can't tell the difference at the moment. "I'm not lying. Come with me and you can hear everything for yourself."

"I'm not going inside that place," she says. "It creeps me out."

"You'll be by my side the entire time. Besides, we're not going that far inside, just a room over from the entrance.

And you're far away from the populace, I promise."

She seems to suddenly believe. Either that or she's trying to avoid entering the asylum.

"Just do what you came to do and I'll wait out here until you're done. You can give me the quick notes and we can discuss the details at a later time."

"Not here," I say with frustration. "It's not that easy to explain like that. I need you to meet Dr. Randal." She notices the intensity on my face and in my words, and is reconsidering. "It's important to me that you know this, and the only way to fully grasp it is by meeting Dr. Randal in person. Our child deserves to know the truth about our family." The child card is played and strategically placed. "You can decide when the time is right to tell the whole story."

"What does that mean?" she asks. "What about you?" Her bewildered look quickly changes to despair as she realizes what I'm saying.

"I may not be around to —. Look, I don't know what's going to happen to me. I just want you safe, our child safe, and that's it. Eventually — . Let's just see how things go here first." I know what I have to tell her, but I cannot do it until she knows the truth about my family. Once everything is out in the open, *then* she can start forming her opinion and future plans with our child.

"Don't talk like that," she says pleadingly. "Of course you'll be around." I can tell that she wants to come closer and embrace me, but the fear of the building and the uncertainty of our relationship are still overwhelming her.

"Please, just come with me inside. You'll understand once the gaps are filled in and you'll feel better about things. I'll feel better about things. Come on, it won't take long."

She appears to be chewing over the information, and a few seconds later asks, "How are we even going to get inside?" I have her. Curiosity has finally nudged the fear aside. "Don't you have to have a pass or something?"

I pull from my back pocket a prescription pad that I found in Fortune's jacket pocket.

"Where did you get that?" she asks with a skeptical look on her face.

I smile and say, "You'll know everything soon enough."

She nods hesitantly and says, "Okay." And then, as if she suddenly remembers, she says, "But what about your uncle?"

"I'll explain that part after we finish here." I leave the subject open on purpose. It will be the last thing I tell her.

"What does that mean?"

"Just trust me, will you? One thing at a time."

She reluctantly accepts my proposal. I scribble down the exact words that Fortune had written for me the first time on the blank prescription. She is still timid, taking small steps toward the entrance. I grab hold of her hand and I feel it moisten as we enter through the gate and up the stairs toward the dark door. She glances up at the tall windows and I feel her hand squeeze mine like we were about to enter a haunted house on Halloween. Only the screams in this place are real.

• • •

The room is quiet. From what I remember, it is set up much the same as the one I was in previously, only a deeper shade of blue paint is peeling from the walls. The room is mostly bare, likely, I deduce, to limit the number of objects that could be used as weapons. The old Victorian style high-backed chairs and the huge ornate mirror, which looks like it hasn't been cleaned since they installed it, only enhance the creepiness of the place. Lesley agrees with my assessment with a nervous nod as she sits in one of the chairs. She hasn't spoken since we entered. I think the stern nurse who lectured us on the way in may have intimidated her even more so than the ominous building and the stories that surrounded this place during our childhood.

I try and speak to her to break the cold, eerie pillars of ice in the room, but she remains quiet with her thoughts, intermittently studying our surroundings and then staring back at the dark-grey concrete floor. I can almost hear the apprehension steaming from Lesley's ears as she drums her nervous fingers on her right knee. She scoots her chair closer to mine and I unfold a half-smile. She extends one back, only hers is saturated with unease.

A few minutes later the double doors creak open and a henchman wearing all white enters the room. Following him is Dr. Randal, wearing dark purple scrubs and a pair of thin black spectacles. His hair is again disheveled, and more grey has infiltrated. Overall, he looks better than before, but worse at the same time, if that's possible.

The henchman waits at the door and crosses his arms while Dr. Randal moves slowly forward, his head hung low. The henchman doesn't give me a time limit, as I was given before. He nods, and I nod back at him. There is only one henchman this time, probably due to either good behavior or cutbacks.

I stand when Dr. Randal is halfway to us and Lesley follows suit. He raises his head and stares at me as he gets closer, not losing eye contact. I stare back, but not in an intimidating manner; I try and present myself as humble and appreciative. He stops a few feet in front of me and speaks first.

"Tryke, right?" he says in a calm, reassuring tone.

I nod and say, "Yes, sir."

"And this is?" he asks, moving his eyes toward Lesley.

I give her a second to answer for herself, but she does not.

"Lesley," I say.

"Nice to meet you, Lesley," he says, his eyes remaining on her.

"You too," she stumbles. She is holding her hands

together, probably to hide the mild shaking.

He finally removes his eyes from Lesley and stretches out his right arm for us to be seated. Lesley and I sit simultaneously, and he takes a seat in the empty chair across from us, his fingers interlocked.

"To what do I owe this pleasure?" Dr. Randal asks.

"I have some disturbing news, I'm afraid," I say. "Your old colleague, Dr. Fortune, is dead."

I am testing the water. I don't look over at Lesley, but her complete silence tells me she is listening — I haven't heard her take a breath.

"How did he die?" he asks, without emotion in his voice.

"Heart attack I believe."

"Maybe it's the meds, but I have to say I'm not entirely upset."

I suspect his memories have caught up with the events. Maybe not entirely, but enough pieces to form a general suspicion about Fortune.

"That's not the only reason I'm here," I say. "I'll get straight to the point." He nods for me to continue. "Here goes." I take a deep breath and methodically tell the story of Fortune and his hypnosis drug, pausing briefly after each piece of new sensitive information. When I get to the part about my mom and what she was ordered to do, he tears up and begins to rock back and forth while staring at the floor. It seems to hit him harder than when I tell him about how Fortune ordered him to kill his own wife and daughter. I presume he's more affected by the news about my mom because he has already accepted what he has done to his family, no matter the reason.

I look over at Lesley and she is wiping her eyes and sniffling. Dr. Randal takes a break from his rocking motion and looks up. His eyes are stained with grief behind his dark-rimmed glasses. He reaches over to the small table next to him, grabs a tissue, and hands it to Lesley. She thanks him and he nods back to her, returning his stare downward. He softly grabs a fistful of his grey hair and begins tapping his feet on the floor. I don't interrupt his thoughts or the process he is using to cope with the information, but I notice the henchman paying close attention. I decide not to intervene unless I see the henchman approach.

After a few tense minutes Dr. Randal finally recovers, and I let out a deep sigh of relief. The henchman grumbles a few times in place, but never moves a foot closer. He crosses his arms, clears his throat, and returns to his stoic stance.

Dr. Randal removes his glasses, and while wiping them with a tissue, he says, "Finally, some substance to my nightmares. I have pieced together certain events over time, but now it all makes sense. I trusted that son of a bitch, Fortune." He shakes his head in disappointment and anger. "Your mother and I did our damnedest to uncover the deceit that was taking place right under our noses. Her more than I. She was the one who came to me. She was suspicious about something, but couldn't quite place it. She wanted to stop taking the pill in session. Actually, she wanted to stop all of her medications. She was trying to convince me to start over with her treatment." He shakes his head. "Dammit man, this life has certainly thrown me down the drain."

I don't know how to respond. I only stare at him. Lesley finally seems to be relaxing a little. At least she is breathing again.

"Your mom would be proud of you," he says in a solemn voice. "You know, you have her eyes." He stares at my eyes and I can see the deep ache encompassing his. He moves his right hand to the top left pocket of his scrub shirt. I can hear Lesley take a deep breath and then shuffle in her chair, as if flinching. "I think *you* should have this."

He hands me a small golden locket in the shape of a heart. "Thank you," I say accepting it. I can feel Lesley's breathing on my neck as she peers over my shoulder. I slowly pry open the locket and my eyes immediately well up with tears as I take in the picture of my little sister. She is smiling and I hear the echo of her giggle.

"I now know why your mom gave that to me," he says. "Why, toward the end, she wanted me to give it to her at the beginning of every session. She was fighting the orders. I never told her to do that. That had to have been Fortune. Oh, please tell me I didn't give her the order!" His voice trails off into a stuttering babble. He grabs hold of his hair again and begins to rock back and forth.

Though Fortune had admitted to it, I can't be completely sure that he didn't give the order. The files in the storage unit had been tampered with by Fortune. But it doesn't matter anymore. This man has suffered enough.

"Dr. Randal, it wasn't you. Fortune admitted to it. He gave the order himself, personally, just as he did to you. He said he implemented the sacrifice command."

"She was trying to fight it, Tryke. She was a good person, and a good mom. You have to know that."

"I do, Dr. Randal. You're a good person, too. You can't help what happened, any more than she could."

"I was her doctor. She trusted me and I failed her. I failed her..."

"That's enough for today, Doc," a rough voice says from the direction of the door. "You have two minutes to tie it up."

Dr. Randal stands, removes his glasses, and wipes his eyes one more time with the back of his hand.

"I'm sorry," he says, and turns and walks toward the henchman standing at the open door.

I stand up and say, "She wrote in her diary that you were her best friend."

His steps hesitate at my words and he stops in place. He turns his head to the side and nods, and then continues toward the exit, never turning back around.

Chapter 29

Lesley and I are quietly sitting in the front seat of my truck in the asylum parking lot. The menacing clouds converging on us match the mood brewing in the cab. This can go either way depending on how I decide to handle things, which I am still considering. Lesley has not said a word since leaving the room with Dr. Randal. If my assumption is correct, the mob of emotions will shield most of her rational thought.

"Now you know the truth about my family," I say, breaking the thick thread of uncomfortable silence.

Her arms are crossed and she is staring out her side window.

"It still doesn't change anything," she says, as if this is an entire waste of her time. She is completely disregarding my efforts to show her my family's secrets, and I can feel the temperature of my blood rising. Lesley has no idea how hard and painful this is for me. Above all, this is my history, the history of my family, and the history of our child's family.

"What do you mean?" I say, tempering the seething frustration now inching closer to the surface.

"Look, I'm only saying that I'm here now. We both are." Her tone suddenly switches to a motherly one and she softly lays a hand on her stomach. "Don't you see, none of it matters anymore. We have a chance to start over and forget everything. We can start *our* family now." Tears are welling in her lower lids.

"I can't forget. I can never forget. It will always matter, Lesley. I can't just start over. It's not that easy. That's what I've been trying to tell you… I wanted you to know everything and now you do. Now you know the truth. I can't live happily ever after. It just isn't in the cards for me."

"Anything can happen if you want it to. You have taught me to believe in things, the world, the universe. There are no absolutes, right? You always say that. There is always a way. Your life is not set in stone. What happened to you, happened, I get that. But now it is our time, me, you, and the baby."

I shake my head, attempting to shy away the sadness creeping in at the mention of our child. I want everything to be all right, I want us to be together, I want us to have a normal family and do all of those things families do, but…

"I'm still running, remember?"

The tears are now flowing freely. "Your uncle isn't chasing you. He never was. It was all part of your —"

"My what? Go ahead, say it. My sickness."

"Tryke, come on, I'm not saying that." She sniffs and I reach across her and into my glove compartment for a napkin and hand it to her. "All I'm saying is that your uncle may have let you go on purpose. Maybe he forgave you."

I set aside the sadness and stifle a laugh at the mention of my uncle being an honorable man. She might as well know why I am so reluctant to see things as she does.

"He caught me in New Orleans, Lesley, and escorted me

back here."

The gears in her head are grinding in full force as she realizes the implications of the situation I had been in. The white picket fence and a perfect family are fading quickly from her eyes.

"Where is he — What did you do, Tryke?! Tell me you didn't; not your own family."

My face reveals too much. I don't know what else to say to avoid the inevitable. She shakes her head and reaches for the door handle next to her and begins yanking on it.

"I want the hell out of here! How could you?! Your own flesh and blood!" The handle isn't budging. I locked it out of habit when we got in. "Unlock the door, Tryke." She looks at me in a way that I have never seen before — a frightened hatred, as if I were a stranger who had just trapped her inside his dungeon.

"You have an unlocking mechanism on your side," I say, calmly. Her eyes dart down at the button. Seconds later she has the door open. "Will you give me a second to explain to you what happened? Please."

Once again I am thrown from what I thought I knew of rational conversation. I thought I had this figured out by now, but the opposite sex has stumped me once again. The rain started a few minutes ago, and in the short time she has been standing with the door open, her hair has turned into a glistening black wave of beauty, and I am brought back to our first kiss under the gazebo: how clumsy and unprepared I was. How I spilled my glass of wine. How so perfectly warm and passionate her lips were when they touched mine. I desperately want that moment back and to start everything over. I want to start my life over and meet Lesley all over again.

"Tryke."

"Sorry," I say returning to the present. I realize she hasn't left yet. She is waiting on something.

"Just tell me if you killed your uncle. Yes or no."

I thought we were past this already. What do I say? She isn't going to listen to my explanation if I tell her I killed him. Do I lie and say I didn't? She'll eventually discover he is dead when it hits the news.

"Yes, but —"

"I can accept you. I can accept your —"

"Sickness."

"Yes, your sickness." There it is, all inhibitions out the window. She is ready to flee. No holding back now. "What I can't accept is you killing your own family. I don't feel safe around you anymore. And what about our baby? Will you kill your own child, too?"

"That's not fair. I would never hurt you or our child."

"How do I know that?" She is ignoring the rain and is now almost completely drenched.

"You have my word." I know it is a rhetorical question, but she has to know I would never hurt her or our child.

"Will you get help?" What's this? "Will you do what needs to be done and go see someone and figure this sickness out?"

Finally, I see what she is doing. It's all spelled out in front of me on the cover of an array of pitiful self-help books. She is giving me an ultimatum I cannot keep.

"After all I have been through, you really want me to seek treatment from a psychiatrist?"

"You have a choice, Tryke. Get help. That's my condition."

There it is. I am still trying to process the fact that she really said it. She is really leaving, and the only thing I know to do is let the fury burn. I want to yell, to scream, but I cannot. I have to restrain the motley of emotions spreading across my insides like a swarm of angry bees. She has changed her mind once again but this time it is different. She wanted out when she left in New Orleans and her request to stay with me was only temporary because of the child. I should have seen through her false plea a few minutes ago. I should have seen through them both. It was all a ploy to clear the conscience and keep it from falling into the deep despair of guilt.

"I guess this is goodbye then," I say.

She isn't expecting this answer, but she seems pleased by it, even if it is hidden snugly behind a waterfall of tears and a slew of running makeup.

"I don't know what to say," she says.

"You've said enough, I think."

"I don't want to end it like this. I love you, Tryke."

I can't tell if there is a new set of tears flowing down her cheeks, or if it's the rain.

"I don't either, but I think we both know it has to be like this. We have different journeys to explore. Besides, I would just be a burden. This way you will be free of me and my dark clouds."

"I don't want this, Tryke. I take it back. All of it."

Okay, now I'm really confused. Was she bluffing the entire time? Was I wrong for the... second or third time in this short conversation? She gets in the truck and closes the door, her hair dripping wet and her saturated clothes soaking into my seats. I grab a t-shirt from the back seat and give it to her to wipe the rain away. She thanks me and scoots next to me. She lays her head on my chest and I can only sit there, quiet.

"I don't want to lose you. I don't care what you did or what you've done. I can't do this alone. I can't raise our child alone. They need their father." She cries softly into my shirt and I embrace her tightly. I still don't say anything and we just hold one another.

"I have made arrangements," I say after a considerable amount of time has passed. She doesn't seem too interested as she doesn't budge from her position. I continue, "You may not like them and I'm not saying you have to honor them by any means. I'm only requesting you give it some serious thought before you make a decision."

I tell her my plan and she doesn't say a word or move her head from my chest. I guess it means she is finally facing the inevitable. We must part ways for now. For just a brief moment, I allow the feelings that I have been trying to suppress a tiny vent to breathe. I hold her snugly against me and I lightly kiss her forehead. We continue to sit a while longer, quietly, allowing the continuous symphonic rain to teleport our minds anywhere they choose. Mine desperately wants to move forward, past the slow moving immediate future of pain and suffering to a time when things are less complex. I usually embrace the solitude and quietness with myself, but for some reason I feel I will not like what is coming.

Where are Lesley's thoughts? I only hope they are searching for somewhere they can be happy. I long for her to see that softly falling snowflake of bliss floating in the far distance. I want her to never lose faith that she will someday catch it. And along the way, I hope she is able to shove off the heavy blanket of darkness and allow some light in.

Chapter 30

Letter No. 2

Dave,

If you are reading this, then you have recovered from your injuries enough to comprehend what I'm saying. It also means you have read the first letter and now know more intimate details about me and my family. Yeah, things in my life have been quite screwed up for a while. Do I suffer from the same sickness as my mom and little sister? I know you have likely pondered that question after reading the first letter and have probably cycled through our time together, attempting to dissect our conversations and events to form an opinion. I'll give you a second to reflect…

The short answer is no, but that doesn't mean it will not manifest later in my life. I am not so naive to think that I am not susceptible; denial is my friend at times, but never naivete. You and I share a commonality, one that involves the opposite sex. We have both suffered in our own ways as we attempt to decipher the emotional hieroglyphics tossed our way. The struggle is real but we both seem to have perseverance — you more than me. We also share something else, a fondness for Lesley, which brings me to the purpose of this letter.

Lesley is pregnant with my child and I have to leave until things cool down. Unfortunately, Lesley cannot come with me, for reasons I cannot explain at the moment. By now, depending on the time you read this letter, the child may or may not be born. I know you have always had a thing for Lesley, but hopefully and more importantly, you consider her a good friend. With me being gone for an unknown length of time, Lesley is going to need a friend and support. She is likely not going to accept my reasoning as she doesn't have all of the details — for obvious reasons. I can only hope that in time she will come to understand and accept that I had to leave.

I know you have your own child to take care of and will probably have some medical obstacles to overcome. Let me go ahead and put it out there: I am not asking you to raise my child for me. I am only asking for emotional support for Lesley and to look in on her and my child from time to time. As our job has taught us, there is a never-ending surplus of dangers in this world and our vulnerable children can use all the help we can provide. And if it's not too much, maybe mention me to them occasionally, and reiterate how hard this was for me. I know she will not understand without more details, but if it is coming from you I know she will at least consider your words, as she trusts you. One more favor: tell my child who their dad is — you know very well how important this is, as you have a child of your own.

I can't believe I'm saying this, but in the unlikely event I am unable to return, you have my permission to pursue Lesley — after of course an adequate amount of time has passed, meaning more than a week, pervert. I will also have instructions and money set aside for them in a secure location if that were to occur.

I love her and my child with everything I am. I hate myself right now for not being able to provide what she needs, but I don't have a choice in my current situation. I apologize for placing you in this situation. You are truly the only one I trust to do this. You have always been a good friend to me and Lesley, and an honorable friend at that.

The prepaid phone I left by your bedside is for me to keep in touch with you; I have my number preprogrammed on it. Not knowing if Lesley will accept anything from me, I will send you money and anything else my child may need. My number may change occasionally, so please listen to all of your voicemails and delete them soon after. If you decide this is too much for you in your current state, or you just don't want the responsibility, I understand and I will not hold a grudge. Either way, please give me an answer.

I will check in on you periodically and see how you are doing in the hospital. If by chance you don't recover and never read this letter, I will not hold you liable from the other side. If you read this in ghost form, you are still obligated.

Your friend,
Tryke

Chapter 31

Approximately five years later...

I finally made it to Florida. I called the panhandle my home for a few years until I felt enough time had passed for things to cool off in Dallas. I kept up with the news feeds until a conclusion was made in the detective/psychiatrist murder investigation. It wasn't until they found my uncle's body in Dr. Randal's storage unit that they unraveled the mystery behind Dr. Fortune's death in New Orleans. I removed the faked documents that Fortune had placed and replaced them with some new, freshly typed ones. It didn't take me long to put together enough evidence to link Fortune to a pharmaceutical company — never specifically mentioning the company's name — and clear Dr. Randal of any wrongdoing. Also, that his family was killed by Fortune. The note pinned to my uncle's shirt was a suicide note that implicated him in the death of Fortune, followed by an insufferable guilt for pursuing him on his own to avenge his brother and sister in-law.

My headaches became less intense and sporadic over

time. My little friend that I thought was attached to my brain was actually never there in the first place. Apparently, I mistook the image on the computer screen for the person who had been scanned before me. Eventually, I got up the nerve to call the hospital in New Orleans and the doctor was decent enough to violate HIPPA laws and tell me over the phone that my CAT scan was clear. I even managed to convince myself to have another CAT scan a year ago for good measure; it was also clear. I suspect the event was all a ploy by the Gamemakers to lower my morale in the fluidly dicey situation taking place in New Orleans.

I have recently moved back to the Dallas area and now live a few counties over from my previous address. I still own my mother's house and periodically go over there to keep it up since I moved back. Dave was nice enough to do it for me while I was away. I work part-time for a small EMS agency just to keep busy, and to search for opportunities that wouldn't present themselves as often if I weren't working as a medic. While in Florida, I managed to make a decent profit on some lucky real estate investments, which have afforded me the luxury of working at my discretion. I was even able to keep one of the properties I purchased in the event I ever need to return.

Though Dr. Randal was ultimately cleared of any wrongdoing in the murder of his family, he has decided to remain a patient at Bolin Asylum. I have tried many times to talk him into leaving, but he is adamant about staying. He feels that the incarceration is a decent ongoing self-punishment that he deserves. I may not agree with his decision but I respect it. I visit him a few times a month and we converse over a game or two of chess, and occasionally we switch to checkers to break up the monotony. The visits help us both in different ways; weary minds need company, and as painful as it is to recall our past, it keeps us sharp and reminds us of our continuous struggles. I suppose his incarceration isn't too horrible since he isn't constantly followed by henchmen and a demanding nurse warning him to swallow his medications. For the most part he is a free man — voluntary incarceration — able to roam the facility during the day. Though the pain is still obviously there behind his haggard eyes, I think the asylum offers him occasional moments of comfort, as he knows the world is safely outside the walls where he can't reach it, and it can't reach him.

Lesley gave birth to a healthy baby girl and named her Katie — spelled a little differently from my sister's name. Before leaving, though she was still upset with me, we agreed on names, depending on the sex of the baby. I see them often, though they do not see me. Lesley completed medical school and now works as an emergency room physician at Mercy General Hospital in Dallas. She purchased a house a few blocks over from her parents, where she and Katie currently live alone. I offered her my mother's house when I left, but she declined. I will leave it to Katie when she turns eighteen.

I am sitting on a bench at the park close to where Katie attends kindergarten. Every Wednesday, Lesley brings her to the park after school and they have a picnic and play on the swings — weather cooperating. I try to attend every week. I pack my lunch and eat my sandwich from behind a paperback book and sunglasses, and I watch from a distance, longing, wishing, dreaming that I could take part in their conversations and be part of their world.

I can hear Lesley's voice as she yells for Katie to come back toward her. I watch them from under the brim of my hat and from behind my dark shades. Katie has her mother's long black hair and piercing blue eyes. I can hear her giggle, and I am reminded of my sister. I picture them running together and playing in an open field — their laughter ringing out in the warm afternoon air as they chase one another in a zig-zag pattern. I smile, but am quickly brought back to reality when I see that Katie has roamed to a bench where a man is seated by himself. He is middle-aged, with a neatly folded paper in his lap. When he sees Katie closing in to his location, he leans over and picks an orange flower from the ground beside him. He says something I cannot hear and then offers her the flower.

"Katie Sylvia, I'm not going to ask you again," Lesley warns. Lesley is marching in her direction, but is too far away to see what I see.

The man curls his lips, unfolding a dark smile from under his mirrored shades as Katie pauses and stares up at him with trustful innocence. He continues to watch her as she runs back to her mother. Lesley waves toward the man in an apologetic manner and the man waves a friendly hand back that says, no problem. When Katie is a safe distance away and Lesley is no longer looking, the man removes his glasses, replacing them with another pair of spectacles — these used for focusing and clarity. He pulls a phone from his pocket, fiddles with it for a minute, and turns it upright. He is filming Leslie and my daughter.

I turn my attention to the swing set where Dave is watching his own daughter being pushed by Elizabeth — the nurse who had been taking care of him in the hospital. They married and have a daughter of their own, but Dave has not forgotten about Lesley. They have play dates often. and Dave has done as he promised and mentions me often to my daughter. We communicate on a regular basis and he knows of my location, promising not to reveal it to Lesley. He repeatedly asks why I have to continue to stay away and I keep my answer vague, only saying it is better this way. He vehemently disagrees with my decision, but doesn't intrude.

"Lesley," Dave shouts. "Come on, we're about to start the swing-off."

Lesley picks Katie up and they move toward the swing set. Katie is staring over her mom's shoulder toward the man with the phone. He is still filming them. I remove my sunglasses and turn toward the man. A few minutes later, he notices me and our eyes meet for a brief moment. He suddenly changes the direction of his phone, as if to divert attention from his secret. He turns back toward me and a shadow of a figure emerges from his face – a blurred image wielding bared teeth and a wide, sinister smile. It retracts itself almost immediately, as if it were an accident, but it is too late. I have seen it and I know it was no accident. Their hubris is their undoing and has become my natural cloak. It is a tease granted by the Gamemakers to allow the chase to begin.

Though my attention is temporarily drawn away from Katie and Lesley, I do not forget what I have come to do. In my hand is an envelope holding two letters — one for Lesley and one for my daughter. The letter to Lesley is simply a reminder of my family's past, especially that of my sister, and the age at which her tragic death occurred. I include pleading instructions on how to proceed. Dave is also aware and has been good about giving me current information.

The letter to my daughter is to be given to her if something were to happen to me, or if the sickness were to manifest itself in her, but at a proper age, of course, when she will be able to understand the words and concepts. I have thought long and hard and have written many drafts, but in the end I kept it simple and short. There are subtle clues in the letter that will ultimately lead to a written guide for her. If she is anything like her father, she will have no problem understanding what I have hidden in plain sight. It is the best gift I know to give, a clear path I wish I had been given. She will uncover hard truths about her family along the way, but in the end my wish is for her to find peace and understanding — something I fear may not exist on this plane.

The swinging contest is underway, so I saunter over to the tree where their picnic basket and bags are sitting. I place the envelope on top of the basket and hurry to the parking lot, where I wait in my truck for them to leave. I continue to watch the man who gave my daughter a flower. He is now strolling the sidewalk that circles the park, clutching his satchel of video equipment and other unknown paraphernalia. I don't want to think about its possible contents at the moment; it will bring only anger, and right now I don't want to be angry. All I want to do is deliver a message.

They return to their place under the tree about ten minutes later. Katie immediately sees the envelope perched on the basket and makes a beeline toward it. Clumsily, she knocks over the envelope and the item that had been weighing it down. The envelope remains on the blanket as Katie picks up the shiny object. She is instantly captivated by it as the sun reflects off its surface. Lesley kneels down and glances at what Katie is holding. A few seconds later, when she recognizes the watch, she stands up and jerks her head around like a perched sparrow on a fence. I sit back in my seat so she doesn't see me, but I can still see her. My truck is different, yet she seems to focus on the one I'm sitting in. A moment later, Katie gains her attention with the envelope by hitting it on her leg repeatedly. While Lesley is focused on Katie and the envelope, I put my truck in reverse and drive away.

Not even my soul is sure I made the right decision, but it has to be this way, for now. It is too dangerous. The Gamemakers will use Katie as a threat, a last nail pounded in my coffin, a weakness to stop me from playing the game. If I get too close to her, as they showed me today, their minions will intervene. They are always lurking, watching and waiting, salivating until the order is given. Being this close to her, I must stay vigilant at all times, but this is also the only way I know to keep her safe.

Until the time is right, I have to remain in the shadows and dwell where the underworld thrives. Maybe one day when Katie is old enough to be on her own, she will know her father. I feel certain that she will seek me out before that time, and unfortunately for reasons I am not proud of. But this is who we are, this is our destiny, and we must embrace it until the end. I have been made to witness many things, seen more than any one man should in a lifetime. There are truths out there. Some can be felt, some seen, and others have no explanation at all. But we know they are there. Dimensions, unexplained senses, the complexity of the human brain and its organic suit — there are no absolutes in this life, which is one of the things that drives me forward each day.

As I have always done, I will carry on, surviving and avenging the innocent by battling the Gamemakers and the horde of minions they place on the battlefield. For every group of evil that enters the world, there are those like me to balance the darkness with the light — a barely warm center, not quite fully dark, but also not quite fully light. We are always watching, always ready to light a candle for the innocent. There *are* decent people out there, but this world is flawed. Until the battle ceases, the streets will run red with tidal waves of the avenged blood.

Chapter 32

Katie,

 You are old enough now to know certain things and how they work. First, I want you to know I don't have all of the answers. I'm afraid no one does. That is the beauty and the curse set upon us while we wait in this dimension. Everything is constantly changing, in this world and beyond. There is an endless supply of knowledge, if one only opens their eyes to find it. You will meet all kinds of people on your travels as a human: some brave, some bold, some smart, some not so smart. There are deceitful ones, clever ones, nice ones, and not so nice ones. But we all share our cluelessness about the universe, which is not always a bad thing; it means we will never stop discovering.

 There is good in the universe, which also means there is an abundance of evil out there, lurking in the shadows and waiting to do us harm. For what reason? That's the rub. There is a battle that has been waging since the beginning of time, and we are stuck in the middle. As individuals we must search within ourselves and discover what it means. Then, and only then, will you come to understand a small fraction of who you are. You can unwrap that piece and play with it as you see fit. It is your destiny to follow, to discover, and to unravel.

For now, trust that I will always watch over and guide you the best way I know how, even with the restraints placed upon me. The watch I left for you is a reminder of the good in the world, the love your mother and I shared. It is also to let you know I will always be watching and thinking of you, no matter the distance between us. My father taught me a great deal, though he was not able to be there in person. He showed me things from up above that were hidden in plain sight. I hope to be able to do the same for you. Enclosed is a picture of my sister — the person you were named after — and my parents and me at the lake. It is one of the fondest memories in my life — next to the moment your mother told me of you. Search for those memories, for they are few and far between. When you find them, hold them close and discover what was hidden in front of you all along.

P.S. Laughing is the soul's only break from crying.

I love you,
Dad

Journal Entries

*I have left the number system in place, mainly for nostalgic reasons. I have seen the soul many times and know very well that it exists.

10

Entry No. 223. 56 y/o male, name: Frank Harper. His apathy for his family and the attempted murder of me has brought the number to a 10. He also threatened the life of Lesley and my unborn child. Family has always been a top priority to preserve and honor, but betrayal erases that connection. These are unforgivable actions and have been dealt with as such.

Results: No visualization, but there was a brief high-pitched noise that sounded like air being slowly let out of the stretched mouth of a balloon. No attempt made to coerce the soul. My family is safely on the other side, but Frank is on a different plane. Though I don't believe he was a player initially, the Gamemakers will likely use him in the future in another form. I will keep this in mind.

8

Entry No. 323. 47 y/o male, name Hal Brandon. His love for children goes way beyond filming them in the park and other outdoor arenas. I knew what he was up to the second I spotted him filming my daughter and Lesley on his phone in the park. He even arrogantly revealed himself in plain daylight to me. I waited close by for him to leave and followed him to his trailer a few blocks from the park. The next night, I discovered an array of short videos on his computer, including the one he took of my Katie and Lesley. There is enough evidence in his home to convict him. I only have to send an anonymous tip to the authorities. But he'll just waste taxpayers' money for a brief stay in jail, and then he'll be out again doing the same thing. He needs to be released, and it is my duty to protect my daughter. So I will.

Results: The release was successful. Not only did I visualize the soul, I retrieved a slew of information about more specimens involved in a huge operation. This should be quite the summer coming up. In preparation, I purchased a few more journals on my way home.

6

Entry No. 225. 45 y/o male, name: Johnny Bosch. His desire for money hasn't shielded the stench emanating from his pores as he unloads another pile of body parts in plain sight at the city dump. He was not terribly clever, as most aren't, allowing his loftiness to hang out, much like the human leg in the black trash bag he was carrying. I feel certain that once he is on the table, he will spout the names of a plethora of untapped suits waiting to be released.

Results: He never released any names, but I did catch a glimpse of him hovering in the room.

5

Entry No. 256. 29 y/o male, name: Andre Davis. His fascination with dogs, particularly the taste of them, is not the only reason for a release. His taste didn't stop with their flesh. He showed a fondness for torture toward these innocent creatures. This one's for Earl. When I told him the details of my plan, he barked and wagged his tail in approval. It was probably just the smell of the takeout box from the restaurant, but it still made me smile.

Results: He left quickly, as I knew he would, fearful of his own cowardly acts. I allowed Earl in the room on this one, and he barked and spun in place once the release was complete. Once again, I wasn't sure if it was the treat in my pocket, or if he was happy that I had avenged his brethren.

5

Entry No. 275. 45 y/o female, name: Josey Schultz. I picked her stepson up from a day care center this a.m. I discovered the bruises during my examination after he fell from a jungle gym. The injuries from the fall were minor, but I transported him to the ER anyway for further evaluation, and to question him about the old bruises.

Addendum: My research turned up a long history of abuse, aimed not only at her step family, but also her own daughter, as well.

Results: No visualization. No sound. A quiet, knowing dismissal from this place. It has been a while since a release has left me uneasy.

3

Entry No. 281. 50 y/o male, name: Trey Mann. I transported him after he plowed his vehicle into a crowd gathered around a grave during a funeral service. His plan, he told me in the back of the rig, was to kill his ex-wife. Unfortunately for his own mother, the alcohol in his system guided him toward her instead of his intended victim, and I had to pronounce her dead on scene. His ex-wife, though distraught, was still very much alive. When I saw the apathy in his eyes after I told him about his dead mother, I knew then what he was. The alcohol was not to blame.

Addendum: The authorities got to him first. I will return at a later date once he is released from jail.

Result:

9

Entry No. 291. 28 y/o female, name: Jordan Spokes. I picked her grandmother up from Twin Oaks NH for a possible OD. Though I was temporarily distracted by her beauty, her false emotions coming from the corner of the room while I loaded her onto the stretcher quickly brought me back to reality. The white residue on the edge of the cup on the nightstand beside her bed felt eerily familiar.

Addendum: Initially, I wondered if Dr. Kimberly had a sister, but after further research there was no connection. Jordan was the only living relative of the elderly lady I picked up at Twin Oaks. Apparently, she didn't want to wait for her rich grandmother to die. I wiped the white powder evidence from her grandmother's mouth on the way to the ER, and kept the discovery for myself. I also uncovered a boyfriend accomplice working behind the scenes.

Results: She was a stunning woman with long black hair and pearl white skin, but her looks did not hide the aged detritus of filth behind the suit as it departed. Still, there was something about this woman that made the experience unique for me. I found her release beautiful as I embraced her with a breath of warm air, which contrasted starkly with the coldness she exuded. When I opened the door for her, she hesitated, but quickly comprehended the situation and understood that we couldn't be together.

5

Entry No. 292. 27 y/o male, name: Sam Bowman. He was the boyfriend and accomplice to Jordan Spokes in the murder of her grandmother.

Results: I wanted to release them together, but their connection was not strong enough. He was not nearly as beautiful a release as Jordan had been. He did not deserve the beauty he had been manipulating. He revealed nothing, not even a smidgen of coolness or a flash of darkness in the dim room. However, I was not left uneasy, as I had been before. This was easy. Every now and then, they allow me one.

A note from C.S. McMillian

I hope you enjoyed Distortion. It has been a long and lonely ride but we finally made it to the end of the trilogy. It was more difficult to say goodbye than I anticipated, but in the end I did it with a smile on my face, followed by a lengthy sigh of relief. All things must eventually come to an end, right? But that just means something else is aching to begin. I can already hear the restless projects I have set aside eagerly vibrating in their loosely bound boxes at the mention of a potential opening. And, as always, I will be unable to resist their allure and charm. The long and lonely nights will start again very soon.

Thank you for your valuable time and support. Please, don't hesitate to connect with me on Facebook and Goodreads: www.facebook.com/darkofthemind and goodreads.com.